A NEED TO BREATHE

Rebuilding Hope Book 1

P.A. WILSON

Perry Wilson Books

CHAPTER ONE

Lena stood at the living room window staring across the river where the industrial buildings lined the river bank. The only indication that the world had changed since they'd moved into the apartment was the lack of crowds. Even two years ago in New Surrey, when it was sunny and warm, people would have been walking the seawall and the sound of kids at play would have drifted up to interrupt the silence.

There weren't many kids anymore, since the global measles epidemic took most of the babies. By the time the doctors had figured it out, it was too late. It only took a few infected kids on a plane to take out almost every country. Kids born now were kept safely inside away from contagion until they were able to be vaccinated. Would they remember? Was eighteen months old enough to realize you hadn't seen the sun — ever?

Lena understood, but she wasn't sure if she agreed. Everyone was vaccinated now; shouldn't that mean babies were safe? But that fear was just another factor in her plan to leave.

The news today about New York City felt like a step through a door to a dark future. She could feel it in her bones. Every day there was a little less freedom, a little more restriction. The world was ruled by people who were afraid, and this city wasn't any different. In New York, they'd declared martial law. People had to share their tiny apartments so that the dwindling resources could be more efficiently used. Rumors had it that there was only a year, maybe a little more, supply of fuel oil and gas outside of the oil producing areas. Fuel was too expensive to transport around the world, and no one seemed interested in finding a real alternative. People had to rely on solar, or wind, or something else, none of which would power a car, a plane, or a ship.

Was she the only person who thought it would be better to leave and start again on a farm? A place they could grow their own food, raise animals, and babies, live with more freedom than they had here.

The sun went behind a cloud and her image appeared in the window. Lena reached back to release the band that kept her braid in place letting her hair fall past her shoulders. Brian liked her hair loose. Maybe that would help convince him, because he would be home soon, and this time she wouldn't back down.

Even in the dim reflection, she could see the contrast between her fair skin and black hair. Was there physical evidence of her dissatisfaction? She had always been thin, and with her height it looked worse. People often thought she was weak, but she wasn't. In her window, she looked the same as she always did, no dark circles of worry under her blue eyes, no twitch of impatience, nothing to give away her plans. That was good because they would have to go in secret when they left.

There was no getting away from the fact that they'd need to take some supplies and the powers-that-be would probably find a way to make that illegal soon.

The sun erased her reflection as it passed out of the cover of a cloud, Lena told herself it was an omen of success.

She turned at the sound of Brian's key in the lock. It was time.

Before he made it down the hall to the living room, she had a glass of wine ready for him. There was plenty of local wine available, it just wasn't as good as the imported vintages she remembered.

He took the glass from her with a puzzled look. It wasn't her usual greeting. In fact, usually she was marking papers, or planning lessons and barely noticed he'd come home. Thinking of her class made her sad. She'd miss them when she was gone.

"What are we celebrating?" Brian asked.

Lena took a sip of her wine. Now that it was time to put into words, it was harder than she imagined. "Not so much celebrating as commemorating. Did you hear about New York?"

Brian took a gulp of wine. "Are we going to talk about this plan of yours again? Yes, I heard. It makes sense for them. They have a huge population. Transporting resources will be easier with people living close."

"It won't be long before that will be us." Lena wouldn't let his blindness to the situation deter her from making her argument. "How will you distribute food to the people living on the outskirts when we finally run out of fuel? That's supposed to happen too soon to find alternatives according to the latest restrictions. And electricity? Water? How long before they get rationed?"

He put his glass on the coffee table and took her hand. "First of all, it's not me who decides how supplies get delivered. You know that's another department altogether. What I can tell you is that there's talk of using horses, and bikes, and all kinds of non-gas fueled vehicles, to make deliveries. We are not going to force people to share living quarters. We, that is the larger towns, we keep the services running. It doesn't take many people to keep the power grid going, and solar is easier. The water system is the same."

Lena was surprised that as much as she wanted to believe her husband, she could only think that he was deluded at best. More likely he was just giving her the party line, and he was so deeply in the leadership that he believed what he said. It just didn't make sense to her.

"I know you believe that, Brian, but I don't." She set her glass beside his and pulled her hand away. "I think we need to find a place where we can build a life."

He gave a little sigh that reminded Lena of her students. It was annoying when teenagers did it, and patronizing when her husband did.

"Let's pretend you are right," he said. "Why do we have to leave? We are part of the solution here. Your teaching job will always be valuable. I'm part of the decision-making level. We have a life here. Those services you asked about? They won't be reliable outside the organized areas. At least not for much longer."

Lena closed her lips tightly to stop the words spewing out. How long before she was told what to teach? How long before books were removed from the curriculum? How long before all she taught boys was how to be good at approved jobs, and girls how to be good wives? But it wasn't time for that argument. "This isn't the life we pictured."

Brian looked away from her. It was his usual way of telling her the discussion was over. Lena wondered if he'd been like that before things had changed. He rose and walked to the window, standing where she had been a few minutes ago. Was he seeing the same thing she had?

"I don't want to talk about this anymore, Lena." He turned from the view to look at her — look down at her. "Can you just stop trying to get back to what we had before things went wrong?"

Lena knew he wasn't ready to see life as clearly as she could. This life they were living was only going to get smaller and more about survival than living. "I'm not trying to get back to before.

I'm just trying to find something that feels more normal. Something with more breathing space." She wasn't going to give up, but Lena was willing to give Brian time. They weren't going to agree tonight. "They delivered some beef today with the grocery allowance. I made a sauce to go with the pasta."

CHAPTER TWO

The next morning Lena made tea with the last of the leaves from the beginning of month delivery. The coffee supplies had apparently been used up months ago. There were rumors that the tea was almost gone too. They were going to have to rely on locally grown herbs to make any kind of hot drink soon.

"Busy day ahead?" Brian asked as he sat at the table. He didn't wait for her answer, just buttered his toast, and kept talking. "I was thinking about what you said. Didn't get much sleep because of it."

Lena didn't want to start the day with an argument. She was doing exam prep lessons all day so she'd be worn out; it didn't help to start with the emotional aftermath of a fight. "I thought the topic was closed."

Brian took the mug of tea she handed him, poured in milk and then answered, "Is it? You know that there are rules about taking stuff out of the city, and about hoarding. You don't want to get in trouble, do you?"

She knew he'd edited his comments. He hadn't said 'and embarrass me', or that the trouble might affect him. She'd noticed he hadn't slept, even if he hadn't been aware that she was awake too. It didn't take much imagination to work out that he'd been practicing his argument, not considering the sense of her plan.

Despite her reluctance to argue, Lena couldn't stop herself from speaking. "When you said that we wouldn't do the same things as New York, did you forget we're already rationing?" She kept her eyes on the contents of the breakfast plate. At least chickens were local, they had eggs, and wheat was grown not too far away, so rations always contained bread or pasta.

"That's exactly why we aren't taking such drastic steps. Rationing now will mean resources stretch as long as we need them. We'll find a way to make it work." He touched her hand to make her look at him. "Lena, don't obsess over this. It's not as bad as you imagine."

She nodded, not in agreement, but as a way to stop the discussion. He just needed time, more indications of what was coming. Eventually he'd realize she was right.

"Good. I don't see the point of leaving anyway. If it's so bad here, where there are schools and hospitals, and a police force, what do you think it will be like on your aunt's farm?"

Peaceful and less like a prison.

"Brian, it's okay. I get your point." She picked up the last of her toast and stood.

"Lena, you won't have anything like the services you get here. If we do go to the farm, how do you plan to run the equipment? There won't be fuel deliveries."

"I forget you never went there. Aunt Mae was a Mennonite. She kept her farm small, and used a horse not a tractor." How had she forgotten that? Brian didn't like to travel outside the state. Even to Manitoba for a week. *He's always said Canada is a foreign country, and I like it here.* "I have to get in early. There will be a ton of questions from the kids. Exam prep, remember?"

"I remember. I'll get dinner at work; you can just relax when you get in."

Lena knew he was being kind. Brian always complained about the food at work. "Well don't stay too late," she said.

Lena grabbed her school bag and kissed Brian on his cheek before she started for the door.

"I'll try," he said. "We're working on how to best deal with people who aren't participating in the community work hours. Can't make it acceptable to laze around while everyone else pitches in."

He didn't even see how that made her case. They weren't that desperate for help that people needed to be forced to work. There were too many of their neighbors still clutched in the agony of losing children. No matter how long it took, people should be allowed to grieve. The government would be using its time better dealing with the gangs that were growing all over the city. Too many kids lived without parents, or with parents who couldn't care for them.

Gangs were targeting kids who had no way of seeing a good future, pulling them into a life of violence. Kids who'd survived the epidemic because they'd been vaccinated. Kids who wouldn't survive long in a gang. There was no vaccination for that.

Lena picked through the box of food staples that had been left outside their door. Was this really all the variety they could manage in the gardens? Before the epidemics, she'd had seasonal local vegetables delivered and there was more choice then. Now, it was whatever the city leaders deemed appropriate. She knew they got more in their rations because Brian was one of the leaders. She'd seen Ava's box often enough, and Ava was a teacher, supposedly important, on top of that, she had two kids to feed out of pretty much the same rations as Lena and Brian got. No matter that he denied it, there was always a little something extra in their box.

This time she saw barely ripe tomatoes, a small bag of dried beans, and a vacuum sealed salmon. It would make more sense to Lena if they ate well in season, but apparently, it was better to preserve the fish and ration it out all year. The rest of the box was dried pasta, canned sauce, and a bag of tea. She wouldn't be able to save any of this for her travel supplies. Perhaps that was part of the philosophy; don't give anyone enough to hoard, or supply an escape from their rules.

When she got to the farm, she'd make sure everyone had enough to eat, and no one would feel trapped.

Lena stepped across to the balcony. Being outside, even in this small space, made her feel free. It was a place she could think, a place where the influence of the city rules didn't seem to matter. She knew she couldn't go alone. Even if she left by herself, the farm needed people. There were only a few she could trust, but she had to ask them. More people meant more skills, more heads to plan their journey. Brian might change his mind, but if he didn't, she wasn't going to let him hold her back.

His key in the door interrupted her mental inventory of what she needed, and how they could transport everything.

"Lena," he called.

She stepped back into the living room, pasted a smile on, and kissed him. "You're late. Busy day?" Let him talk about his job and he'd have no reason to ask her questions.

"Not too bad. It's getting harder to keep people engaged. Well, that's probably not the word. It seems like people fall into the blues easier these days. Too many call in sick. The kids don't seem interested in anything but joining gangs." He hung his coat on one of the hooks beside the door. "I don't know where they are getting the supplies to make these new drugs."

Lena opened a bottle of wine. One of the good bottles. Their stock was getting low, but if he was in a bad mood it was worth the cost. "You'll figure it out soon. I can try to ask around the school, if it would help." Her students would know where the drugs were coming from, but she didn't think they would say. It was just something to make Brian feel like she was involved with his problems.

"No. That's not your role." He took the glass from her and sipped. A smile of appreciation crossed his lips. "We all have to keep to our assigned roles; otherwise things get complicated."

Since when had he called her job a role? Lena's stomach clenched at the thought that they were closer to the future than she feared. No. Not feared, knew. This was what happened when things got tough. People in charge got more powerful. She'd seen examples in every society, from Bountiful with its polygamists, to whatever the last terrorist group was called. When people had power, they didn't hand it over.

There were still cans of soup left from the last food box, she opened one and heated it in a pot while Brian changed from his work clothes. She needed a reason to be out of the house in the evenings. She needed time to plan and gather people for the journey. It was going to be harder to make small talk all evening when her mind was on the future.

Brian set the table and poured the rest of the wine. "I have some news for you." He took the bowl of bread from her and placed it on the table.

Lena nodded for him to continue as she ladled the soup.

He sat and unfolded his napkin. "That news you heard."

His pause made her want to ask what news, but she kept quiet. Brian would spool out the information at his own pace.

He tasted the soup, chicken noodle. "Delicious."

Lena nodded although she thought it too salty. If they gave her chicken she could make better soup.

"New York," Brian said. "The rumors aren't true. Some dissatisfied anti-government propaganda. The citizens are still free to live where they want."

Lena shook her head. Brian couldn't be right. The news had been so detailed. "How do you know that the denials aren't propaganda?"

"The mayor got it directly from the government communications." He broke a slice of stale bread into pieces and dropped them in his bowl.

"What government communications?" Lena hadn't heard that the cities were coordinating information. Was it good that they were? Or would the bigger cities sabotage the smaller ones? If they needed supplies, it was an easy way to get information. Or was she being paranoid?

Brian chuckled. She hated that sound. It made her feel like a child. As though he'd been amused by her unworldliness. The old Brian wasn't this patronizing. When had he become this irritating man? Was that why she convinced herself that it was vital to leave? She tried to push the thought away, but knew that there might be truth in the nagging thought that she was using her fears to cover the fact that she really wanted to leave her husband.

"Did you really think we were muddling along by ourselves?" Brian pushed his empty bowl away. "The mayors share ideas and experiences. We are still part of something bigger."

"That doesn't mean they don't lie to each other."

The cheerful light went out of Brian's eyes. "This nonsense of yours is just that. I think you need to let it go. It could be dangerous to talk about leaving."

"Why? Aren't we free to do as we see fit?" The patronizing was bad enough, now he was talking to her as if she was dangerous. No, not even that, as if she was a rebellious teenager. Perhaps it really was more about leaving Brian, than leaving New Surrey.

"I didn't mean that," Brian said. He'd heard the anger in her voice and knew his argument wasn't working. "I meant the gangs might hear and who knows what they'll do."

It was a weak statement and Brian knew it. Lena shook her head. She needed the conversation to end before Brian stumbled onto her doubts. "Fine. I won't bring it up again."

His smile returned. Lena couldn't believe he'd been fooled

into thinking she'd drop her plans, but if he stopped talking, she would get the space to work out her feelings.

Pushing up from the table, Brian wiped his lips on the napkin. "Good. Now, I have a late meeting to get to. I'll probably be home after you're asleep." He bent and kissed her cheek before heading to the door.

Brian didn't usually have meetings after work. Lena couldn't decide which was worse. The thought that Brian was getting deeper into the government, or the thought that he was having an affair. Either way, she didn't want to fight for him.

CHAPTER THREE

Lena could see the papers sitting outside all the doors on her floor. She was usually the first one home of her neighbors, and that meant always seeing what had been delivered. Brian never gave her advance notice of these changes, probably knowing she'd argue with him. She would, even if there was nothing to be done. The notices, printed on yellow paper to get people's attention, were never up for discussion.

She bent to pick up her copy before unlocking her door.

Three pages.

It wouldn't be good news.

She dropped the papers on the table and changed out of her work clothes before settling down to read the contents. She hadn't slept well for the last couple of nights. She'd been trying to work out if Brian was right. That she was turning the changes necessary for survival into attacks on her freedom because something else was wrong in her life.

If she was right, the proof would come too late for her to act. If she was wrong? Well, leaving for the farm wasn't a bad choice no matter what the rules were in the city. The farm would be self-sustaining. She'd make sure they had someone who could hunt, and teach others. And someone who could dress the meat so they could save it for the future. She'd done her research on farming, and she'd hidden away all the books she could find about agriculture.

She checked the clock. Brian would probably be home in an hour, and he'd expect her to comment on the notice. If she didn't, he might suspect that she was going to leave. She didn't think he'd report her, but she couldn't take the chance.

The first page was a lengthy explanation of the reasons for the new rules, and what was supposed to be a reassurance that the city leaders were looking out for the citizens. To Lena, it was all a little too much rationalizing and too little reasoning. The second page listed the new rules.

1 All citizens will be in their homes by nine pm on weeknights, and eleven pm on weekends.

This was to keep the gang activity under control. Lena couldn't suppress the feeling that she was grounded.

2 Any citizen found to be hoarding more than a week's worth of resources will be required to work extra hours on the labor teams equal to the number of days hoarded.

This was supposed to manage resources fairly, but she knew it would be just an excuse to put people on hard labor.

3 Any citizen found to be organizing protests against the city leadership will be assigned to one week on the labor teams.

And that one turned Lena's suspicions into reality. It wasn't too late, but she would have to be more cautious than she planned when it came to recruiting people.

The list continued with petty rules about nuisance behavior and expectations for civic responsibility.

Brian was part of this and he said he couldn't see what the problem was with a few expectations. The man she married wouldn't have put up with this. Whether he'd been brainwashed, or was so afraid of the future that he was willing to give up his freedom, she didn't know.

She put the papers away and turned to prepare dinner. There was another can of soup, and a few slices of bread. The weekly delivery was due tomorrow. She'd find a way to add part of it to her secret stash. The first order of business would be to find a black-market contact for more food.

Lena gave a bitter laugh at the thought of a black market. She knew it would be a neighbor who grew extras on the balcony. It wouldn't be long before they were shut down, or required to provide their crop to the city stores. Or, worse, shorted on the weekly delivery and deprived of their crop.

CHAPTER FOUR

Two days had passed since the new rules went into effect. Four of Lena's students had been caught running drugs for one of the local gangs. Now, instead of learning something that might help them escape from that life, they were digging out concrete and exposing soil — most of which wasn't arable because of contamination. She looked at the stack of papers she needed to mark. Half of them were on homemade paper, and all of them were too short.

Her mind wasn't ready to focus on the essays, so it wandered to her progress on leaving it all behind. She'd managed to tuck away some medicines and bandages. Her supplies were growing, but there was only enough food to get her a few days away from the city. She couldn't rely on strangers to feed her. The farm was a day and a half drive away, but she would never get her hands on a vehicle. It would be whatever she could carry, and maybe drag along in a wagon.

At least Brian hadn't raised the subject since the crap about New York City. It was hard not to relax and believe she was clear of his suspicion, but Lena knew her husband hadn't let it go. He was hatching a new plan.

If it was time to start recruiting people to join her, Lena had to decide who to approach. She only had one person in her life who she trusted to keep the secret. Ava Walker, her best friend. Ava was worried about her kids, and Lena couldn't blame her. If it wasn't the gangs, it would be the government, but her kids would be swept up in something that would kill their future.

The classroom door opened, startling her out of her planning. Brian was there. He never came to the school.

She smiled and waved him in. "This is a nice surprise," she said, hoping he would buy the sweet tones.

"We've been invited to a party." He leaned over to look at the stack of papers. "Are you going to be working long tonight?"

"Another hour." Lena picked the top paper off the pile. "Is the party tonight?"

"Yes. It's at the mayor's house, for dinner." He pulled a chair from behind the nearest desk and sat facing her. "Can you leave this until tomorrow? I know it's late notice, but a lot of influential people will be there. I may be up for a promotion. It's important to me... to us."

Important to his career. She didn't want to be noticed by influential people. She needed to be running under the radar, not helping Brian raise his profile. "These papers are important too." She couldn't bring herself to say no outright.

"The security chief said he was looking forward to meeting you. Lena, you know my job requires some socializing." Brian waved at the papers. "How hard can it be to mark these? How different can they be from every one you did before?"

How important can they be when you really want all the kids stupid and compliant?

Lena realized that the anger boiling at his dismissal of the value of her job was not the only thing shortening her breath. Fear was slithering through her nerves. Was this dinner party a way to investigate her actions? Did someone know about the tiny stash of supplies? Was she going to be put on the concrete-breaking chain gang?

"They are always different, Brian. But I can do them after the party. How long do I have to get ready?"

He smiled and stood. Now that he had the answer he wanted, Brian would get back to what he deemed more important. "I'll be home in two hours. We can leave then."

She watched him go. What did he expect her to do that would take so long? She'd finish the papers before leaving.

Brian gave her a little wave as he turned to close the door. Lena knew that even if this was really about Brian's career, she wouldn't be able to recruit people if she was the wife of an important politician. Right now Brian was low enough on the ladder to be safe. If they were looking to promote him, it would be fast, and her chance to leave would be gone forever.

It had taken a long sleepless night, but Lena had a plan.

The dinner with the mayor had been fine on the surface. Brian's colleagues were good at small talk and making the person they were speaking to, at the time, feel important. Under the surface things were very different. The Head of Security spent a lot of time asking her about the students she thought had the most potential. So much so that she suspected there were plans in the works to take the brightest students out of the system.

A couple of times she noticed Brian talking to the mayor, which wasn't odd. What concerned her was the way they looked at her when their conversation paused. The wives were no better. Not one held a job. The mayor's wife asked Lena why she bothered to work. It had taken all of her control to not to tell the woman she didn't want to leech on the work of others.

There was no longer any doubt in her mind that she had to leave, and it had to be soon. She needed to make Brian think she'd given up on the idea — more than given up, that she was on his side in his bid for promotion. And she needed an excuse to be away for hours at a time.

"Morning," Brian mumbled as he joined her in the kitchen. "I should probably have stopped at the third glass of wine."

Lena handed him a glass of water and two painkillers. "You should probably have stuck to wine. That twenty-year-old scotch put you over the top."

He leaned in and kissed her cheek. "I couldn't say no. Who knows when we'll have an opportunity to get more. Thanks for coming. I know it's not really your thing."

That was the opening she needed. "It was fine. I guess I'll be going to more of those kind of events in the future so I can be a good political wife."

Brian looked in the pot of oatmeal she was stirring. "If things go well, we'll be able to have more than porridge for breakfast. Bacon and eggs, coffee, butter, how would you like that?"

Much better if everyone had access to it.

"Some variety would be good. Will we have to host a party? I'm not sure how I'll get enough food together from our rations."

"Not soon, and by the time we need to, there will be enough food available. The mayor knows that some people get less than others. He doesn't like it, but it's important to have perks for the people who commit their time to the betterment of the entire city. And no one is starving."

Not yet.

"I wouldn't want to let you down."

Had she gone too far? Lena glanced at Brian, afraid he'd be suspicious of her easy agreement. He was reading the paper. Reminding herself to be careful not to overdo it, Lena ladled out the breakfast and joined Brian at the table.

"If there's anything I can do to help, let me know." She sipped the tea before launching into the second part of her plan. "Actually, I've been thinking about what some of the wives said last night."

He looked up, suddenly all attention now that she'd mentioned someone who might help him move ahead.

"The wives are a good group for you to get involved in."

She nodded and let Brian think she was agreeing. "They all seem to volunteer for things. I thought I'd find a cause I could help."

"I can ask around for you," Brian said. "Find out the best group. No point in spending time volunteering for a cause that doesn't work in our favor."

He said 'our'. He'd bought it, but she couldn't let him find her a volunteer opportunity. It would be something his buddies could check up on. She'd be gone soon, so it wouldn't hurt to let him think it was a good idea. "I'm sure that will be the best. In the meantime, I thought I'd work with the library. They are always looking for help, and I can leave when you find something more suitable."

Her body was tense with anticipation. This was critical. If Brian accepted her idea, she'd have access to the books she'd need for research. She'd be able to take them out of the library. And she could eat two meals on the city's dime; it would be a while before their rations got cut because of it. She'd be able to stock up more food in the meantime.

"Good, it will show you are willing. It might take a few days to find the right opportunity for you. The library will be perfect."

Lena took a spoonful of oatmeal to hide her smile. The library was also a great place to meet other people. She'd get Ava to come there today.

Brian took his bowl to the sink. "Don't book too much time with the library. I think it's a good idea for you to start socializing with the wives. You'll need to fit in with them, so starting early will just make that easier. I'll see if I can arrange something after work. Perhaps a card game." He moved toward the bedroom to get ready for work.

Lena's heart dropped into her gut.

So much for a perfect plan.

Belle, the librarian, had jumped at the chance to get help, and set Lena to cataloging a heap of donated books. This was one of the better ideas from the government. People were encouraged to drop any copies of books they no longer wanted at the library. Some had printed out copies of ebooks before paper had become precious, and when the internet worked reliably.

She was sitting at a table in the back corner of the basement hidden behind rows of shelving containing old magazines, damaged books, and academic papers. None of it would be thrown out now. Nothing could be replaced. It was creepy, but at least no one else was there. Belle didn't have any expectations of production, so Lena could work at her own pace. When she went home, she'd let Ava know to visit her and they'd have all the privacy they needed. A notebook sat open on the table beside her, ready to tuck under the current pile of books she was supposed to catalog if someone came by.

Her plans were basic right now, and she figured it would never get much further than that. She didn't have the luxury of time. They needed the weather to cooperate, and the longer they delayed, the more likely they would get caught. Lena was certain that Brian's position wouldn't stop the mayor locking her up.

The notepad listed the number of meals per person she needed to supply for the trip. She figured it was going to take anywhere from a couple of weeks to a couple of months. They would have to find a way to supplement their supplies if it took more than the couple of weeks. Since people had been on short rations for a while, she hoped two meals would cover it. They'd be walking and hauling their supplies, hard work, but not too difficult. They only needed to travel fast for the first few days. Get far enough so no one would bother looking for them.

They needed guns. Hunting and defense were things that they

would have to take care of themselves. Her mind wandered to where she'd find weapons, but she pulled it back to the task. All she had to do was make the list. Everyone who joined would have access to different resources. If they couldn't get things on the list, then they'd have to do without until they could buy, or earn, them outside the city.

A loud laugh from the other side of the basement startled her. She tucked the notebook away and started cataloging again. The laugh had been a little manic and a little lustful. She realized that other people would want the privacy of the basement. Teenagers looking for a place to engage in what came natural. That would be fine, she could ignore their fun as long as it stayed away from her corner.

The other activity might not be so easy to avoid. Gangs would find this a perfect location to sell drugs. If they hadn't already, it would be soon. Their customers could come to the library without anyone questioning it. A drug dealer would be more likely to search the whole area than a horny teenager. Another reason to be fast and get out.

Tomorrow, Brian had arranged an after-work tea party with some of his colleague's wives — although he'd called it a social event. She couldn't duck it, he had to remain convinced that she'd dropped her plans. It was a waste of time because none of the vapid women would be useful on the farm. The thought of how many more days would be wasted on keeping Brian happy filled her stomach with acid.

CHAPTER FIVE

Lena took her notebooks off the kitchen table and tucked them into her purse. It was dangerous keeping notes, but she couldn't remember everything without the prompts. It was in code but there was always a chance that someone could decode it. Keeping the books with her was the only way she could feel secure.

Ava would be waiting for her in the library after work. It was the first step to actually getting away. Lena knew they would need more people and every person she recruited came with the risk of exposure.

"Where are you rushing off to?"

When had Brian come home? When had he started to sneak up on her? Lena hoped he hadn't noticed that he'd startled her. She turned with a smile and went to give him a kiss on the cheek. "I'm helping out in the library tonight. I won't be late."

"I set up a meeting for you with Cindy. You know Cindy Maclean?"

Lena couldn't help but think Brian was joking. Cindy Maclean was the wife of the deputy mayor. Lena didn't need that kind of visibility right now.

"Did I forget to mention it?" Brian asked.

His innocent act didn't fool Lena. Brian was hiding something, but was it just his ambition, or was he suspicious of her? If she met with Cindy, Lena figured she could find a way to dodge any obligations that Brian was setting up.

"When is the meeting?" *Please make it tomorrow.*

"I said you could see her at five. She's at city hall for a committee meeting." He turned away as if there was nothing more to say.

Lena bit her tongue on the anger that was pushing her to fight. "I'll make it, but please don't set up commitments for me again without talking about it. I'm busy, and I can't always be available at the last minute." It wasn't the meek agreement that it sounded in her head, but Lena hoped the frustration she heard in the words was only because she could feel it.

"I am sorry. I thought I told you that I was trying to get you involved."

Yes, that conversation had happened, but Lena thought it was a general discussion and not an agreement. There was no point in keeping the conversation going, the longer she stayed to argue, the less time she'd have with Ava.

"Okay, I guess I'll see you later. I'll get some work done before I head out to city hall," she said. Then, not able to resist a final dig, she added, "I don't know what time I'll get home, so you'll have to make your own dinner."

Brian looked up from the pile of papers he'd put on the table while she was talking. "Oh, don't worry. I had a big lunch, so I won't need dinner. Have a nice time."

Lena picked up her bag and left the apartment. As she walked away, she muttered, "Have a nice time? What the hell is he up to? What the hell am I going to do if he keeps interfering?"

Lena sat at her desk in the basement of the library watching time pass on the wall clock. Ava was late. In her head, Lena had worked out the best way to talk to her best friend about leaving. But that conversation needed more time than she had. If Ava didn't show up in the next five minutes, Lena would have to reschedule, and that meant a delay that she couldn't afford.

"Hey," Ava called as she rounded the last row of stacked books. "I was beginning to think I was lost."

Lena laughed, Ava had a sense of direction like the old GPS devices. "It's kind of nice down here," she said. "Well, until kids sneak down to make out, or the occasional drug dealer uses it as a trading post."

Lena checked that they were really alone and then pointed to the folding chair she'd cleared for Ava.

"So, what's the latest crisis?" Ava asked. "You and Brian fighting again?"

"I need to talk to you about something that might be dangerous."

"That sounds ominous," Ava said. Leaning forward, her straight black hair falling to frame her face, she added, "I promise to keep it a secret even if you need help burying Brian's body."

"Not yet," Lena said. "I'm just going to come out with it. I think we need to get out of this place before it becomes a prison. I think we'd be better off living on my aunt May's farm."

Ava pulled back. Lena expected a laugh or snort of disbelief. This Ava was calm and thoughtful. Her brows furrowed in thought, and her eyes unfocused as though she was running an internal analysis of what she'd just heard.

"I need to know what you think," Lena added to fill the silence. The meeting Brian had set up was pressing on her mind and it felt like she was running a race to get everything done. Lena tried to tell herself to calm down, that time wasn't the important thing. That Ava's response was the most critical piece. She would always find a way to explain it if she was late to the meeting with Cindy Maclean.

"Is Brian coming?" Ava finally asked.

"No. He's too happy playing with his pals in the government. I'm not even asking him."

Ava looked around. "Is it safe to talk? Really safe?"

"Yes. We'll hear anyone coming, but I have to go meet someone soon. I know you need to think it over, but can you tell me if I'm being crazy?"

"Who else are you bringing with you?"

"I don't know yet. We need to figure out what skills we lack and then who we can trust with the information."

Ava nodded slowly. "Is this because of that news from New York?"

"Not just that. It's just another straw. Do you want Maya and Jason to grow up here with all the gangs?"

"I haven't had a choice until now," Ava said. "I'm in. I just want to know my kids won't be in more danger on the road than they are here. At least here we know what's dangerous."

Lena glanced at the clock again. She had five minutes before she had to leave. "I haven't thought out the details, and one of the things we'll need to acquire is weapons. But we need someone to join us who can hunt, and defend us." She pulled the notebook toward her. "We need someone who can teach us to defend ourselves."

Ava turned at the sound of voices, but they passed. "We have time to learn things too. We need skills for the journey, and skills for the farms," she said, adding to Lena's list.

Lena made some notes and then shoved everything in her bag. "I have to go meet Cindy. We need to talk again soon. I know there's a lot to plan, but we can't wait forever to get started. The longer we take the more we risk getting caught."

"Yeah, that's true. I know none of this is actually illegal until we steal supplies, but I'm sure the police will find some reason to lock us away for just thinking about it. I wonder why they don't just let people leave."

"It's not people, it's the right people. They don't want to lose teachers and workers, but if a gang member ran off, there wouldn't be a problem."

"Not so sure about that, Lena. Gang members can always do hard labor. Have you noticed there are more arrests every day?"

"Another reason to go." Lena led Ava to the stairs. "When can we meet again?"

"I'm tied up tomorrow. How about Wednesday. Here?"

Lena flicked the light switch off when they reached the bottom of the stairs. "After work. I'll let the librarian know you're helping me so she won't get suspicious."

Lena ran up the steps to the front door of city hall. She had no idea where to find Cindy. Perhaps Brian had left that out on purpose, but the building wasn't that large.

Pulling open the door, she was relieved to hear voices coming from the first conference room on the right. It seemed like the committee meeting was running over. Maybe Cindy wouldn't notice that she was late.

The door to the conference room opened and four people walked out, still talking. Lena knew two of them from the cocktail party. The other two people seemed familiar, but she couldn't place them.

"Are you looking for someone?" one of the strangers asked.

"Cindy Maclean. She's expecting me." Lena tried to sound excited about the opportunity.

"She's just finishing up. Go ahead. I'm sure it's okay." The woman pointed to the conference room and left.

Lena wondered what kind of meeting Cindy had in mind. A conference room wasn't the most inviting place to chat. Was she about to be handed a list of jobs to do? Jobs that would look good to Brian's bosses? She peeked into the room. Cindy Maclean was writing in a leather-bound notebook with an elegant pen. Signs of luxury that would set her apart from the common rabble.

"Cindy, hi," Lena said to get the woman's attention.

She looked up and smiled superficially. "Come on in. I'll just be a minute. We can go get a drink while we talk."

A drink wasn't what Lena wanted. "I need to get back home soon. Can we just talk here?"

Cindy's smile faded for a second then came back. "Oh, don't be silly. Brian can fend for himself while we chat." Cindy was good at getting what she wanted.

"Sure. Can you give me a hint about why we need to chat?"

Cindy didn't answer. She made that last note, snapped the cap on her pen, closed the notebook, and dropped both in a briefcase. Standing she gestured to the door. "Let's just get to that when we are sitting comfortably."

In the bar, Lena waited patiently while Cindy ordered wine and a plate of snacks. It seemed the rationing didn't apply here, but then this was a private club for what was quickly becoming a ruling class.

When their order was placed in front of them, and the waitress had returned to her station, Cindy raised her glass. "Let's raise a cheer to our new friendship, Lena."

Lena clinked her glass with Cindy and then waited.

"I wanted to meet you, Lena, to give you a few pointers on how to get along with Brian's social circle. I'm sure you want to be successful and help him rise." She looked at Lena and then took a sip of her drink, as if expecting Lena to put two and two together. When she didn't respond, Cindy continued, "The thing is we haven't seen you around."

Lena sipped her own wine before answering. "I teach, so I'm not always available for socializing." Why did she feel like one of the high school mean girls had pulled her aside?

"That's very noble of you, but you need different priorities now that Brian is being promoted."

Another thing Brian hadn't mentioned. Although he'd hinted at it, and, perhaps, Lena could admit that the subject had passed her by. "I understand. I appreciate your help."

Now Cindy's smile was genuine. "Wonderful. We'll get you set up with some committees soon. We know you need time to unwind yourself from the little things you did before. Give notice and that kind of thing."

Get out of New Surrey and that kind of thing.

"Thanks. Is there something I can do now to help?" When did she become such a good liar? Usually Lena would feel the blush heat her cheeks as soon as she considered lying, but tonight nothing happened.

"Well, you might want to think about your friends. I mean, to think about if they are the right people to help you now."

"I see," Lena said. Cindy didn't seem to notice the ice in her tone. "Are there any that I might keep?"

"Only you will know that, Lena." Cindy finished her drink and checked her watch. "Oh, I have to run. You can stay as long as you like. I'll take care of the tab on the way out."

She didn't wait for Lena to reply.

Swallowing back the rest of her wine, Lena considered staying and thinking over who she needed on her team, but the place stank of privilege and she couldn't wait to leave.

CHAPTER SIX

Lena noticed the silence and looked around her. It was time to put her classroom in order and lock up so she could get together with Ava in the library.

After the meeting with Cindy, Lena had avoided talking to Brian by claiming a headache and crawling into bed. By morning she'd been able to shed the unpleasant feeling that lingered from contact with the woman. She reported to Brian that they'd had a nice chat, but nothing concrete had come of it.

Brian seemed satisfied with Lena's account of the meeting and said he'd follow up in the next few days. Now, two days later, she was still waiting for him to tell her that he'd volunteered her for something complicated.

"Ms. Custordin? Do you have a minute?"

Lena turned to see Mellow, one of her star pupils standing in the doorway. She seemed poised to run away rather than enter.

"Of course. Grab a seat."

Mellow was pretty in a way that hinted at more than just physical beauty. Her blue eyes showed an intelligence that teenage boys sometimes found intimidating. She wore her long dark blonde hair loose and little makeup. Lena had never seen Mellow with a boyfriend, or many friends at all.

Sitting in the chair across from Lena's, she placed her backpack on the floor and her elbows on the desk. "I don't know what to do."

"Is it about your marks? Or your homework?" Lena didn't want to stand in for a parent. If it was about sex, or anything else personal, she was uncomfortable. But Mellow didn't have parents. She was one of the new orphans. The measles plague had taken her baby brothers at a year old. Her father killed himself for listening to the antivac propaganda. Mellow's mother had just faded away over time, becoming less able to take care of herself let alone a young girl. She'd died when Mellow was only thirteen.

"No. I don't know what to do. I guess I need some advice, and if I go to the counselor, she'll make a fuss. I know I have to make up my own mind, but I have no one to talk to." She took a breath and sat back with her arms crossed.

Lena couldn't turn Mellow away. It was too easy to see the girl's future. "You can tell me. I might not have good advice, but I'll listen and I won't make a fuss." She would break that promise if Mellow was in real trouble, but the girl was sixteen and nowadays that meant she was almost an adult. The fact that she was still in school was unusual; more than half of Lena's teenage students had dropped out to support a family, or start one.

Taking a deep breath, Mellow nodded as though she had come to a decision. "There's a gang that keeps following me, and saying things. I think one of them wants... you know. I don't want to be in a gang. At least I don't want to be one of those girls. If I have to be in a gang, I'll be the leader, not the sex slave." She gave a little laugh at the end of her speech.

Lena wasn't fooled. She knew Mellow well enough to understand that gang life would destroy the girl. She was too strong-willed to bow down to a gang leader and that meant she'd likely be dead within days.

"What do you think you can do?" Lena asked, hoping Mellow had a good solution worked out and just needed to be told she was right.

"I think I have to get away." Mellow tossed her head to clear her hair from her face. "I don't know how else to stop them. I know if I fight, I might win, but I don't want to take that chance. And I don't want to spend my life fighting."

Lena wanted to tell the girl that everything would be okay, and that they would get away together, but she knew that a heart-breaking story wasn't a good reason to join their group. If it were, she'd have a hundred people to take and no way to say no. "Do you think you have to decide today?"

"Probably not. I mean, I think they're going to get more aggressive, but I wasn't planning to run away tonight. I can kind of throw them off for a while by taking different ways to school, I guess."

Lena needed to talk to Ava. She needed another perspective on who they would invite along. "Let me think about it for a while. I might be able to help you out."

Mellow screwed her lips, she wasn't happy that Lena didn't give her an answer. She didn't push at Lena to help, she just grabbed her backpack. "Sure. Um, please don't tell anyone. I'm not sure if running away is okay. I don't want to end up on a work gang just because I... I don't know because I have the bad luck to be pretty."

"It's never bad luck to be pretty, Mellow. Will you tell me who these guys are? If I know maybe someone can stop them."

Mellow was standing now, and it looked like she was about to run from the room. "No. If I get them in trouble, things will only get worse. Promise you won't tell anyone?"

"I promise. Please don't do anything until we talk again."

Mellow nodded and then left. Lena couldn't help but think the girl was in too much danger to wait even a day.

. . .

Lena stopped by the office on her way out of the school. The administration staff had left hours ago, but Lena knew where the key was kept for the student files.

Ten minutes later, Lena arrived at the library, still trying to figure out what to tell Ava about Mellow. The promise didn't matter since she was trying to find a way out for the girl, and Ava wasn't just anyone, she was part of Lena's group — her escape plan buddy. Lena laughed and recognized the taint of hysteria in the sound. Things were going too fast, and not fast enough. They had no viable plan, but here she was recruiting a teenage girl.

As she rounded the corner to her desk, she saw someone there already. For a heartbeat, she froze and then, recognizing Ava's dark hair and easy smile, kept going.

"You are five minutes late, missy," Ava said in her best schoolmarm voice. "Detention for you!"

Lena tossed her bag onto the floor. "Yeah, yeah. If I have detention, you'll have to supervise me."

Ava pushed a pile of books aside. "Maybe detention hall would be a good place to plot our escape. A less dusty one anyway."

"Not as good as this," Lena said. "Too many students getting sent there these days. I swear detention has become a mark of achievement in some of the classes."

"Better than some achievements they're getting outside school," Ava said. "My kids aren't the only ones who are two steps away from gang membership. Maya and Jason are lucky that they have me. Some of the kids see the gangs as a family. There's just too many teenagers living on their own."

Lena couldn't add anything. The city leaders were more interested in setting rules and getting rich than finding a solution to the problem of kids with no parents. Kids like Mellow. "I need to tell you something."

Ava held up a hand. "Me first. I need to say something so we can have the fight and then get on with business. I told my kids we were leaving."

Lena's body went cold. Had she heard right? Ava's kids were too young to keep a secret. "Are you trying to get us punished?"

"I couldn't leave them in the dark until we left. You know there's too many people preying on young kids. I needed to give them a reason to stay straight." Ava's eyes shone with tears.

Lena realized that Ava had been living with this fear for too long. She reached over to hug her. "I wish you had told me. I would have helped," she said. Then letting go of Ava, she added, "It doesn't matter. It's done and you know your kids. If you think they'll keep it secret, then I'll believe you." She didn't feel any easing of the worry that Ava's announcement brought, but it did help her with Mellow's problem.

Lena dug out her planning notebooks. "We need to figure out who to invite along. People who will say yes, or at least we can trust not to go to the police. And I have someone in mind already."

Ava leaned forward, interest plain on her face. "Who? No wait a minute, we should talk about what skills we need first."

"No. I mean, yes we need to talk about skills, but no I need to know what you think about Mellow Jannsen," Lena said.

"She's in my gardening class." Ava frowned and then nodded. "Yes, she'd be great. She knows a lot about growing food. We need that knowledge, right? It's not a good idea just to rely on me for making a farm work."

"She's in trouble. Well, she's almost in trouble. Someone in a gang, probably one of the leaders, seems to have taken a liking to her. I want to ask her along, but I'm afraid my heart is making the decision."

Ava shrugged. "From what I know she's capable and she doesn't have any ties. She doesn't flinch at the dirty work like some of her classmates. She'd be good."

"Okay. I'll talk to her tonight. It'll help to have a third opinion when we plan this out. But we won't have a lot of time. If we leave too late, we'll get to the farm and not be able to plant. It will be a hard winter and spring without crops."

Ava grabbed a sheet of paper and started listing dates. "To get there in time to plant, we need to be gone by mid-June, right? Unless it's in a different growing zone?"

"No, or at least not that different."

Ava continued, "So in the next couple of days we have to figure out what we need in the way of skills and supplies. Then we'll have some time to fill in the gaps. Both of us can lift books from the school, and there's probably useful stuff down here that no one will miss."

Lena looked around at the mess of the basement. There was probably knowledge on everything they might need right in front of her, but it would take more than three weeks to organize it, let alone learn anything. It all felt hopeless, but Lena couldn't let that stop her.

CHAPTER SEVEN

Lena passed Brian on the stairs to their apartment the next day. She was leaving to meet Ava and Mellow. He was coming home from work. He was an hour earlier than usual; in fact, he'd been an hour early for the last three days.

"New shift?" she asked.

"No, just a light work week. I don't need to be in the office all the time now." Brian looked at the bag hanging from Lena's shoulders. "Where are you headed?"

She'd counted on being out of the house before Brian got home. If he was early more often, she'd have to have excuses. "The library. I go there most evenings for an hour or so."

He made a noncommittal noise. Lena moved a step down, hoping their conversation was over.

"Lena, I hope you aren't making a commitment to this book thing."

Lena shrugged, determined not to get offended at his attitude. "You wanted me to get involved with something. I thought this was helping you get ahead."

He went up one stair. "Hiding in the library isn't showing

anyone that you are supporting me. I'll talk to Cindy tomorrow to get you something more visible."

Brian didn't wait for her to respond. He marched up the stairs and through the door to their hallway.

Having to dodge Cindy is just another problem to solve.

Mellow and Ava showed up in the basement ten minutes after Lena had settled. They came in together, chatting. Mellow looked more alive than she had yesterday. When Lena had knocked on her door in the evening, Mellow looked like she'd aged a year. Before Lena could explain the risks of her plan, Mellow had burst into tears. The gang members had been on every route she'd tried to take to avoid them, and she knew she was running out of time. The girl had agreed to go with Lena and wouldn't hear any of the potential problems.

"We can talk," Ava said. "Mellow's set a stack of old magazines up as an alarm. There's no way anyone can sneak up on us without knocking them over."

Lena smiled. If every recruit was this resourceful they would be on their way soon.

"I've been thinking, we need someone with some medical skills, and someone who can help us to find meat. We'll have plenty of vegetables on the farm, but only a few cows — if they've survived."

Mellow pulled a list out of her jeans. "I started thinking last night. We need two lists; what we need to get us there, and how to get through the first year."

Lena reached for the paper. "Be careful who sees this," she said.

Mellow glanced at Ava. "If anyone asks, I'm doing an assignment on how the rural areas might be surviving."

"It's believable," Ava said. "The people here will be farming their own stuff soon enough."

How had she never noticed this talent in her best friend? "You have a bright future in politics if you can lie so easily. Are you sure you want to come along, Ava?"

"I'm happy to stay an amateur in that area," Ava said. "Mellow is better at it than me."

"We'll see. So, let's get everything on the table. I'm sure between us we've thought about all the details we might need."

Getting through the various lists made Lena sure that she wouldn't have been able to do this alone. Mellow and Ava had two completely different takes on what was needed. Between them, they'd identified another ten skills that would be valuable.

"We're never going to get all of this in time without pulling in fifty people," she said when they'd exhausted their ideas.

Mellow moved the lists around as if reorganizing them would help. "Some of it we'll have to learn. Some of it we'll have to do without. How many people do you think we can take?"

Thinking about it in numbers gave Lena a sick feeling. It was like she was choosing whose life to save and who to abandon. It wasn't that bad, she told herself. Some people would thrive in New Surrey.

"It could take us a couple of months to walk to the farm," she said. "We can't take a vehicle; it's too valuable for the council to let go without a fight. I figure we can do this with five or six of us and whatever kids they have. I just don't know who to trust."

"I don't know too many adults," Mellow said. "I can't add any names to the list." She picked up a fresh sheet of paper. "Why don't you two talk about people. I'll go through the books and articles here and see what we should bring with us."

Ava watched her go. "That girl is amazing. How many of your other students would be smart enough to think about those details even if they had a week to come up with ideas?"

"If you'd asked me last week, I would have said none. Now, I'm not sure I know any of them well enough to guess."

Ava turned back to the task. "I can only think of one person we should approach."

That's a hundred times more than me.

"Who? Maybe they'll have someone to add."

"You aren't going to like it," Ava said. "Keith Boatman."

"That guy who runs the outdoors store?" Lena started to say that he wasn't the right person, but changed her mind. "The one who goes fishing and hunting? The guy who brings a ton of the skills we need to survive?"

"Yeah. And the guy who will bring Deb, the useless spoiled ex-cheerleader."

Deb Boatman never had a nice thing to say about anyone or anything. Because she couched her judgement and criticism in sweet words some people never noticed how mean she could be.

"What made you think of him?"

"I get the feeling that he's afraid of something. He's been acting weird. Or weirder than usual," Ava said. She leaned in closer to Lena and whispered, "You know that guy who was found dead a week ago?"

"In your building? Yes. Have they found out who did it?"

Ava shook her head. "I saw his wife talking to Keith a couple of days earlier. Her face was badly bruised. I think her husband was beating her. I was going to talk to her, but then he turned up dead."

"You think Keith did it?"

"I don't know, but if he did, it would be good to have someone along who could do that kind of thing to defend us."

After another hour, they hadn't come up with any new names, so Lena sent them home. It would help with Brian if she came home earlier than expected. Maybe he would get off her back if she paid a little attention to him.

She smelled tomato sauce as she opened the door to their apartment. "Did you make dinner?"

Brian looked up from the pot he was stirring. "Yes. I got a few extra supplies yesterday. You've been so busy lately, I thought I'd start being more self-sufficient. So, I made a big pot and then I can reheat what I need."

Was that a dig at her? If it was, then she'd ignore it. Brian was so eager to get her involved in the social lives of his colleagues he probably hadn't thought about what that meant for her time. "That's a great idea. Sorry I was so late last night."

"No problem. I don't mind an occasional evening alone. Are you hungry?"

On edge, waiting for the other shoe to drop, Lena nodded.

"Go change. I'll get everything ready and we can have a little talk."

There it was. Lena didn't want to fight with Brian, but the constant juggling of half-truths was exhausting. Maybe they could hash out this problem and she could find a balance that allowed her to get ready to leave.

She was about to pull on her favorite pajamas when she decided that a little concession to Brian couldn't hurt. A quick shower refreshed her, and pulling on her blue sweater that Brian loved, along with her own favorite worn out jeans, helped to separate the worries that were tightening her muscles. She'd focus on Brian tonight, and then worry about how to approach Keith tomorrow.

Returning to the kitchen, Lena saw Brian dishing out the pasta which was already covered in sauce. She leaned in and gave his cheek a kiss. "This smells great. I forget how good a cook you are."

He rested his hand on her arm and leaned in for a longer kiss. "I should probably treat you more often. Sit. I also got a little treat from the club."

Lena couldn't stop herself from wondering how she could take advantage of Brian's new found power to get food. They would need much more than she could skim from the weekly rations when they finally left.

The little treat was a bottle of imported wine. The government must have a private cellar. No one could buy French wine any more. It was another thing that the powers that be considered not worth the effort of transporting — at least to everyone.

"What have they got you doing at the library anyway?" Brian asked.

"Sorting through the stacks in the basement," Lena answered carefully.

"How about changing to something a little more visible? Maybe volunteering with the after-school programs? A few of the wives do that one day a week."

So, this was the little chat.

"I spend all my working days with kids, Brian. I don't know if I have the energy to spent my free time with them."

He topped up her wine. "Well, if not that, maybe something at city hall? They are looking for someone to help organize some of the events."

I'll have to give in on something. "I could probably find the time to do an activity one day a week. I really like the library, Brian."

"I'm a little worried about your reputation," Brian said. He kept his eyes on the plate of pasta in front of him. "When people don't see you now and then, they start to think you're up to something."

Was that true? Lena hadn't thought that anyone would care. "I'm not up to anything but helping to catalogue what's in the library. I don't want to over commit my time. I need to be here for you."

"We both know I can muddle through on my own. In fact, I'll be out more in the evenings too. I have a few committees to lead now."

So how much could her hiding in the library be hurting his

career? "Okay. I'll look into some other stuff. I'll cut down my time at the library and see what I can do about helping with events." And maybe she could meet with Ava and the others — there would be others soon — somewhere else.

"I appreciate it. I'm sure Cindy can help you work it out. She's anxious to get you up to speed."

Up to speed on what? On who her friends were? On what she did every minute of every day? "Lovely," Lena said. "I'll call her to arrange a time."

"I'll take care of it. You can wind down your efforts at the library while I set something up."

"What kind of things do you think you'll find?" Lena asked. She hadn't meant to ask him anything. She'd meant to keep her mouth shut and find a way to dodge all of Brian's plans.

"Nothing you'll find hard. I want you to succeed. So we'll start with a little function or a small committee." Brian picked up his empty plate and took it to the sink.

He couldn't even look at her while he patronized her. Lena could feel her control slip. It wasn't the time to start a fight, but her logic was being swamped by the anger at being treated like a child, and maybe not fighting was more suspicious. "Brian, if I'm going to use up my time with these people, I should be doing something worthwhile."

He turned slowly. Lena could see he wasn't angry. He was patient. "It's more important that you succeed. We'll get you working on more important things later. Are you finished with that?"

Lena looked down at her plate. She couldn't eat any more of the food, no matter how much she hated to waste it. The conversation was twisting her stomach. "Yes. I'll do the dishes." If she kept busy, maybe she'd stop pushing the fight.

Brian nodded and took his glass of wine to the living room. "Is there something you would like to do?"

Turning on the water, Lena avoided the question. As she

washed the plates, she turned her mind to a plan. She needed Brian to get off her back. Was a fight a good idea? It would feel good to get her fears and frustration out, but it was dangerous. If she let herself get too angry, she might say something wrong.

"Are you washing the pattern off?" Brian interrupted Lena's thoughts.

She'd been washing the same plate the entire time. "I guess I'm thinking. What happens if I get too involved with these functions and committees? I might not see you much."

"It will be worth it in the long run," he said then flipped open his paper.

"What's the long run, Brian?" Maybe it was something she could live with.

"You and me living well no matter what happens. I don't want you to worry about things."

"I do worry. I can't do what these women do, Brian. I won't live 'well' when people I know are starving, or hurt, or in danger. I can't be part of that."

Brian put down his paper. "You would rather be like everyone else? You'd rather eat old pasta and canned beans than fresh vegetables and the occasional steak?"

The way he confirmed her worst fears burned in Lena's gut. This was not the man she'd married. "Yes. If that's what everyone else has."

"Oh please, Lena. You are just saying that. Calm down. It wouldn't be a good idea to show up to help with that kind of attitude."

"Then maybe you should stop trying to get me to help out with those vapid social climbing idiots." There her temper had ripped the skin off the emotions, and she hadn't said anything about getting out.

Brian looked hurt. Despite the fact that she wanted to hurt him, the look still dug a knife in her heart. Lena sealed her lips to stop the apology slipping out. If she said sorry, he'd have her serving tea to socialites within the week.

"I had no idea you felt that strongly. Of course, if you'd rather not help out, then I won't push. Stay with your library, and I won't mention it again."

That was more like the old Brian. He hated confrontation. He always withdrew, at least for a while. If she handled it right Brian wouldn't raise the subject again for days. He'd also refuse to talk to her and that meant she'd lose any information on what was coming from city hall; a good compromise.

"Thanks," she said. "I will."

He nodded and picked up the paper again.

The silent treatment was starting.

CHAPTER EIGHT

Lena stood outside Keith's shop. There were a few people on the street, so she couldn't just stand around. Turning to stare in the window while she collected her thoughts, Lena noticed the fishing supplies arranged around a fake campfire. She'd been inside a couple of times before. Brian had taken up the idea he'd go fishing, so she'd bought him a rod, a reel, and a box of brightly colored lures. He'd never gone and the equipment sat in the closet alongside a baseball bat and glove, and a set of skis. She'd eventually given up on the challenge of finding activities for him.

Now she was going to test her ability to recruit someone to the cause. Her only plan was to sidle up to the topic by asking about some of the gear Keith sold. If she thought they could get away with it, Lena would buy tents and travel food for the trip. But even if Keith didn't report them, Lena couldn't take the chance that someone would get curious about the purchases and tell the authorities.

She tried to believe it was only paranoia, but in the core of her being she knew that if that kind of surveillance wasn't already being done, it would be soon.

She couldn't delay any longer, so Lena pushed open the door and stepped inside. It smelled of dust, some kind of oil, and pet food. The walls were stacked with camping equipment. There were aisles of everything you would ever need to go fishing, and behind the counter, locked securely and guarded with bars, were the guns. Seeing them on the wall made Lena realize that they needed Keith no matter how much she disliked him. And that the world outside the city was probably a place where everyone needed a gun.

"Can I help you?" Keith called as he came from the back room. "Oh, Lena, right? Fishing."

Lena shook her head. "I'm here for something different this time."

Keith leaned against the counter waiting for her to go on. He was old, maybe in his fifties. His face and head were covered in a short, grey stubble of hair. His age didn't make him look weak. Keith Boatman looked like he could take on a bear. He was compact and hard like he'd lived life in the mountains.

"Do you want me to guess?" he finally asked.

"Sorry, no. I need information on camping," she said. Was that too blatant? "I was thinking of proposing it as a section of the life skills classes."

Keith rummaged around under the counter and then came up with a ledger. "I've got some stuff, but you know I can't restock any more. No shipments from manufacturers, no glossy catalogues. You know how it is."

She nodded. "Are there basics that we can get for the class, or information on how to make do with... I don't know, whatever is around?"

He stared at her. Was he trying to figure out if she was doing something wrong? Lena knew too well that if she wasn't careful she'd fill the silence and make a mistake. She'd used the silence tactic with her students often enough. Knowing how it worked didn't make it easier to keep her mouth shut.

"You are talking survival skills not camping." Keith flipped open the ledger. "You know enough about it to teach?"

"I don't know anything about it."

"You think kids will need to survive outside the city sometime soon?"

Was it an opening, or a trap? "Things are changing. Who knows what these kids will need to face. If I don't teach them something, they'll end up in gangs, or addicted to drugs — or both."

"I've thought about getting out and living in a cabin myself." He started making a list.

"Why don't you?"

"Deb. My wife, she wouldn't like that. She's too fond of the luxuries that we can still get, and I'm too fond of her to take her away."

"What if you didn't have to live in a cabin?" Lena tossed the words out and kept her eyes on the merchandise.

"Like another town?"

"Yeah, a town in the country. Or a farm. Maybe a community farm. You'd get to be part of something without all the rules and stresses of living here."

"I might be able to get Deb to agree to that," Keith said. "People here are getting nasty. It'll take a lot of rules and enforcement to keep us from heading to anarchy." He pushed the list toward her. "You'll need these things. I got some in stock, and I can show people how to make do. You want me to teach?"

The offer was way beyond what Lena had expected. If the classes were real, Keith would be a great teacher — well as long as someone else was there to make sure he didn't scare the kids.

"I'll ask about it." She put the list in her pocket. "What you said, about people getting nasty. I've been worried about that."

He leaned in and lowered his voice. "You worried about your kids?"

"I don't have any."

"Me and Deb decided not to have any either. We didn't see much future for them, so why bother."

It had been the same for Lena. Brian didn't care one way or another about kids. Lena had her students. No matter how much she cared for them, they moved on and she didn't have to feel accountable when they chose a bad path.

"A farm would give kids a future," she said.

"Your husband is that Brian Custordin guy, right?" Keith straightened and his eyes hardened with suspicion. "He's getting up in the security side of city hall."

Brian wasn't in the security force. As the words formed to deny it, Lena realized that she didn't know if Brian had changed careers. "I'm not my husband."

"You here to trick me into saying something? Is the law trying to take over my shop?"

Something she'd never considered. Would they take over all of the shops? It would be a great way to control people. And it was another good reason to get out.

"I don't know." Lena looked over her shoulder to make sure there was no one else in the shop. "It's not beyond them. Keith, I'm looking for people to join me in leaving. I hope you'll come and, if not, I trust you won't tell anyone. I know you've taken justice into your own hands and I think you did the right thing."

He pulled back. Lena's heart stopped. Had she misjudged?

Keith walked to the front door, flipped the open sign over, and turned the lock. When he came back he beckoned Lena into his back room.

Inside, the small office was crammed with supplies.

"I've been planning for a while but had nowhere to go," he said. "This won't be enough for a big group for long, so I need to know more."

Lena moved a stack of books off the chair and sat. "We don't have much of a plan. I have a farm. It was left to me by my aunt."

Could this be so easy? Lena kept her doubts quiet as she listened to Keith work out some details that she would never have considered.

CHAPTER NINE

Tik stood in the shadows watching the runners move between the stash of items and the junkies and users. Their job was to barter items for hits of the drug of the day. Today that was heroin. Tik's job was to make sure no one got out of hand.

The other supervisors took their frustrations out on the junkies. They'd ask for higher value items all the time. The junkies did what they always did, stole something so they could get their hit. Tik knew that was a bad idea. More theft meant more complaints and eventually the cops. If the cops came down hard on them, business would stop for a while. Keeping the cost down and the thefts under control meant that the trade kept going.

Junkies didn't think past their next high. Tik figured it was up to him and the rest of the gang to do the thinking.

He wasn't usually stuck here with the runners, but he'd pissed off the chief and was doing penance.

The kid, Jason, was hanging around again. Tik hated recruiting. The gang always wanted more kids, but if everyone was in the gang, who would buy the drugs, or gamble, or pay for sex?

Jason wouldn't take the hint. Tik had scared off that two-niner who'd tried to get the kid to deliver some crack to a customer. That's one of the easiest ways to get a kid into the gang. The two-niners were supposed to keep to the east of the city, but they didn't often obey agreements.

"Hey," Jason said.

He'd snuck up while Tik was thinking. Not good. What else had he missed.

"Get lost." Tik shoved Jason with his elbow.

Jason dodged and then came in closer. "I need to talk to you."

"No, you don't. You don't want to join the gang. You have a mom and a sister. You need to get back to them."

Jason didn't move. "Yeah, I know. That's what I want to talk about."

If Jason was determined to be initiated, then there was nothing he really could do. If Tik didn't take him in, Jason would find someone else. "I can't go anywhere. Say what you came to say."

"It's a secret. You have to promise not to tell."

The kid was still young enough to think a promise would hold. "How do you know I can be trusted?"

Jason looked around him. "I keep a lot of secrets about you. If you break your promise, it'll be bad, but it'll be worse for you to have the cops know what's going on here."

So not so naïve. "Be careful who you threaten, kid."

"I'm not threatening you. It's kind of like insurance."

"I'm not sure you know what insurance is," Tik said. Jason had caught his interest. How bad a secret could an eleven-year-old have? "I promise."

Jason moved close and whispered in Tik's ear in the same way a runner would if he wanted advice on a trade. "My mom and some other people are leaving New Surrey soon. I think you should come with us."

What the fuck? "Why would I go with you?"

"You don't want to stay here, Tik. These guys'll kill you. Besides you saved my life that day. I owe you."

Tik didn't take any of the drugs his gang sold. It was a matter of pride, and survival, that he stayed away from that life. Once you were hooked, you were in forever. That's the only reason Tik knew that Jason's offer was real and not some drug fueled dream.

"Does your mom know you're here?"

Jason looked out to the street as though his mom was standing there. "No. She'd kill me if she knew."

Tik's mother had died when he was three. His dad lived until six years ago when Tik was twelve, then he got killed at work. The thought of there being someone in his life who cared about where he was, or what he did, hurt.

"What if she says I can't come?" Tik couldn't let Jason pull the offer away. The kid was right. Tik didn't really fit in, and one day that would kill him.

"She won't," Jason said. "We need people. We need guys. But it would be good if you could contribute something." He said it as though repeating words he'd heard.

"What do you need?"

"All kinds of stuff. You should probably talk to mom's friend. She's kinda in charge."

So, it wasn't even up to Jason's mom. Tik had something to use as leverage on her. Saving her son's life should buy Tik into the group. But if the decision was up to some stranger... Tik decided not to worry about it. If they said no, his life would be the same. And he could just take off alone now that Jason had put the idea into his head.

"Yeah, so when do I meet her?"

"I'll let you know." Jason ran off.

Tik returned to watching the runners. No one seemed to be dead or fighting so he hadn't missed anything important.

. . .

"I don't know about your loyalty, Tik," Basso said.

Tik didn't want to be here. The message arrived just as he was handing over the corner to his replacement.

"See the boss." It was said in a monotone, but Tik knew a threat when he heard one.

Now he stood in front of Basso. Three enforcers stood behind Tik so he couldn't leave until dismissed.

"I'm as loyal as I was before. What's the problem?" He was glad his voice was steady. Inside he knew that this was going badly. If Basso had noticed Tik's lack of enthusiasm, then it wouldn't be long before Tik was lying in a pool of blood somewhere dark and dirty.

"You need to recruit. That's how I know you are loyal. You need to bring in a new member soon, Tik. I want you to sit at my right-hand. I can't have that if you ain't loyal. I don't like not getting what I want. You get me?"

So, an ultimatum with a juicy reward at the end. Tik knew death was the unstated option. If he got promoted, he wouldn't have to recruit, he wouldn't have to stand on corners watching the sad progress of addiction. But he'd still be part of the destruction. "Only one, boss?"

Basso smiled and waved his fingers as if what he wanted was a trifle. "One particular recruit, yes."

Tik knew the name before Basso said it.

"I want that Jason kid. His mom is a teacher. It will get us into the school, and then we'll have them lining up to join."

The police were useless except around the schools. The parents — the few that cared — made sure the gangs couldn't enter. The cops did what it took because it was easier than dealing with parents.

"Dangerous, but I guess it's doable," Tik said. He had to stall for time. Whatever Jason had in mind for an escape was looking like the only option. Tik knew he wouldn't survive on his own. He didn't know how to find food, He didn't know how to build a

house. All he knew was gang skills, so he'd end up trading his old
gang for a new one. At least in Basso's, gang Tik knew the rules.

"I guess you want to use the kid against his mother? It'll take
time to set up."

Basso lifted a glass in a toast. It looked and smelled like cheap
whiskey. The guy could get his hands on the good stuff, but he
seemed to prefer rotgut. "Take all the time you need, Tik, my
friend. As long as it's done before school's out."

That gave him until the end of June. "Consider it done."

He turned to leave, hoping the enforcers wouldn't make a big
deal of it. They stood aside and one opened the door.

There was nowhere to go but home, so here he stood in his one-
room hovel, staring at his stash of supplies. It was the only thing
he had that might buy him into Jason's plan. Probably not enough,
but a start. He could get more from the gang's hoard, but only at
the last minute. There would be retribution if Basso's guys could
find Tik after he stole from them.

When he met this woman in charge, Tik figured he'd need two
things. One, look less like a gang member. She probably knew he
was, but if he looked respectable, then maybe she wouldn't say no
right away. If he had time, he could talk her into taking him. That
was a gang skill that might be valuable.

The other thing; an estimate of what this stash contained.
He'd never really checked it before, just eaten the food that
wouldn't last and stacked up the merch. If he knew how many
people would be going, he could estimate how many days he could
supply. And he'd know how much more he needed to take from
the gang.

Tik cleared a space on the floor and started sorting his loot.
Cans of soup, fruit, and vegetables. Dried beans and some stuff
that said MRE and Astronaut Food on the label. If this was just
for him, he'd make it last a month. He knew how to get by on low

rations from when he first joined the group. Runners didn't get much of a share.

He had clothes in his stockpile, but how many of them would fit his size? He was skinny and tall. Well, maybe someone in the group would know how to make the clothes work.

What he needed from the gang were weapons. He had his knife. He could ask Basso for a gun, but then it might be suspicious. And if they couldn't find bullets, a gun wasn't going to help. More knives and maybe a few bats would help. There were things like bows and arrows in the gang storehouse. Tik didn't know how to use them, but maybe there was someone who did.

Tik blinked away his fatigue, but it kept pushing back. He needed sleep. If he showed up at this meeting and passed out, it wouldn't look good. He dragged his sleeping bag over and curled up between the two piles. One that he'd offer as payment for his future, and the other would be left for whoever found it. The second pile was bigger.

CHAPTER TEN

Jason found him the next day.

"I know where we can meet with mom's friend." He grabbed Tik's arm and started walking.

Tik pulled away. "First of all, never touch me like that. Second, stay away from this neighborhood unless you want to join up."

Jason frowned at him. "Yeah, I know this is a bad place. Mom would kill me if she knew I was here. But I don't know how else to find you."

The kid had a point. "Fine. What did your mom say about her friend?"

Jason looked at the ground. If he couldn't lie convincingly, Jason would be a problem. Not the kind of problem you get rid of permanently — unless you were in a gang. "When you're going to tell a lie, look the person in the face."

"I wasn't going to lie," Jason said, staring at Tik. "I just didn't tell my mom. I said she would kill me if she knew I was here. She'd kill me more if she knew I talked to you. I wouldn't get a chance to tell her how you saved my life. She'd kill me and then come after you."

Tik grinned at the thought of an angry mother attacking

Basso's right-hand man. Maybe she'd have a chance. "So, this friend of hers. What does she know about me?"

Jason kept his eyes on Tik. "That you are a good guy and deserve to be with us."

Now he couldn't tell if the kid was lying or not. *Fast learner.* "She didn't ask any questions? Does she know about the gang?"

"No." Jason reached for Tik again and then seemed to think twice. "Look, we can meet her in the library. She's in the basement. Let's go before she leaves."

If he was going to escape with these people, Tik knew he had to trust them. It was hard to find that inside him.

The basement of the library was empty. The air was dusty and smelled moldy, like someone had left things sitting damp for too long. They worked their way around shelves of papers and broken books to the woman sitting behind a desk piled with more books and papers. She was staring at them as though they'd broken into her home. Tik figured that was a good reaction. Until they left, anyone would be a threat. Maybe he'd be good as security.

"Jason," she said. "What are you doing here?"

The kid coughed and looked up at Tik. When no help was offered, he turned back to the woman. "Um, Mrs. Custordin, I brought Tik to talk to you. I think we need to take him."

"Jason, did you tell people?"

The kid took a deep breath and then started talking like he was afraid of any interruption. "Just Tik. I promise. He saved my life, and I think he needs to come with us because I'm afraid he might not be okay."

The woman looked at Tik. "I don't know what you did to save Jason, but holding it over him like a debt isn't the act of a hero."

Tik stepped forward and held out his hand to shake. The woman looked at it but didn't respond. Okay a test. "I'm Tik Allan. I didn't make Jason bring me. I saved his life by keeping him away from my gang. I don't expect anything from him, or you."

Lena nodded. "Lena Custordin." Now she held out her hand.

Tik shook on the introduction. So far there was hope. "I do want to join you, and I have things I can bring."

Lena looked at Jason. "I don't care who you think you owe, Jason. Don't tell anyone else. Now, go home. Tell your mother what's going on."

When Jason opened his mouth to respond. Lena looked at him with that teacher expression. Tik remembered it from when he was a kid. You didn't argue with that look.

"Don't pretend she knows what you did. Ava would have told me."

Jason ran from the basement. They heard his footsteps as he stomped up the stairs. Tik wasn't sure if the stomping was about anger, or just the speed Jason was going.

"So, Tik. How do I know I can trust you?"

Tik had been practicing this answer since he'd woken up. He figured this group was another kind of gang. One that was more interested in survival than power, but it would still have a leader and a set of rules to follow.

"I need to get out. I can't trust anyone," he said. Then pointing to his clean shirt and jeans. "Don't let this fool you, I'm in a gang. I don't want to be, and now I'm being forced to decide on something that will make it impossible for me to leave. I need to get out. Nothing can be as bad as what I'm in now."

"I'll have to figure out how to verify it. But this isn't a joyride, Tik. I need people who can contribute. What can you bring to us?"

"Okay, Mrs. Custordin," he said.

"Lena," she said shaking her head. "Just Lena from now on."

Tik figured she had a reason for dumping her married name, but it wasn't important right now. "I have supplies; things you need and can't get. I'm good at keeping people safe. I figure I can do that while we're on the road as easily as I can do it on the street at night."

Lena moved some papers around on the desk. Tik could tell she was arguing with herself. It was the same way with users. They really wanted to do one thing, not take the drug, but they were hooked and they had no choice.

"You need to prove what you have. I really don't like this, Tik. Jason took away my options when he talked to you."

Relief made Tik dizzy. It didn't matter if she was unhappy at being forced to take him. He had time to show her that he could be trusted. She was saying yes.

Proof would be easy. Tik ran home to get some samples. He'd show that and give Lena an estimate of the total. He'd even tell her where he lived so she could check herself. For the first time in as long as he could remember, he felt like things were going to get better. Soon he'd be out of Basso's reach and then he'd get to live without looking over his shoulder for the violence he knew was just out of sight.

A quick glance around before he opened his door showed the hallway clear.

Inside, Tik knew exactly where there was a bag big enough to hold the things Lena would value. He'd take those MREs for sure and some of the cans. Lena would know what else they needed. What else he could get from the storehouse.

"Tik, we been looking for you."

The voice belonged to Nigel. Tik didn't need to look up to know that he'd brought Al and Dicko with him. Every time Tik got something, Nigel tried to take it, or destroy it.

Tik stood and then turned slowly. He had no weapons on him except his fists. Nigel likely had a knife or a set of knuckles. "Basso want me?" Maybe they were here on orders — not likely, but a guy can hope.

"Not as such," Nigel said. His buddies kept silent. "I'm taking it on myself to insert a little urgency to your task. Basso doesn't know what we do."

He didn't want to ask. Nigel would eventually tell him. The guy could never keep his mouth shut. That's the main reason Tik rose faster in the ranks. Basso didn't like talkers.

"I'm working on it. I know it's important to get this kid in before all his friends end up on their summer work program," he said.

Nigel giggled. "It's not the kid. It's the mom. Basso is going to use the kid to get the mom to sell in the school."

"That won't work," Tik said. It didn't make sense. Yeah, Ava would probably do whatever Basso wanted to keep Jason safe, but she would be caught right away.

"You saying the boss is wrong?"

The words came out innocently as if the question was valid. There was only one safe answer that would work for Basso. Nigel was just playing games. Even if he'd made up the reason, Tik knew that Nigel had another agenda.

The three thugs were spreading out as much as they could in the small space. This visit was just an excuse to give him a beating. Nigel wanted to be the one to bring in Jason. Tik knew he didn't have much chance to avoid injury, but he'd try.

Dicko was closest. Before he had a chance to start swinging, Tik bent and picked up a can smashing it into Dicko's face. He went down. Tik knew it wouldn't be for long.

Al was on him before Tik could rebalance for another swing. He ducked but not soon enough. Al's fist caught him on the shoulder.

Tik kicked out, connecting with Al's knee. Not hard enough to put him out of commission, but enough to hurt.

Nigel stayed back while Tik dealt with his friends. Nigel would step in to do his damage as soon as the other two had immobilized Tik, if he kept to his usual practice.

Al punched him in the kidneys just as Dicko got to his feet.

With two thugs on the attack, Tik had no chance. Al and Dicko were showing off for Nigel and trying to pretend they hadn't been hurt.

He warded off the first few blows, but Dicko landed one to the side of his head and Al hit Tik's hip. He went down in paralyzing pain.

Then Nigel stepped in and all three were kicking and punching, sometimes connecting with each other rather than their victim.

It seemed to last forever, but he was still conscious when they stopped.

"No need to kill him, boys." Nigel was wheezing with effort. "The boss needs to hear it from him."

He leaned down and whispered, "You tell Basso you're too hurt to get the kid. Look at you, anyone with a drop of sense would run away before you can open your mouth."

One last kick to Tik's ribs then Nigel led his mini-gang out.

CHAPTER ELEVEN

When he was alone, Tik tried to stand but his arms couldn't support him enough to push him off the floor. There was no grind of broken bones, so he knew it was just the effect of the beating. He had to talk to Basso.

He crawled to the small shower and turned on the hot water. Still on the floor, he stripped his clothes and pulled himself into the stall. He still couldn't stand, but the warmth of the water was bringing life back to his arms and legs. He could feel the stinging where the beating had broken the skin, but it was mostly bruises. It would fade fast, he hoped. His skin wasn't dark enough to hide the bruise, but it wasn't light enough to make them look real bad. He pulled some of his hair over his face, hoping to cover his bruises, but the touch of it on his black eye was too much. Pulling it back in an elastic wasn't a great way to hide the damage, but at least he wasn't blinking through the curls.

By the time the shower ran cold, he'd managed to stand and clean the blood off his face. Turning the water off, Tik stepped in front of the mirror above his sink. It was steamed over.

Taking his towel, and fighting the pain of moving his arms,

Tik wiped the glass. They'd managed to do little damage to his face. A black eye and a split lip wouldn't get in his way.

The rest of his body was battered and he could see the places where bruises would form over the next few days. He'd be stiff, and in more pain than a few aspirin could solve.

He'd manage.

Tik wouldn't touch any of the available painkillers. It was too easy to slip from needing them for pain to needing them for escape.

A half hour later, he was dressed and standing outside Basso's office. Nigel was nowhere to be seen. Tik could only hope he was nursing his fist and toes from administering the beating.

The office door opened. Tik walked through to see Basso lounging on the couch drinking a beer and checking a gold necklace; one that looked like it was made from heavy ropes.

"Shit, what happened? The kid fight back?"

Everyone laughed. Everyone always laughed when the boss said anything that might be funny.

"Not the kid. Did you send someone to do this?"

Basso sat up, dropping the jewelry onto the couch. "No. If I want you beaten, I'll bring you here so I can enjoy it. Who did it?"

"I'm not a rat," Tik said. He was half hoping that Basso would make him tell, but didn't need the new beating it would take. "Just let everyone know to leave me alone so I can get on with it. It's going to be harder to approach the kid now that I look like I'm a fighter."

Basso glanced at his closest henchman. "Make sure the message gets out." He stood and looked closer at Tik. "How bad is it?"

"I'll live. I'll get the kid for you."

"Make sure you do, Tik. If you fail, what you feel right now will be easy compared to what I'll do to you personally before I kill you."

He tried not to flinch, but he couldn't help it. Basso was unpredictable and liked to remind people of that. He was capable of carrying out the threat even if Tik did bring Jason in.

"Why this kid, boss?" It couldn't hurt to ask, or it couldn't hurt much more than he already did.

"Not your business," Basso said. "Just get me the kid."

Tik nodded and turned to leave. Maybe Nigel would get the message and maybe not, but the boss was alerted to the problem. That's all Tik needed.

Tik had to get the samples before he met Lena again. He was supposed to be back in the library by now. He figured being late was better than going empty handed.

When he approached his door, he could see that it was open. He'd locked it before leaving. If Nigel had come back to punish Tik for going to Basso, then he'd get a surprise. Tik had weapons stashed outside.

He retreated to the end of the hall where there was a loose panel in the wall. He pulled the panel off and took out a set of knuckles and a crowbar, an extra-long one he'd taken from a firehouse. This time he'd be the one walking away.

He kept close to the wall as he returned to his door. The floor was less likely to creak if he stayed away from the center of the hallway. Also, creeping up to the open door would let him react if someone came out.

No one challenged him. Tik listened before he used the crowbar to push his door wider. There was no one there.

He stepped inside, pulling the door closed.

There was nothing inside.

All of his supplies were gone.

Tik's head got light. He leaned on the crowbar as if it were a cane.

Don't panic.

It was easy to say that, but panic has a mind of its own. Tik could feel the adrenalin in his system burning through his veins. Trembling started in his fingertips and spread out until it felt like his heart had stopped beating and started flickering.

Don't panic.

There was only one thing to do. If he didn't go meet Lena and tell her what happened, he'd never convince her to trust him. He knew that not showing up would be like a betrayal, and Lena would worry that he was turning her in.

He drew in a few deep breaths, ignoring the stab of pain from his bruises and put the crowbar on the floor. He was keeping the knuckles in case he bumped into someone.

At the library, he made his way to the back of the basement. Lena looked up and frowned. It wasn't a frown of anger, it was concern.

She started toward him. "What happened?"

Tik shook his head. "Just a little disagreement. Look, I have to tell you something."

"You don't have the supplies," Lena said like she'd expected it.

For a second, Tik wondered if she'd had someone steal his stuff, but only for a second. If he expected her to trust him, then he'd have to trust her.

"They got stolen. I can get more. I can get enough."

She cocked her head and looked him up and down. "How do I know that won't suddenly get stolen?"

"I'll hide it. I'll give you the key so you know where it is. You can take it or move it or whatever," Tik could hear the desperation in his voice. "Just, please, don't say I can't come."

"Do you have something to help with the pain?"

The question startled Tik. "Yeah, some stuff."

"Okay. You have to replace your supplies fast. I need to see them, Tik. We can't rely on last minute changes. I have to know that we have enough to get us on our way." She looked at him again. "Can you get enough food for up to ten people for a week? Only what we can carry. I don't have access to a vehicle."

Tik swallowed the lump in his chest. He didn't like this feeling of being dependent on someone. "Yeah. Uh, thanks."

"Don't thank me. We may be worse off out there than we are here." She snorted a laugh. "We might all be making the worst mistake of our lives."

"Maybe of your life, Lena. There's nothing worse than the life I have," he said. "Can I find you here when I have the stuff?"

Lena looked around her. "In my den? Yeah. I'm here almost every day after school. If that changes, I'll leave a note."

There was only one way to get his stuff back fast. Tik had to see Basso again. It wasn't a good idea to keep going back to him. If Tik was trying to be his right-hand man, would he find a way to get the stolen goods back alone? Probably, but that wasn't an option. Now Tik had to go in hard and demanding.

He didn't wait to be announced, just pushed past the guard, and shoved the door open.

Basso was talking to someone. He looked up at Tik and the other guy turned around.

Nigel!

"What do you want now, Tik? Do I have to hold your hand through this? Did I pick the wrong guy?" Basso wasn't really angry.

Tik figured it was just a show for Nigel who smirked at the words.

"I don't know, boss. Shouldn't being your right-hand guy mean I get some respect? I mean, disrespecting me is really disrespecting you, right?"

Nigel paled. Tik didn't need to rat him out, the guy had no poker face. He'd be confessing at the slightest pressure. Any other time, Tik would have pushed, but now he just needed his stuff back.

Basso watched both of them, kind of like a snake in the shadows deciding who to bite. Then a smile crossed his face, "Yeah, Tik. That's exactly what it means. What happened?"

Tik watched Nigel as he spoke. "My place got robbed. All my shit is gone. I want it back."

Nigel swallowed. Tik wasn't sure that he'd been responsible for the theft, maybe Nigel was just worried he'd be blamed.

"You know who did it?" Basso asked.

"No. Even if I did, I told you I'm not a rat." Tik saw a twitch start in the corner of Nigel's right eye. The guy knew he'd made a mistake, and now he owed Tik a favor.

"You know anything about what's been going on with Tik?" Basso asked Nigel.

"No, boss. It looks like he's had a run of bad luck. You need me to protect him?" Nigel's words were smooth, but Tik saw the twitch increase. The boss saw it too.

"Yeah. Well, I'll leave you to figure out what to do. But I expect Tik to get his stash back today. I don't want word getting out that people can't rely on each other in my gang."

Basso kept his eyes on Nigel. Tik had to give it to the man. Nigel didn't sweat or mumble. The only evidence of his growing fear was the twitch. "I'll get my guys on it."

Tik stayed with Basso as Nigel swaggered across the room to leave. They stood in silence for a few minutes. Tik knew better than to speak or try to leave without permission. He'd won the battle, but he was still making the boss deal with things.

"Is this how you'll be when I promote you?" Basso asked.

Basso wasn't looking at Tik. He was sorting through a pile of jewelry and gems that likely came from the last shift of runners.

Tik wasn't fooled. Basso was focused on him. The message was plain. *Don't bother me again until you have what I need.*

"It's just competition, boss. I figured you needed me to concentrate on this Jason kid. When I'm promoted, I'll be able to focus on keeping order." Tik waited. Just because the answer was reasonable was no guarantee that Basso would accept it.

"Was it Nigel?"

Was this a test? Ratting was one thing that danced the line between loyalty to the boss and loyalty to the gang. "Do you really need to know, boss?"

Basso looked up. "You need to figure that out, Tik."

There was no hint in Basso's voice about which option Tik was facing. "I'll take care of it, boss. If I think it's something you need to know, I'll tell you. But first I need to get my shit together so I can go after this kid."

"Fine, Tik. You go now. Don't come back unless you have the kid in tow. Understand?"

Tik nodded. Whatever the real plan was, Jason would be gone before Basso realized he'd lost his easy way into the school.

Tik didn't go home right away. He didn't want to run into Nigel for one thing. And he had to find a place to keep his stash. If he did that first, maybe the stuff would be there by the time he got home.

On the east side of town there were a bunch of half completed condos. The developer had abandoned his project when the suicides had started. Maybe he was one of them. Tik didn't care. One of the condos would work as a storehouse. He stopped to buy the tools he needed to install a lock and then went to pick out a location.

It took him until dark to get the right place locked up and more secure than his apartment. By the time he got home, his place was full again. He spent the next few hours carting the stash to the condo. When it was done, his body was too stiff for him to do anything but lay on his bed.

The next day, Tik stayed home. Basso wouldn't expect anything to be done. It would be the most painful day for Tik, but instead of resting and letting his body get more and more useless from the damage, he stretched and kept busy with little chores. It hurt like hell, but tonight he'd be mobile and tomorrow he'd be almost back to normal.

As soon as he heard kids passing his apartment on their way home from school, Tik showered and dressed so he could meet Lena.

The library basement was quiet as usual. Tik knew that this was a prime location for selling anything — at least until the librarian clued in and called the cops. It would be good for their purposes as long as Lena could explain her visitors.

She was there at the desk writing something on an index card. Tik guessed that she had a real reason for being here that had to be done once in a while.

"Hey," he said quietly.

Lena jumped. "Oh, Tik. Sorry I was miles away. Not a good idea, I guess. So, did you get the problem solved?"

He dug out the key. "Yeah. The address is on the tag. I'll add to the stuff as long as I can. Let me know if there's anything specific we need."

She pocketed the key. "Okay. Ava's going to be here soon. Do you want to meet her?"

Tik touched his black eye. "Maybe when I look less like a gangster. I need to tell you something."

"About Jason? About why you want to protect him so much?"

She was smart. Maybe that would help. "I don't like what the gangs do to kids. For some of them, it doesn't matter; they have no one else to look out for them. At least with the gang, they get food and protection. Jason has a mom; he has a chance at a future. That's why I stopped them trying to recruit him."

Lena sighed. "I wish the world wasn't like this, Tik. But even before this there were gangs, and plenty of kids who saw that life as a way out. You did good. I hope that will continue."

"There's more." Tik didn't want secrets to get in the way. "My boss — my gang leader — wants Jason for some reason. He sent me to get the kid. I can hold him off for a while, but eventually he'll send someone else."

"How much time?"

Tik was surprised that she didn't ask why. "A couple of weeks, maybe more. Basso knows this has to be handled delicately."

"Do you know why?" she said it like she knew the answer. Like it was some kind of pop quiz.

"Not really. Maybe something to do with his mother."

Lena nodded. "Ava is a teacher and she's involved in the gardening program. It doesn't sound like much, but she connects with a lot of important people. My guess is that your boss is looking to take over the town. Let's not tell Ava about this."

He agreed. If Jason's mother reacted to the news it would draw attention. He'd take care of protecting the kid.

Tik worried that he'd missed something with Basso. He hadn't thought that far, but Lena's guess made sense. Someone would try to take over, and Basso was ambitious.

CHAPTER TWELVE

In her empty classroom, Lena gave up the struggle to keep her mind focused on the student papers. The library wouldn't work any longer. When Belle commented on how many people seemed to need something in the basement, Lena knew it was only a matter of time before she came looking to see what was going on.

Tik's condo might be a better idea, but it was across town in a deserted area. It might be just as bad to have people dropping by all the time. Maybe Ava's place would work. It was all about planning now. They didn't need to bring anyone else in. Eight people were enough and probably all they could support until the farm was back in shape.

It had been vacant for a while. Most of the cows were sold off, the few left were managed by a neighbor, and the land let fallow. From her reading, Lena knew that was good for the soil, but for anyone trying to live off it the immediate result was backbreaking work.

The real problem with using Ava's place was Tik. If his gang was watching, they'd expect fast results if Tik had access to Jason's home. And if anyone else in the building saw him coming, they'd report it to the police. Tik couldn't pass for anything but a gang member right now.

Lena stacked the papers she'd been marking and locked them in her desk drawer. She didn't have to solve this problem alone. Ava was busy with the after-school gardening program, but Keith's store was still open. Maybe he would be able to suggest a place.

Lena waved at a few teachers who were still elbows deep in end of term papers as she left. Turning right from the school, she headed for Keith's store. Brian wouldn't be home for another hour. Lena figured she had plenty of time to see Keith and still be home to make soup for Brian's dinner.

He was still giving her the silent treatment, but it didn't mean he wouldn't notice if she didn't follow her usual routine. Keeping Brian from getting suspicious was almost as important as planning their escape.

There were no customers in Keith's store. Lena wondered how he made any money, but that wasn't her concern. It wouldn't be his for much longer either.

He looked up from a magazine. "I didn't expect to see you so soon."

There was something about him that made her read insinuation that she wasn't capable into every word. She couldn't put her finger on it, and worried that is was more to do with his wife than Keith. Deb annoyed everyone for exactly the same reason. She was entitled and whiney. When she couldn't get what she wanted, she pouted and acted like a spoiled teenager. Mellow was far more mature. Lena couldn't help but wonder if Keith liked that about his wife. What kind of man was attracted to that kind of woman?

"We have a bit of a problem. And I think we have all of our team," Lena said. If she treated him like he was a good guy, maybe she'd start feeling that way about him.

"How many?"

"Eight. Four adults including Deb, two kids and two teenagers. What did Deb say when you told her?"

Keith gave Lena a thin smile. "I haven't told her, and I won't until the last minute. Gives her less time to worry about it."

And gives them one less risk to deal with. What Deb didn't know she couldn't screw up. "Good idea."

"What about your husband?"

"He's not coming. He doesn't know about it."

Keith nodded. "I figured. He doesn't strike me as the kind of man to leave a cushy life for a farm." He closed the magazine. "What's the problem?"

"We need a place to meet. The library is too public for all of us and we, the adults, at least, need to get together."

"When you say the adults, you mean just the three of us?"

"No," Lena said. "The two teenagers as well. They are too old to just let us tell them what to do."

"Too many for my back room," Keith said. "There's an empty apartment in our building."

Lena explained about Tik.

"How will we leave? I mean, what side of the town?" Keith pulled a street map from under the counter.

Lena glanced at it. New Surrey used to be a medium sized city, now most of the neighborhoods were empty. "It's something we have to figure out. My recommendation is across the west bridge. It's in the right direction and it's not far for us to go at night."

"Okay. There'll be something around the bridge where we can meet. Leave it to me. I'll let you know."

A part of Lena wanted to say no. That it was her job to deal with it. The more rational part was happy to pass the task along. "Okay. Tomorrow? We need to go soon."

Keith folded the map and put it back. "Tomorrow morning."

Brian was late. Lena couldn't settle until he was home. She needed to judge his mood so she could keep him from interfering with her time. When he'd been home early, there was a hidden agenda, now he was late, there must be something else. She needed her routine back. There was enough stress involved in the escape without having to deal with Brian's plans.

An hour after she expected him, she heard his key in the lock. At least dinner wasn't ruined. Soup kept well.

He stepped into the kitchen and sniffed the aroma. "Smells great. I'm sorry I didn't let you know I'd be late."

He was being too nice. It did not make her feel better. "Go change and I'll heat it up."

He kissed her cheek and headed for the bedroom. Lena's stomach churned with acid from the tension. It was hard to marshal her argument against what was coming when she didn't have a clue what exactly she would have to deal with. All Lena knew for certain was that it would be bad.

She stirred the soup pot and tried to calm herself down. Brian wasn't like the guy Keith had to deal with. She didn't have to worry that he'd go off the rails. He definitely needed something from her, but maybe it wouldn't be big.

When he returned to the kitchen, Lena was dishing up the soup. "Hard day?"

He sat and smiled as she placed the meal on the table. "Long. I had a meeting with Cindy at the end of it. Melanie Jones was there as well."

"She's the tall one with all that red hair." *The bossy one who doesn't speak to anyone who can't help her with some event or other.* Lena took a spoon of soup to mask her reaction.

"Yes, that's right."

"Anything interesting?" *Please say no. Please don't put me with them.*

Brian leaned in as though sharing a secret. "Not for me, but I think I've found the right job for you. You are so great at organizing."

Oh, god, here we go. "I'm kind of swamped with end of year things at school. Exams and helping with the prom committee."

"I know, but this won't get in the way. I got them to agree to let you organize the end of session party. It's in a couple of weeks and they don't have anything ready. You'll come in like a hero."

He'd already said yes for her.

Lena wanted to argue, to tell Brian he couldn't make commitments for her. That she couldn't take it on, and that he would have to tell the two women to look for help elsewhere. The problem was that the old Lena would have said yes. And saying yes now would save a lot of aggravation and worry. It would also make Brian think she was on his side, and that was what made her bite back the angry words. If it kept Brian from wondering what Lena was doing, then it was worth the effort.

"Did you tell them how to get in touch with me? Or did you arrange a meeting for me?" She couldn't just let it go. Even the old Lena would have been annoyed that he'd committed her without asking.

"I thought you could meet them over lunch — tomorrow." He didn't look at her as he spoke.

"Fine. Do I go to city hall? Or will they come to the school?"

"Cindy said you knew where the club was, and to meet them there around noon."

Lena finished her soup and left Brian at the table. She needed to get to Ava before this lunch meeting. And maybe all the work on this would be during the day. If she had to spend her nights on this stupid party, she'd never get any sleep.

Lena thought about how hard it had been for the students to get food and drink for the prom. They'd had to work in the town for no pay to increase the rations. They'd given up all of their free time for months just so they could have a celebration that every kid had enjoyed before. Lena couldn't imagine Cindy or Melanie, or any of the other council wives earning the treats for their party.

. . .

Keith had come through. Lena found a message from him in her inbox at school. There was an abandoned house near the bridge. He'd give her enough keys for everyone and they could meet there as well as store their supplies. He didn't explain how he'd managed to get keys, but Lena figured that with no one around, rekeying a lock wouldn't be that hard.

She passed the information to Ava at recess and brought her up to date. Now she was on her way to the club to find out about this party she had to help organize.

Cindy and Melanie were sitting at a table in the middle of the room, martinis in oversized glasses at their sides. They were on display, pretty, happy, and clearly important. Lena wondered who they were preening for, everyone in the club was part of their circle. Glancing around she realized that didn't matter. They were at the top of the pecking order. Everyone else needed to be reminded of it. If Keith were part of the government, Deb would be right there with them.

"Lena," Cindy called. "Over here."

As if I could have missed them.

"Ladies," Lena responded with a smile. This could only take forty minutes. Lena knew she could be pleasant for that amount of time. No matter how much she wanted to be anywhere else.

Cindy air kissed both of Lena's cheeks. "You know Melanie, I think."

Lena endured another air kissing before she sat. "Brian says you need me to help out."

"All business. That's great," Melanie said with a smile that conveyed completely the opposite.

"I have to get back to school soon, so I need to get right to it."

Cindy waved to the waiter. "Just go ahead and bring our order." She turned to Lena and added, "We ordered for you, I hope that's okay."

Lena smiled and hoped they'd ordered something she'd eat. The waiter put roast beef sandwiches on a platter in the middle of the table along with a bowl of salad that he proceeded to serve them.

When the serving ceremony was complete, Lena said, "Can we talk and eat at the same time?"

Melanie looked to Cindy before saying, "Of course. What do you need to know?"

Were these women completely nuts? Or had Brian forgotten to give her some information? "Let's start with what kind of party you want."

"Oh, the usual," Melanie said. "You know, nibbles, lots of drinkies, and music. We want to dance."

Lena felt like she was pulling teeth. At least the food was good, what she could bite between short answers to her questions. "I've never been to one of these, so I'm not sure what the usual means. Why don't you go into more detail?" They looked at her like she was speaking Latin. "I mean, what kind of music, how late do you need it, who are your usual caterers, do you need security?" She ran out of ideas. Her only experience with party planning was the prom and that likely wouldn't cut it.

Cindy started talking about last year's event. It wasn't a party; they were looking for a gala. Lena ate and took notes. By the time Cindy was finished rhapsodizing about last year's party, Lena had finished her food, made two pages of notes — and had an idea.

"So, some of the people you used last year aren't available."

"Yes, it's unfortunate, but there is a fair amount of violence in some areas. We'll need a new caterer — of course, we'll provide the supplies — and I'm not sure what happened to the man who did the music."

"I think some security would be a good idea too, Cindy," Lena said. "You are so right about the violence. I'd hate to have the party disrupted by some undesirables."

Cindy beamed. "See, Melanie. I told you Lena was just the right woman for the job."

It was an effort not to roll her eyes. "Do you have a date for the party?"

"I'll be going with my husband," Cindy said then laughed. "Oh, you mean a day. Yes, June thirteenth. We'll start around six and go until we drop. Usually it ends around one or so."

Lena checked her watch. "I have to go. Shall I meet you tomorrow about the details. That will give me enough time to touch base with a caterer and security person."

"And music," Melanie reminded her.

"Yes, music too," Lena said. "I'll drop by tomorrow at lunch. Here?"

When Cindy agreed, Lena took her leave.

Ava for catering, Keith and Tik for security, and Mellow for music. Perfect. They had a legitimate excuse for meeting and maybe a chance to divert some supplies.

CHAPTER THIRTEEN

After lunch, Lena had passed the news on to Ava. It was important that all of them meet the next evening at the latest. By the time Lena met with Cindy and Melanie, everything needed to be in place. They would leave the night of the party. While it was in full swing, and no one would notice they were gone for hours.

At ten the next morning she walked up to the house they'd use as a base of operations. A house like every other on the street; attached garage, empty flower boxes on the windows, an unkempt patch of garden, and beige and cream paint. If things hadn't fallen apart, the curb appeal would have been very different.

Everyone was arriving separately so that it wasn't apparent they were meeting. Lena tried to keep a grin off her face. For the first time, she was certain that they would make it.

The door was ajar, and she could hear the quiet murmur of voices. No one seemed to be arguing. She'd take that as another good sign. Shutting the door behind her, Lena stepped into what had been the living room, well the space that would serve that function. The whole floor was open plan. Ava stood by the fireplace, Mellow perched on the kitchen island countertop. Keith kept to the shadows, his eyes on the street. Tik was looking through the kitchen cupboards. Everyone looked up as she appeared.

"Morning," Lena called.

Tik stopped his rummaging and leaned beside Mellow on the counter. No one spoke.

Realizing they expected her to talk, Lena said, "So, I guess Ava told you about the party. We leave in thirteen days."

They nodded but still no one spoke.

"We're here to make the plans. From now on we'll be working toward one goal."

Keith broke the silence, "We need a lot of supplies. There's nothing here."

"I've got them somewhere safe," Tik said.

Keith looked at Tik, suspicion all over his face. "Why should we trust what a gangbanger says?"

Tik straightened up, his chest puffing out. "Same reason we should trust an old man, I guess."

Lena dropped her bag. It hit the floor with a thump, the notebooks and other planning tools adding weight to the canvas. "Stop fighting. Let's start by getting our stories out. We need to know more about each other, so we can get to a level of trust."

The silence was heavy. Keith and Tik staring at each other over a testosterone-filled gap.

Ava sighed and stepped between the two men. "Cut it out. We're in this together. We all have reasons for being here. No one is along for fun."

Keith returned to his post by the window. Tik relaxed back against the counter. Lena wondered how much of his machismo was about impressing Mellow.

Ava continued, "I'm here because my kids need a future. Jason is in danger of being drawn into a gang. Tik knows that's not just a mother's worry."

Mellow told her story and then Tik. It was striking for Lena to hear how gangs had affected so much of the group. Another reason to get out. The gangs were getting ready to do something that wouldn't improve the lives of the people in this town. Whether that was coordinated or a gang war, ordinary people would get hurt or killed.

Keith looked at Lena. She wanted to be the last one to speak so she raised her chin to him. He glanced at the street again before turning to the group.

"I killed a man. It's only a matter of time before I have to face the consequences." It wasn't news to Lena, or Ava. They'd both suspected that he'd killed the wife beater. Lena watched Tik and Mellow. Would Keith's admission affect them? Mellow was still just watching.

Tik finally spoke, "You win, old man. I've never killed anyone directly. What did the guy do to deserve it?"

"Beat his wife one time too many," Keith said. "I don't want to do hard labor for applying justice. My wife needs me around."

Tik gave a small nod, whether in approval, or respect, Lena couldn't tell.

"So, you think it's okay to do what you want? What if one of us does something you don't agree with?" Mellow asked.

"Don't beat on people weaker than you, and we'll be fine." Keith turned back to the window. "Why are you here, Lena? You have it good. You don't have kids to protect. What secret are you hiding?"

Lena was suddenly embarrassed. Everyone had a dire reason to go, she just wanted more than she could have in New Surrey. "I don't like what's happening," she said. "I guess I don't want to deal with the problems. Most of you know my husband is part of the government. I don't want to live a good life while others get nothing. I want a community that helps."

"So, you want us to follow you to this farm," Keith said.

Why was he being so obstructive? His reasons for being in the house were as valid as anyone's. Lena didn't think he was planning to leave, but he wasn't trying to make the group solid either.

"Yes. My aunt's farm."

"What if it isn't there any longer. What's plan B?" Keith asked.

The others looked at her. This was the hard part. She had no plan B. "I don't know. All I know is that we need to get out of here. If the farm is already taken, then we'll figure something out."

Keith nodded.

It wasn't what Lena had hoped when she walked into the room. Everyone seemed to bristle with suspicion. No one was leaving, which was good on two fronts. They didn't have time to recruit anyone else, and she had no idea how to stop someone from leaving and tossing the group to the authorities.

She felt the fool standing in the middle of the room. There was no place to sit but the floor. It was better than standing. Keith was invested in his role of watch keeper, but maybe if everyone else was sitting on the floor with her, she could get them to start cooperating rather than this weird antagonistic competition.

She lowered herself to sit cross-legged on the laminate flooring. "Can we at least talk about what needs to be done? We'll have plenty of time to work out plans B, C, and D on the road."

Ava dropped to sit across from Lena. Mellow shrugged and hopped down from the counter to sit with them. Tik followed Mellow. Keith marched to the door. Lena held her breath for a moment and then released it as she heard the lock click. He returned and lowered himself beside her.

"We need to work out how much we can carry when we go. It's not just food. We need seeds and tools." She pulled out notepads and pens and handed them around.

"I think we need to talk about skills. What is Deb going to do?" Ava asked.

Keith snorted a laugh. "I know what you think of her. I'll take care of her and carry her supplies, if needed. She'll come around."

Ava wasn't going to let it go. Lena knew that expression. She wanted more than assurances. Lena couldn't blame Ava. They couldn't afford passengers on the road.

"Wasn't she trained as a nurse?" Lena asked to intercept the argument.

Keith nodded. "Yeah. I'll make sure we have what she needs to do her thing."

Tik looked at Mellow and then Ava. "I guess we all have some training. What about Jason and his sister. How will they contribute?"

Lena knew he was trying to make the point that Deb wouldn't be the only weak link. Ava wasn't going to like the implication.

"I'll make sure they aren't a burden," Ava said. Her voice was cold.

Lena could feel the little control she had over the group slipping away. It felt like there needed to be an argument and no matter what anyone did, it would happen.

"The kids can carry their own packs," Lena said. "We'll be training on the road. Keith knows a lot about hunting and fishing and other outdoor activities. Ava has the knowledge we need for the farm. If Deb is going to be our nurse, then she can train us all in first aid."

Mellow looked up from her lap where she'd been inspecting her nails. "I can cook. But maybe we should bring more people in. I have a neighbor who is a nurse so she'd have the practice."

"Yeah, I've got a buddy who's a carpenter," Keith said. "Maybe we should do like the kid said. We should bring on people with the skills we're lacking."

"No. We need to go as soon as we can," Ava said. "My kids are in danger. I can't wait for more people to get on board. We need to go and deal with what we're missing when we're outside."

Tik stood. "She's right. I can only hold the gang off so long. Two weeks is going to be hard enough."

"We can't risk our future for a couple of kids," Keith said. "If we go too fast, we'll make mistakes. We'll be found and dragged back."

Lena pointed Tik back to the floor. "Sit down and stop arguing. We can't take everyone. Yeah, it makes sense to find someone who can do everything we need, but that will never happen. Every person we approach is another delay and another possibility to let our secret out." Mellow started to say something, but Lena held up her hand. "I'm not asking you to be friends. I'm asking you to cooperate so we can all get away."

She was shaking. All the fear and anger of the last weeks had come out with her words. She felt empty. If the others couldn't work it out, she'd leave with Ava and the kids tonight.

"In two weeks I can learn a lot about building stuff and first aid," Mellow said. "We should all try to learn as much as we can. Lena's right. We need to go."

"What about Deb, we need her to do more than just be a nurse." Ava said.

Lena knew she was thinking 'and a mean girl'. Deb had been part of the cool kids in school and never grew out of it.

"I won't put up with anyone sniping at my wife," Keith said. "But I think Lena's right too. We should get our shit together and make a plan."

The tension between everyone was thinning out. It was still there, but Lena was pretty sure there'd be no more arguing.

"I have to go meet these two women in a little while. I figure if you all take on a role in this party, we'll have a reason to meet, and we'll more or less be together when the time comes. And Deb can babysit Maya and Jason here."

Lena looked at Keith. "You'll have told her by then, right?"

"Don't count on it. I don't like you picking on her, but I do know her. I'll tell her when I go get her. Find another way to take care of the kids."

"Okay, so no one wants to leave us, right?" Lena needed to

hear them commit. This was the last time she wanted to have this discussion.

No one wanted to leave, or perhaps no one wanted to say so, but Lena felt like the storm was over.

She relaxed and set them on the task of listing their skills and what they thought they could learn. While each of them were writing their list, Lena moved around the group so she could talk with them one on one about their cover story for the party. She started with Tik.

"I think you can take on the security role. I don't want you actually doing the security, because you won't be able to leave. Are there a couple of people you can trust not to make a problem?"

"Yeah. Will they get paid? It will make a difference," Tik said.

"I'll make sure that happens. We won't get paid because I'm not waiting around, but the people doing the actual work will." She liked Tik when they talked like this. "What do you think we can get for the group under the guise of security?"

Tik laughed. "We'll get better weapons from my stash. Don't worry about that." He glanced to where Keith was making his notes. "I guess I can talk to Keith about what he has, so we don't bring the same things. He'll have hunting and fishing stuff, right?"

Lena nodded. It was a relief to know they wouldn't have to divert weapons. It had been the thing she'd worried most about. "Keep working on your list."

She moved on to Ava. "So, you'll do the catering coordination. Can you divert food?"

"It will all be perishable. We'd be better off eating before we go if we can get into the party." She made a note on her pad under Jason's name: surveillance.

"Jason?" Lena asked.

"Yeah. He drives me nuts the way he just goes in and out of places. Half the time he startles the shit out of me by popping up unexpectedly."

"Okay," Lena said. "So, anything else at the party you think we should divert?"

"I'll try to get us a few bottles of vodka, and some wine," Ava said.

"I don't think we can afford to drink."

"You'd be surprised what a good bottle of wine can do to raise morale. And the vodka is for medical purposes. We might not be able to get our hands on anything to clean equipment. Vodka will do it."

"Do you know anything about catering?"

"I can figure it out, and my home skills class will have a ball catering the party."

When she got to Mellow, the girl was ready. "I know a couple of guys who can do the DJ. They only have a few of their own records, so maybe just getting their hands on more will make it work."

"No, they'll get paid," Lena said. She didn't want any records going missing and bringing attention just when they were sneaking away. Payment might go a long way to stopping a little petty theft.

"Fine, I'll babysit for Ava that night and bring them here."

Keith was the last one she needed to talk to, and she was running out of time. "Can you coordinate security with Tik? Be a mature face for the committee?"

"Yeah. I don't know the wisdom of bringing a gangbanger in on this, but I said I'd trust you."

"Okay. I've got ten minutes before I leave. I'll try not to get you involved with the committee, but if they want to meet you, I'll set it up. Tik, can you dress like a security expert for that?"

"Yeah, just need some notice. If I dress differently, Basso will want to know why. We don't want him asking questions."

A remnant of the feeling she'd had coming into the house was still there. They might not be a team yet, but she'd find a way to forge them into one. It wasn't just the journey. It might be harder on them living together at the farm. Hard work and close quarters could push everyone to the edge.

"We need to pull this information together. And we need to see what Tik has in the way of supplies," Lena said.

Mellow started gathering the papers. "I'll create a matrix and then we can see what the gaps are. Maybe I can work with Ava on that?"

Ava nodded. "We'll make it part of that fictitious project. I can work with Tik to inventory the food he has so we know what to stock up."

Lena felt her load lightening. She'd started this thing, but it needed a leader and that wasn't something she felt able to do. Leadership meant hard decisions and she'd avoided those all her life.

"I'll coordinate with Ava and Tik about supplies," Keith offered. "We can't keep coming here, but when we've got the lists in shape, it's going to be a good place to store everything."

Lena looked around. The front window was large and didn't afford much privacy. They'd arranged themselves in sight of anyone passing by. A mistake she wouldn't make again.

"We'll need to move stuff here at night," she said.

Ava nodded. "It'll be good practice to see what we can carry. It would be great if we could find a way to, I guess to be honest, steal some transportation."

"Unless anyone can think of a way to hide the theft, it's better that we carry what we can. I get the feeling no one will really come looking unless we take something valuable."

Mellow stood and dusted off her jeans. "So, when do we meet again?"

"Can we be here on Monday?" Lena asked everyone. "I'll have something arranged with Cindy and Melanie by then. And you'll have time to do everything we agreed."

"Not here," Keith said. "What about the condo where Tik's stuff is?"

Lena didn't like the idea of heading off to the deserted condo, but she saw the wisdom of having lots of locations. "Okay, just everyone be careful when you go there. After school. Around four?"

"Sure," Mellow said. "You know I think you have the hardest job. Ava said you're meeting Melanie Jones. I worked for her last school break. Don't be fooled by her airhead act. She's sharp and mean as hell."

CHAPTER FOURTEEN

Lena couldn't believe she was standing in her nicest dress at the back of the ballroom. The party was underway and everything was going smoothly. The last two weeks had been a blur of planning and lying, and running from one fake meeting to another very real one.

Mellow had been right about Melanie. The worst part of the set up was convincing her that they had it in hand. The woman had constantly harped on how different everything was from when they used the usual people. The security was easy since there wasn't a regular company. Eventually, Lena had won out and impressed the bitch.

Tik's gang members were at the door. Big bulky guys dressed in black pants and turtlenecks. The way they looked was deterrent enough to Lena. Tik had managed to avoid bringing Jason in for initiation. Although a new set of bruises had been evident this morning on his face.

Keith was on his way to get Deb. Lena crossed her fingers that there wouldn't be a problem. How would she feel if it was Brian dropping this plan on her at the last minute? The thought churned the acid in her stomach.

Mellow had set up her friends with the music and then slipped out to pick up Maya and Jason. Ava was giving the final instructions to her students who were getting ready to start passing trays full of hors d'oeuvres. Ava was scheduled to leave as soon as the first tray went out.

Now all that was left was for Lena to find an opportunity. She couldn't just slip out. Brian was here and if she didn't find an excuse he'd come looking for her. And he'd said they would want to thank her at some point in the evening. All of these stupid things were getting in the way of her escaping. It felt like everything that had gone right in the last two weeks had to be paid for tonight.

Ava whispered goodbye on her way out. Now Lena needed to take action. She looked around the room. Cindy and Melanie were standing with their husbands like royalty in a receiving line. People casually dropped by to say something, making the women smile and the men look proud. Brian was talking to the mayor and wouldn't appreciate being interrupted.

She made her way to the two women.

"Lena, darling," Cindy called as she approached. "Bob, this is the woman who made all of the arrangements. We must do something lovely for her."

"No, it was a pleasure," Lena said. "I'm glad it came off."

Melanie smiled, the expression Lena had come to think of as the sour lemon smile. There was no pleasure in it. The woman had probably been hoping it was a flop so she could hold it over Lena.

"We must at least thank you in the speeches," Melanie said.

"That's kind of you," Lena said. "I didn't know there would be speeches. When do you need the music to stop so you can do them?"

"Now. Let's get them over with, so we can start the fun." Cindy whispered something to her husband and then started gathering people.

Lena went to the DJ station and asked them to hold the music until the politicians had finished. Then they could go until someone told them the party was over.

She was about to find Brian when he stepped to her side.

"Thank you," he said. Then, putting his arm around her waist, he added, "we'll have time to dance after this."

Lena winced to set the scene for her migraine excuse. "How long are they going to talk?"

He nuzzled her cheek. "It will be short. No one gets a refill on their glasses until it's over."

The tactic seemed to work. To her relief, there was no review of the year, no promises for next year. Just a round of thanks for everyone's hard work — yeah right — and a nice thanks to her and her team for a great party. It took all of five minutes.

Lena rubbed her temple and started to say she needed to go home, when Brian's arm tightened.

"Let's call this our song," he said and moved her to the dance floor.

The song was one of those repetitive beat electronic ones that always seemed to go on forever. This one was slow beats. Everyone was dancing close and moving only in small circles. Lena forced herself to concentrate on not tripping.

When the song ended, she tried to pull away, but Brian was intoxicated enough to want to continue dancing.

After the second, a faster beat this time that allowed her to move out of his arms, she nodded toward a group of men talking. "Shouldn't you join in. This is really a work function; you don't want to miss out on anything."

He reached to pull her into an embrace. "I've missed this side of you. The fun side." He pulled away. "I guess I should go mix in. Come with me?"

Even if she wasn't trying to leave, Lena wouldn't have gone near the group of powerful people. "I'm getting a headache. I need to go lie down."

"But you'll miss the fun."

This was the Brian she'd married. A man who knew how to enjoy himself. But that was only a veneer now. She watched him glance at the men. Her excuse was feeble, but Brian didn't care.

"If I get an hour's quiet, I can come back. You go do your career thing and I'll return before you miss me."

She watched as Brian made his way to the men. He seemed to forget about her as soon as his back was turned. He was really focused on his career. Maybe because he wanted more for her, but Lena had a sour feeling that it was all about Brian.

The room was busy with people talking in small groups, couples dancing, and a few sitting at tables looking determined to get more than their share of the free booze. Lena made sure to catch Cindy's gaze and smile before slipping through to the back room where Ava's students were trading empty trays for full. They were working together like pros. Ava would be proud. Lena could only hope that having this skill meant fewer of them would be dragged down to the streets after graduation.

The back door led into the alley. It was poorly lit, but Lena had scoped it out earlier. There were only a few obstacles between her and the street outside. With luck, the presence of the security team inside had kept the dangers from piling up outside.

A rat scuttled across her path just as she reached the street. Lena had to stop and catch her breath from the scare. If she reacted like this in familiar territory, how could she hope to succeed on the road? It wasn't a productive thought. Lena pushed it away and hurried home.

In the apartment, she changed into jeans, t-shirt, boots, and a warm jacket. A few sets of clothes were in her stash, hidden in the basement of the building so that Brian wouldn't find it. The dress she'd worn to the party was beautiful, but it would just take up space if she took it along. When would they have an opportunity to party like that at the farm?

She stood at the door looking around for the last time. They'd been happy here in the beginning, but this is where they'd grown apart. Lena noticed that the furniture was to Brian's taste, as was most of the art. When had this become his apartment and not theirs?

Lena closed the door behind her and locked it.

There was no one around. Most people went to bed soon after the sun went down. They worked hard and needed their rest, but it didn't mean she could be careless. If she ran into anyone, they might ask awkward questions.

The basement was dark, but Lena knew the way to her pack by feel. It was just inside the utility room, tucked into a space between the boiler and the wall.

Everyone else should be at the house by now. Lena was the last to leave the party because she was the most known of the group. That meant she was the last to arrive, and when she did, they would go.

She shouldered her pack and headed upstairs to the lobby. As she rounded the short hall that led to the door Lena heard voices. Harsh words, which was unusual in this area. Lena knew that no matter who this was, if they saw her with a backpack on at this time of night, they'd know something was up. She moved back inside the doorway to the basement.

"I don't like it," one voice said. A man, his rasp disguised his age, but Lena knew he didn't live in her building.

"You do what you're told to do. He said we need to send a message. Nothing big, just enough so Basso knows we've been here, and his turf isn't so protected." The second voice was young. This boy hadn't had a chance to grow up yet.

"So, we find an empty apartment and take the stuff?" raspy voice asked.

"No one gets hurt. We just need to make a statement."

Lena fought the urge to step out and send them away. She couldn't take the chance that they'd stop her. But she also couldn't leave her neighbors to become victims. Slipping her backpack to the ground, she pulled the hood of her jacket up, and hunched over the way she'd seen junkies move. Then she shuffled to the edge of the lobby again, making sure she was noticed.

"You got anything for me?" she whined. "I got money."

The two men were both just boys really. The youngest had a scar running across his right cheek and held his arm as though he had to protect it. The older one was thin and his face was boiling with acne.

He spoke. "Get out of here." He was the raspy one.

"Basso would give me something," she whined.

"We don't work for Basso," the younger one said.

"Why are you here? Basso is gonna want you dead if you ain't one of his." She scratched at her arm, knowing that was a sign of withdrawal.

The tall one stepped toward her. "You live here?"

She pretended to look around. "Not now. But I used to."

The younger one pulled his partner's arm. "Get rid of her. We're in a hurry."

The raspy voiced one shook the hand off. "I'll give you something if you tell me who lives here. Who important lives here."

Relief calmed Lena's nerves as they took the bait. "There's a guy in the government here. Is he important enough?"

It was hard to watch his reaction without exposing her own face, but Lena could see the pull of a grin on his cheek.

"What apartment?" He dug into his pocket as he asked. Then he held out a tiny plastic bag. Inside there were some grey crystals.

Lena held out her hand. "Four ten."

The thug dropped the bag into Lena's hands and then pulled his partner toward the elevator.

As soon as it started to rise with them inside, she ran for her pack. The drugs went down the first storm drain, and Lena started walking to the house.

CHAPTER FIFTEEN

Lena ran up the steps and entered the, now unlocked, house. Inside she could hear the murmur of voices coming from behind the basement door in the kitchen. The chance that anyone would come in and listen to them was slim, but that didn't stop fear from stealing her breath. They were so close it was vital that they didn't make a mistake.

She opened the door and blinked at the light. This was the main reason they were in the basement, no windows meant they could light one of the lanterns and no one had to sit alone in the dark.

"Keep it down," she whispered. When her eyes adjusted, Lena checked on everyone. Ava and her kids were standing together, the kids wide-eyed. Mellow was checking her pack and Tik was watching her. No sign of Keith and Deb.

"What happened?" she asked. "Has anyone heard from them?"

Tik stopped watching Mellow and shook his head. "Keith told me he'd be here, but we have to go, right? We were talking about how to deal with not having him with us when you came in."

They weren't even on the road and people were missing. "We can wait a little longer." She told them about the gang members in her building. "When Brian gets home to find the apartment robbed, he'll deal with that and not come looking for me. We'll probably have a few hours more than we thought."

"Yeah, but that means we could be a few hours farther away," Ava said. "I don't like leaving them either, but Keith can catch up."

"We wait," Lena said. "Tik, do you think you can go look for them?"

The door opened before he could respond. Tik moved toward Mellow, standing between her and whatever threat was coming.

"We're here." Keith pulled Deb after him.

She was dressed in sturdy camo and didn't look happy. Although it was hard for Lena to judge, Deb always looked like she'd just tasted something sour. It didn't fit on her delicate face. Deb had that kind of pretty that relied on youth, but she'd managed to keep herself trim and knew how to use makeup to hide the fine lines around her mouth. Her hair was dyed a rich auburn, that would fade and grow out without maintenance. She was going to find farm life hard on her image.

So, who's judging now?

"We had to avoid a few people," Keith continued. "And Deb isn't used to sneaking around."

Lena wasn't sure Deb would ever get used to it. "We can get started," she said.

"No," Deb said. "I don't know anyone here, and I'm not going anywhere until I get introduced. Keith, you can drag me around God knows where. I get it, you think we're in danger. I don't know why, but I'll come. I just won't go blindly."

Lena sympathized. She'd feel much the same way given the circumstances. In fact, Deb was being more compliant than Lena had been with Brian's plan to get her involved in his career. It was just the pouty way she reacted. It didn't work for a woman her age to be sticking her lip out like that.

Ava stepped forward. "I don't know what Keith told you, but

we all have reason to leave. I've got kids to protect. Mellow wants a future and so does Tik, Lena is scared about what's happening. I think Keith can tell you why he's ready to go if you don't already know. We can do the rest of the introductions on the way."

Deb's pout hadn't disappeared, but she relaxed her shoulders and then looked at Lena. "You're the one who organized that party tonight?"

Lena nodded wondering what complaint was coming. "I didn't make up the guest list."

"No, but I bet you wouldn't have invited us anyway," Deb said. Then at a look from Keith she added, "I was out when Keith got home. I was outside the hall, listening to the music. I miss music. Anyway, some guy came out and saw me. I thought I was in trouble and I didn't want Keith to know. He asked about you, did I see you, and stuff."

Lena held her breath.

"Tall guy, broody looking?" Deb persisted.

She was clearly looking for an identification. "Probably my husband."

Deb smirked. "Yeah, I notice he's not here."

"Deb told him she'd seen you. And that you headed to the park," Keith said. "She didn't know about this plan. I told her when she got home. Would he believe that? You going to the park at night?"

"Did he seem to believe it?" Lena asked.

"Maybe. He went back inside anyway," Deb said. "I guess he doesn't care what you do."

That would be a dig at her relationship, but Lena knew it was probably true, at least tonight.

She left the words hanging and picked up her pack. "We should leave now," she said. There was time to let Keith know about the activity at home later. "We don't want to risk losing the dark while we're still in sight of the city."

Tik snuffed the lantern and they all stood waiting the few

moments for their eyes to adjust. There was only a little moonlight coming in from the street. A waning moon would give them
plenty of cover, but it hid things they needed to see as well as
their own passage.

Keith checked the street before they all slipped out. Staying
together in a group, holding to the shadows as much as possible,
they made their way toward the bridge. Lena felt like every step
they took rang out like a bell. Being this close to the bridge was a
blessing. She didn't know how they would have survived the walk
from farther inside New Surrey.

The streets were empty, which was normal, and what they
counted on. Lena couldn't get her mind to accept that maybe they
were going to just go and no one would challenge them; not that
they'd seen any of the patrols. Her stomach burned with acid as
her tension increased. The food she'd eaten at the party wasn't
sitting well, but she kept swallowing the urge to throw up. Was
she the only one feeling this way? Taking a second to glance
around, she saw that everyone was tense. Even Jason and Maya
seemed to know that this was the riskiest part of the plan.

Keith was leading with Deb right behind as though she would
be of use. Maybe it was better that she stayed with her husband
and out of the way.

The bridge was in sight. One more block before they could
run across. Lena saw the shadows that would cover them as they
passed. The moon slipping from one cloud to another, cast light
patterns in the inky night.

Suddenly Keith's arm went up, the signal to stop. The group
huddled together behind the stairs to a grand home. Lena trusted
his judgement, but she couldn't see what had alarmed him. She
leaned toward the edge of the stairs trying to glimpse the problem. She heard a shuffle of feet, then two men struggled into
sight.

They were fighting. Moonlight flashed at the edge of a knife
then left them in the dark as it passed to the next cloud.

Ava moved to block the sight from her kids. Tik stepped to stand with Keith, both men protecting the women and children. Lena would talk about that later, right now she appreciated the gesture and they all needed more defense training.

The two fighters grunted with effort. It was fast. They slashed and dodged the swipe of a blade at the same moment.

Lena watched in fascination. They were making enough noise that she hazarded a whisper, "What the hell are they fighting about?" As if anyone would know.

Tik leaned over and whispered, "Turf. What you saw earlier isn't the only clash. That's one of ours... I mean one of Basso's. The other guy I don't know."

She watched the fight, one of them was bleeding, but not enough to slow him down. "Does this go on a lot?"

Tik glanced around. "A bit. It's what keeps any gang from getting big enough to take over. It's unusual that there's no witness."

The injured man stumbled a little and received another wound while he tried to get his footing. Now the blood flowing from his body was enough to drain his energy. Lena saw his swings weaken, his opponent dodging easily and reaching to add another cut.

"This isn't a fight," Tik whispered. "This is a contract. That's why there's no one watching."

Lena wished she didn't have to see this, but they couldn't move until the way was clear.

Keith pulled them back tight to their cover. "Will the winner just go?" he asked Tik.

Tik shrugged. "I've never been there when this gets ordered. But there's no reason for him to hang around." He glanced at the fight again. "It looks like Basso's guy will win this time."

Keith turned to Ava. "The kids will need to walk past a body."

"It probably won't be the last," Ava said. "But is there any way we can avoid it?"

Lena checked on the kids. They were facing the wall, ears

plugged. They knew something bad was happening, but they kept quiet and did as Ava told them. A good sign.

"Tik, what will happen to the body?" she asked.

He pointed to the fight. "It's only going to take a few minutes now. I don't remember hearing about anyone finding bodies. The winner will take a trophy. Then maybe he tosses the body in the river. That's what I'd do. Then the cops won't get suspicious and start poking around."

Deb shouldered her way from behind Keith. "If that doesn't happen, you and Keith go throw it over the wall. I don't want to see a dead body either."

It took longer than a few minutes.

Lena knew that the injured man was going to die. There was so much blood on the road that he couldn't possibly survive. But he seemed to think it wasn't inevitable. He managed to wound his opponent a couple of times. Then the fight slowed down. Both men pulling away to circle and search for weakness in the other.

It was like a dance now, not a swift and bloody flicker of movement, but a slow shuffle. Both fighters drained of energy, knowing only one of them could win. All they had to do was hang on long enough for nature to take control so the victor could take a trophy.

Lena wanted it to end, but felt guilty knowing that she was asking for a man to die. Would it be like that out on the road? Would they be fighting anarchy all the way to the farm? If it was like that, it would mean Brian was right to believe in the rules and restrictions that kept the town safe. It kept this kind of violence to gangs, and kept the gangs contained.

When they'd danced earlier tonight she'd remembered the beginning, when they fell in love. Was that Brian still there? She was convinced that he'd changed, but maybe it was her. If she went back to get him, would he come? Or would she stay?

The grunts from the fight were deeper. Someone was about to lose everything. Lena moved to get a better view. If she was going to be part of this journey, she couldn't be squeamish.

Basso's man was kneeling at the side of the other fighter. Lena heard him laugh as he raised his knife for the final cut. He stabbed down as the other man stabbed up. Both knives found their target. Basso's man fell onto the blade of the other. There was sound of air expelling from lungs, and then silence.

The whole group was stunned. Then the odor of death found them. Lena had never smelled it before but there was no mistaking the stench of blood and feces.

The two bodies were right in front of the entrance to the bridge. "There's no time to clean up the evidence. We need to go," Lena said. "Make sure the kids don't look."

Keith pulled Deb away from the wall. Lena heard him say, "close your eyes and I'll make sure you get there."

Lena followed, moving past the bodies. She held Maya's hand and pulled her along. Maybe it would be a good idea for someone to find the dead men in the morning. Something to distract everyone from realizing her group were missing.

Lena wished that someone was leading her because she couldn't help looking at the bodies. Like the people who would slow down to look at an accident before, when there was traffic. It was a compulsion.

Seeing the blood spreading slowly as it leaked out of the dead men didn't help. Neither did seeing the faces. While she was at a distance watching the fight, they seemed like men. It didn't make it better, but men would have known enough to realize the risks of a knife fight. These two were younger than Tik. Fourteen or fifteen years old. They should have been doing homework, not killing each other.

Then they were on the bridge running along the edge of the parapet where the shadows were deepest. The breeze was cold, but it blew toward New Surrey so it wasn't tainted with the reek.

Lena wanted to look behind, to see that there was no one there, but the pace Keith set was too fast for her to turn without stumbling. Tik was behind her and Maya, Keith at the head of the line. She had to trust that they would know if there was pursuit.

The bridge was wide, built to allow for rush hour traffic coming in from the suburbs. The stone work was intricate, as if it came from an older era. When craftsmanship was valued over speed. Lena turned her attention away from the death behind her and tried to focus on the future they were building.

The weight of her pack was dragging at her. The adults were running in a bent position to stay below the parapet, and no one had trained for this. Lena swore silently at the gap in their preparations. What else was going to come along and bite them in the ass? She'd hoped they could make it to the farm in a month, but they weren't fit enough for that. They would need more rest at the beginning of the journey.

She was lost in her thoughts when Keith stopped them. Lena realized they had crossed the bridge. They were out of the influence of the city.

They were on their way.

"Stay low," Keith said. His voice was quiet but no longer a whisper. "There's a park nearby. I remember it from when I was a kid."

Deb elbowed him. "You weren't a kid."

They'd been together a long time, probably longer than she'd known Brian. Maybe enough time together made it hard to see their faults. Or maybe they just didn't matter after a while.

"Will we be able to rest there?" Lena asked. "I don't want anyone getting hurt by pushing too hard."

Keith beckoned them around the corner of the bridge. They would be invisible to anyone looking across from home and hard to see if there were anyone on this side. Lena didn't fret; these suburbs were deserted. Everyone had moved into the city without thought, looking for security.

"It's too close for us to camp. If anyone comes looking they'll find us right away. But we can rest for a little while." Keith shifted the backpack on his shoulders, the one holding his and Deb's belongings. "I haven't worn a pack this heavy in too long. Anyone else feeling the weight?"

There were a few groans from the group, and Lena didn't feel quite so bad. Then she saw him straighten without trouble and realized that he was trying to make it easy for the rest of them.

The park was bigger than Lena expected. She'd spent her free time in New Surrey in the years before. Thinking like a real urban snob that the suburbs were places to shop and that was it.

There was a kid's area right at the front. Swings still hung on their chains, but someone had taken an ax to the teeter totter and the slide. Past that were trees. Birches that stood like sentinels. The trees thickened and changed to evergreens a few steps inside. There was plenty of cover, but little comfort on the hard ground. There was no soft layer of grass here. The trees didn't allow enough light in for undergrowth.

Keith led them deeper and suddenly Lena stepped through the trees to a lake. The shores were stony, but there was a sense of peace and privacy that helped calm her frayed nerves.

They arranged themselves in a circle, sitting on their packs rather than the cold stone. It was too dark to see the far shore of the lake.

"Do people live here?" Lena asked.

"Not anymore," Keith said. "There are some cabins farther along."

"And some clearings," a man said from the cover of the trees behind them.

CHAPTER SIXTEEN

Lena grabbed a loose stone as she turned toward the voice. Keith and Tik were already moving to where the person must be. Her chest was strangled with fear. They hadn't even got through the first night.

"Hey, I don't mean any harm," the voice said. A shadow pulled away from the trunk of a large fir tree. "I saw you come into the park and you looked like you were running from something."

Lena moved forward, stone still ready to throw. She pushed between Tik and Keith trusting them to protect the rest of the group. The shadow resolved into a young man, about Tik's age, maybe a little older but no more than early twenties. There wasn't enough light to make out more than his height and build. He was taller than Lena, maybe five foot eight and he was rail thin. And he had a mess of curly brown hair.

Lena knew she was looking at him to assess how much it would take to fight him, and wondered when she'd made that transition. "Who are you?" she asked.

"Name's Scott Haverst. I'm a traveler. Who are you? And why are you here?"

A traveler. That might explain his thinness. If he was out on the road, he'd probably not had a full meal in a long time. Lena heard a shift of a foot on the rock behind her. She couldn't take the risk to look, but she hoped it wasn't one of the men deciding to punch first and ask questions later.

"We're heading out west." Lena stepped forward and offered her hand. "I'm Lena Custordin. These are my friends."

Scott shook her hand and Lena felt hard calluses on his palm and fingers. He nodded to the people behind her. "You planning to spend the rest of the night here? It's going to get real cold in an hour or so."

Lena looked back at her group. They weren't prepared to camp out here for a few hours. If they broke out the sleeping bags and tarp, they'd get a little rest, but then they'd have to pack and move on so they wouldn't be seen.

"No just a rest and then we'll leave."

He grunted in acknowledgement. "You can camp with me if you want. I'm far enough in that no one can see my campfire. You'll be safe until you're ready to move on." He looked over at Keith and Tik. "I'm alone, so you don't need to worry. I should be more worried about you."

This wasn't something that she could decide on her own. "Give me a minute," Lena said. She didn't wait for an answer.

She joined the group, asking Keith to keep watch while they talked. "You heard what he offered."

Deb was the first to speak, "Yes, and a warm fire would be nice. We can wait with him until tomorrow night. Then we can leave in the dark again."

And, that would give her time to find a way back, Lena thought. She wanted Deb as far along the road as soon as possible so there was no going back.

"Maybe he can give us some tips," Ava said. "I think spending even a few hours in his camp would be good. We're all kind of running on the adrenalin of that fight. I'm not sure how much farther we can get tonight."

Keith and Tik agreed. Keith adding, "Tik and I can take care of him if we need to."

Lena's stomach turned at the thought of more violence. "No, I don't want to start out our journey that way."

Keith chuckled. "I didn't mean take care of him permanently. Ava's got a point. Look at your hands."

They were trembling. "Okay. We'll rest up with him."

Scott led them from the edge of the lake to a clearing a few minutes away. It was deeper into the trees and they were almost in the clearing when Lena heard the snort of a horse and smelled the embers of the campfire. No one would find them without being noticed.

The kids ran to the horse, petted him, then sat next to the glow of the fire. The animal was hobbled at the edge of the clearing where there was plenty of grass to nibble. Beside him was a wagon, big enough to carry all of their packs and still have room.

"Where are you headed, Scott?" Lena asked.

"West, like you, but only because I'm coming from the east. I don't plan much, just follow the road until I get bored. Then I find a new road."

He made it sound good.

Could that work for us? No. The kids needed some kind of stability. They all wanted a future, and living the way Scott did, pretty much guaranteed a short life. One injury or illness and he'd be dead.

Jason ran to join them. "What's the horse's name?"

Scott flicked a glance at the animal. Maya had gone back to patting it. "His name is Starbuck. Don't get behind him until he gets to know you. His kick is pretty hard."

Jason ran back to relay the message to Maya.

Scott looked around at the group. "I'm going to check my trap lines. We need a couple more rabbits for breakfast now I have company." He rose, picked up a woven grass basket then slipped out of sight.

Lena didn't understand how he could trust them so much. All they had to do was remove the hobble from Starbuck's legs and they'd be gone with all of his stuff and the wagon before he could know.

"You know how to hitch the horse?" Tik asked.

"No. Why do you ask?" Lena suppressed her own thoughts of taking Scott's only possessions.

"You aren't the only one thinking it would be easy." Tik pointed to Starbuck. "I don't know how to get the horse attached to the wagon, but I'm pretty sure you'd need some kind of harness. There's nothing on the horse."

Is this how we start? By robbing someone we don't know? Someone who showed us kindness.

"It might be in the wagon," she said. "But I'm pretty sure we'd get trampled or kicked or something just as painful."

Lena watched as Ava settled the kids. They didn't seem worried at all. It was like they just trusted that Ava would take care of them. Lena hoped they were right. It was one thing to plan their escape, and another to be sitting here in the woods, in the dark, cold, and hungry.

Keith and Deb settled next to Tik. Mellow sat beside Lena, and Ava joined them to form the circle. It was clear everyone wanted to talk while Scott was away.

"Okay, what is it?" Lena asked. She had her own idea, but didn't want to influence anyone. She wasn't going to take on the role of leader out here. It was going to be more about ability than authority, if she had anything to say about their future.

Keith looked around the group, when no one spoke up he started the conversation. "If we travel with this Scott for a while, we might be better off. The wagon will come in handy for people who need to rest. He can give us some advice on how to find food and what the dangers might be."

Mellow spoke next. "It would be good if he came with us all the way. We could get more supplies if we had the wagon. There'll be places we can work to earn supplies, or scavenge, I'm sure."

Tik was scowling at Mellow.

"Ava? Deb?" Lena asked them directly because it shouldn't just be one or two of them making decisions.

"Whatever Keith says is best, I'm fine." Deb's voice was sullen.

Lena wondered if Keith was going to have to pay for making her come, but that was his problem.

Ava looked at her kids again before saying, "If we can trust him, I think we should join up. Even if it's just for a few days. We need to get used to being outside so much. I can't help remembering how nice it was to get home and close my door against the world."

They were looking at Lena to make the decision. She knew someone had to say the words but it weighed on her to be the one to do it. "How do we know we can trust him?"

Mellow tossed a twig into the fire. "He didn't have to bring us here. He left us alone. He trusts us, so why don't we trust him?"

"Don't confuse trust with a test," Lena said. "I guess we can talk to him about it in the morning. I don't think we should decide something like this when we're tired and stressed out."

By the time Scott returned, only Lena and Keith were awake. They'd agreed to take turns keeping watch. Scott had three rabbits in his bag. He cleaned them, laid the fur across a small frame to dry and put the meat in a pan of water to cook in the embers.

"It'll be ready for breakfast. We'll be awake just after sun up. There's no way to keep the light out when you live outdoors." He rolled himself in a well-worn camouflage sleeping bag. "If you like, we can travel together. At least, as long as our paths go the same way."

CHAPTER SEVENTEEN

Keith scraped the last of the stew from the pot and handed the serving to Jason. The kid was polite enough not to say anything, but Keith could see that he was hoping for more. In the week they'd been on the road, Scott had been finding rabbits and squirrels and other small edible animals. Keith knew they needed something bigger. That meant staying in one place long enough to hunt and dry the meat so they'd have enough to eat for a week. Lena wouldn't like the delay, but she knew they needed food.

"Scott, you ever go after a deer?" he asked.

The guy was quiet and he seemed to be okay, but Keith couldn't quite settle in to trusting him. As the man of the group, although Tik and Scott were almost men, they were still kids compared to him, he was responsible for making sure they didn't starve to death. And he had to admit that Deb was getting on his nerves a bit. That usually meant a weekend in his cabin, here it meant a couple of hours hunting.

"I don't usually need that much. I don't know how to preserve the meat either." Scott stood and wiped his hands on the seat of his jeans. "You know how?"

Keith nodded. "This is good hunting country." They were in what was once a state park. The hills were lightly wooded and there was a slow-moving river that wandered along beside the trail they were using as a road. "It's a good place to camp a few days too."

Scott looked around. "Yeah. You got enough guns? If the ladies and kids stay here, the three of us could go hunting."

Keith grinned. "I like to use a bow and arrow, but yeah, there's a couple of rifles for you and Tik."

He left Scott packing the rifles and ammunition and went to find Tik. It would be good to have his opinion of Scott. Keith had to admit that the ex-gangster was turning out to be useful.

"I think someone should stay here," Tik said when Keith asked.

Keith suspected he was staying to be close to Mellow. The girl didn't seem to have a clue that Tik was attracted to her, but that wasn't Keith's problem.

If he couldn't get Tik to come, at least this was an opportunity to get his take. "What do you think of Scott?"

"Seems okay. So, you're going to check him out now, after a week? How long do you usually take to know if you trust someone?"

"I'm still figuring that one out, kid." Keith asked again for Tik's opinion. "I don't want us to get careless around him."

"What if you decide you don't like him?"

"It's a long road and plenty of opportunity to part ways," Keith said. "Why won't you tell me?"

"No big deal. I like the guy, but he's got a different idea of what he wants. Since we all took off from a pretty comfortable place, I don't think it's up to me to judge his choices."

"Okay," Keith said. "We'll be back by nightfall. Make sure there's a fire going so we can have roast venison."

Deb was helping Mellow do some laundry in the river when he found her.

"I'm going hunting."

"Do you have to go? What will I do here if you aren't around?"

Keith appreciated that Mellow ignored the conversation, choosing to concentrate on the t-shirt she was rinsing. "You can tell them how to dress the meat. We'll gut it, but I don't want to hang around to dress it on the spot."

"If I come with you, I can do that."

Deb was going to have to learn to get along with Ava and Lena. Keith knew it wasn't easy for her, but they were planning to live on a farm together. If Deb couldn't fit in, it would be hell.

"No. I want to talk to Scott. You let them know what to expect and I'll bring back a deer."

She deflated and Keith felt like an asshole, but she'd only slow them down, and make too much noise. He'd tried to teach her to hunt a couple of times, but the deer had run from the chatter and he'd brought nothing home either time. Deb was really good at dressing the meat. She knew how to treat the skin so it could be used for clothing and she knew how to salt and preserve the meat so it was edible.

He hugged her and gave her a kiss. "You'll be fine, Deb. I won't be gone long."

It was too early for them to find much in the way of game, but Keith figured it would be good to talk before they focused on the hunt. That way he'd have a chance to see if he could settle the bad feelings he got when Scott was around.

"We should head for the top of the hill," he said, pointing to the left where the land rose toward the top of the tree line and the road. "We'll get there in time to poke around for sign of deer."

Scott shouldered his rifle and started walking. "What kinds of signs?"

At least he could follow orders. "Scat, trees nibbled on, prints, that kind of thing. What do you look for when you search for rabbits?"

"Same kind of stuff, but I can tell by the land. Is it the same with deer?"

For an experienced hunter. "Yeah, for me. I just need to figure out how to train you and a couple of others how to do it."

Keith rolled his shoulders releasing the tension he'd been holding. They passed through the tree line and the shade cooled him.

Traveling in the open where anyone could see them had been hard on him. The one time they'd heard someone coming was enough to convince the rest that the road might be an easy way, but there was too much risk for the few days gained on the trip.

As they'd crouched in the thick brush beside the road, he'd had his hand on the trigger, ready to solve whatever problem came up. A single horse rider trotted by, focused on his path.

Scott had identified the rider as a messenger. A few of the small communities sent information back and forth. "It's mostly about crops, or raiders. They won't mention us even if he noticed."

The assurance hadn't stopped them from crossing to the lower path. The wagon was able to manage the short distance across the rough terrain and then the smooth grass seemed as useful as the paved road.

Scott stood beside a large tree. "What other kind of game is in here?"

"Maybe some wild pigs. At this time of year, most of the other game is higher up."

"Would it be better to go for a pig?" Scott asked. "I'm guessing that was what ripped the bark off the tree."

Keith looked where Scott pointed. The bark was scraped away at about knee height. "Probably right, but we go after deer, not pigs." He started walking uphill, if Scott didn't follow him, then he'd learn something.

Scott caught up to Keith a few minutes later. "Why not? They are smaller and we can carry a pig back."

So, he'd seen wild pigs, and deer. That wasn't what he'd pretended. "Yeah, but deer don't charge you and they don't have sharp pointy tusks. We'll get a deer small enough to carry. We won't get hurt so easily."

Keith didn't wait for Scott to respond. They were getting close to where the deer were likely to be. There were no pigs around — the stench would give them plenty of warning to get out of the way.

Scott was pretty quiet. Keith waved his hand behind him in a signal to slow down and step even more quietly. When Scott was standing beside Keith, he leaned forward and pointed. When Scott was looking in the right direction, Keith whispered, "There's tracks near that stream. They come here a lot. If we wait for them, we'll get our pick."

Scott opened his mouth to answer, but Keith shook his head. Looking around he found a place downwind and far enough away that they could talk quietly and not spook their prey. He pointed and headed toward the spot.

When they settled, he nodded for Scott to talk.

"I don't feel right about this, we should just get ourselves a bunch of small game, enough for a few days and then get going. I don't like sitting around in the open."

"I get that, but you were alone before. We all look out for trouble and we protect the group. A bunch of small game is hard to preserve, unless you've figured out how to do it without making the meat inedible. Venison will keep a while and we need some stock of food. What happens when we aren't some place we can hunt?"

Scott tipped his head at some sound and then shook it. "I cook the meat and then it keeps — well not long, but it does keep. We can have ten rabbits in the bag before we even see a deer. If we did that, we could find a better place to spend the night."

Keith wasn't going to budge. The kid wasn't thinking about being part of the group. If he could only see life as something you lived alone, there would be trouble later. Scott would run when it got hard. He'd leave them some place and take the horse and the wagon, and their supplies.

Keith caught a whiff of the wild pig pack, but it was a long way off. There was no need to give up their spot. "Pigs."

If he was right about the deer, then maybe they could get more than one. He could leave Scott with the carcass and get help to bring it to camp.

"Should we move?" Scott asked. "How close do they have to be before it's dangerous?"

At least the kid wasn't rash. "Not yet."

"But if one of us gets hurt, how will we be able to kill something, let alone get it back to the group?"

"The pigs are far enough away. Now settle down. The deer will want water around dusk, we've got about an hour." Keith needed to think over his assessment of Scott. Was the guy a loner, or was he just so used to taking care of himself that he couldn't think beyond the current day?

"If it's going to take that long, I can go get some rabbits. I'll do it quiet." He started to rise.

"No. Wait here with me," Keith said. He couldn't go looking for Scott when the time came and a few rabbits could cost them a week's food.

"Look, I know you think you're some kind of mountain man. That you know how to survive out here, but I've been doing it for a long time," Scott said.

He didn't leave so Keith figured he had more to say. When Scott didn't speak, Keith said, "You think I just read books on this? I hunted so Deb and I could have enough meat to stay healthy. They ration the food. I wasn't planning to let someone else decide what I could eat."

Scott shrugged. "So, you spent a couple of nights in a cabin alone. You always had a place to go back to. And feeding your wife isn't the same thing as feeding this group. They are depending on us, and we need to be sure that we don't go back without anything."

The kid had no idea how hard Keith worked to do that very thing. "There's risk both ways. We do it my way so we get enough. If we miss the deer, you can go get your rabbits and we'll try again in the morning. The deer will be back around dawn."

"No, old man. We won't get any rabbits to take back for dinner. They hide at night and you have to trap them. That takes time."

Old man? "Listen, kid. Don't talk to me like I've never done anything but sit on my ass watching the world go by. I know how to hunt. I know what it takes to feed people."

"Sure you do." Scott sniffed the air again. "The pigs are getting closer. Will the deer come if there's something else here?"

Keith bit back his answer. He'd let Scott get the best of him. If he kept going, they'd be shouting and scaring off all of the game. Maybe he was wrong about Scott. Maybe he could try trusting the kid. "We need to move fast. I don't think the deer will be discouraged. But if the pigs don't turn away, we might have to take one of them."

"I thought you said that was too dangerous."

Keith wanted to tell him just to listen, but it was his job to train not push around. Tik would probably question everything too. When they were back at camp, there would be plenty of time to straighten out Scott's attitude — maybe starting with an apology, although it wasn't on the top of Keith's list. Right now, they had to work together.

"It was too dangerous to hunt them, but if they come to us,

we'll take what we can. They hunt in packs, so keep an eye out. And use the gun."

Scott swung the rifle around and held it ready. "This was a stupid idea. We should have brought Tik and maybe one of the women."

Keith couldn't argue with that. Maybe the only thing that would come out of the trip was that he'd stop suspecting Scott and learn something about living on the road.

CHAPTER EIGHTEEN

The stench was getting closer. Keith's nerves tightened in a familiar alertness. It was a race now between the pigs and the humans.

A doe stepped out of cover and dipped into the river. Following her were two young deer. One of the fawns would be perfect for their needs. There was no need to worry about over-hunting these days. There were so few people that the wildlife population was going to boom.

He elbowed Scott. The kid turned to look and a smile crossed his face. They were probably both thinking the same thing, Keith thought. They'd bag one of the deer and be done before the pigs arrived. They just needed to be gone, the pigs wouldn't follow.

Scott straightened and raised the rifle. Keith pressed his hand on the barrel and shook his head. The bow and arrow would be better. No noise to attract anyone or anything. Wild pigs might not be the only dangerous animal in the hills.

Scott looked from Keith to the deer. He frowned and mouthed 'are you sure?'

Keith nodded. He took the bow from its carrier and notched in an arrow. He had more than one bow, but this one was compound. As long as it lasted, it was going to be his choice. When it broke, they'd have no way to repair it.

He motioned for Scott to take cover behind the tree. Keith didn't want to worry about anything getting between him and his target. He straightened and aimed for the closest deer. The bow was oiled so no sound would come from it when he let the arrow loose. A second more and the deer would be at the water's edge and motionless.

Keith took in a slow deep breath, preparing to release on the exhale so that there was no jerk when the arrow shot forward. This had to be perfect so that Scott would understand that Keith knew how to survive. The deer dipped his head, Keith loosed the arrow and it found its target. The rest of the animals froze for a split second before bounding off into the trees.

Keith turned to tell Scott to come with him. Scott's arm shot out from behind the tree and pulled at Keith.

He struggled away. Scott's grip loosened and Keith fell, a pain shooting through his leg as his right knee twisted.

"Shut up," Scott yelled as Keith swore.

A shot and another, and a squeal and another shot.

Then Scott came around to kneel beside Keith. "How bad?"

"I can't stand. Why didn't you just tell me what happened?" Keith tried not to show the pain that was ripping through his leg.

"You were about to step into the herd. Didn't you smell them?" Scott placed his hand on Keith's knee. It was gentle, but for Keith it was like a knife stabbing through. "It's swollen already. We'll have to get someone up here to help."

"Did you kill one of them?" Keith didn't argue. He'd crawl over to the deer and start gutting it while Scott brought help.

"No, I shot to scare the herd. They scattered." He looked to the carcass. "That's going to attract scavengers."

Keith nodded and tried to get his breathing under control. "I'll deal with it."

Scott looked at Keith. "How do you plan to get over the boulders?"

"Crawl." Keith tried to shift. "You should have just warned me."

Scott placed the rifle against the tree. "Maybe, but I didn't know if you would argue or act. I'm sorry this happened, but at least you're alive."

Keith knew that if the pigs had reached them, Scott would have had to run, and the deer would be unusable after the herd was done with it.

"Next time. I promise I won't argue." He tried to make it a joke, but this was serious. If they didn't get the deer to Deb for dressing, the carrion eaters would come. First birds, eagles and vultures. Then wolves. And none of them would turn down human flesh. Wolves would be happy to finish him off. A rifle wasn't much good for close in fighting.

"Keep the rifle. You won't be able to use the bow," Scott said. "I'll carry what I can down with me. We'll lose a bunch of it, but maybe there's more than a few rabbits worth of meat to be saved."

Keith figured he deserved the dig. Hunting wasn't a sure thing, so maybe they wouldn't have found any small game either. "If you can get me over there, I can keep working on the carcass while you're gone."

Scott put the bow and remaining arrows in the case. "No, I'll go light and fast. You'll be safer here, away from the meat. Maybe the wolves won't come looking for you."

Did he have to keep digging at Keith's expertise? "You are an asshole sometimes."

"Yeah, I guess." Scott took the tarp they'd brought to carry their kill and hurried to the downed animal.

"Take the legs," Keith called. No need for silence now. "That'll leave the organs intact." The leather would be a loss, but it was meat they needed right now.

It wasn't elegant. Scott clearly didn't have his skills at butchery, but the kid did get the legs off and in the tarp. He didn't say anything when he was done, just ran downhill. He was out of sight in seconds.

Keith watched the sky through the gaps in the tree cover. It wasn't much, but at least he'd have a chance of seeing something circle before landing. Maybe he could keep the birds away for a while. He wouldn't be able to take the kick if he shot, but the rifle would work fine as a bat. As long as Scott came back as quickly as he'd gone.

There was no way the kid was getting away with leaving Keith to die.

He wouldn't abandon his horse and wagon. And even if he did, Deb would eventually make someone come looking. Lena would want to know there was nothing to do to save him, no matter the story Scott gave.

Fuck! How had he been so careless?

Anywhere else, he'd get a doctor's opinion. He knew that his knee would repair itself with some rest. Keith knew he'd ride the wagon for a couple of days, but it was just a wrench — he couldn't accept that it was more. Who needed a cripple at a working farm?

A screech ripped Keith's attention back to the sky. Eagles. He used his arms to shift into position, wishing he had a shotgun.

Regardless of the pain, if he could keep the birds in the air, then the wolves would take longer to find the deer. He lay back and aimed for the sky, with an angle on the gun so he wouldn't end up getting the bullet in his eye when it came back down. That would be the last straw.

Keith shot both barrels in rapid succession, the recoil burning a pain through his knee. He saw a flash as a bird circled wider. Nothing landed on the carcass. If they were very lucky, the rest of the animal would be fit to bring back when they came for him.

It was working. Keith fired another round. The birds had stayed away from the meat. But now he was out of ammunition.

It wouldn't be long before the birds tried to land and there was no way to stop them. Once they started attacking the carcass it would be contaminated.

Scott wouldn't be back in time, so the only option was to get up and move to the deer. Keith used his arms and good leg to raise himself against the tree trunk. He needed a crutch and the useless rifle was the only thing in reach. When he was standing, Keith hopped to the first obstacle. The rifle was too short to be of much help, and every few hops, his bad leg got jostled driving pain through his body.

"You are a stubborn fuck," Scott said.

Keith looked around and saw Scott standing at the edge of the clearing holding a branch long enough to actually support his body. "Sometimes that's all you can count on," Keith said.

Scott handed him the crutch and took the rifle. "I guess we're both stupid. If we're going to get to this farm, we have to give up what we had before."

Keith hopped toward the deer. "You planning to stay with us the whole way?"

"I told you, I don't plan. But I don't have any plans to take off either. And I promise I'll tell you if I decide to split." Scott walked beside Keith.

"Anyone else coming?" They wouldn't be able to carry much, but if Tik was on his way, they could protect the meat until he got there.

"No. I left the legs with Deb and came back. I figured you didn't have time for me to explain and get a rescue party together."

Keith leaned on the crutch. "Yeah. I guess that was the right decision." As he finished speaking the first bird landed beside the deer. It ripped the stomach and pulled out a rope of intestine.

"Next time, we won't fight so much," Scott said. "We could have had a lot more food if we hadn't been testing each other."

CHAPTER NINETEEN

Tik looked at the campground. They'd been on the road almost a month and the monotony was getting to him. Find food, travel, find food, travel. There was rarely anyone else on the road and when they heard someone approach, Keith or Scott usually made them hide.

It was like there was no one else left. They'd come through a couple of deserted small towns, most of the supplies had already been scavenged. They'd picked up a couple of tents, and a camp stove in the last one. If Scott left them, they'd lose any equipment they couldn't carry, but Lena didn't like leaving stuff behind.

Now, Lena wanted them to rest. He'd been surprised at the amount of energy it took to walk all day. Unless someone was sick, or injured, only the driver rode the wagon. Tik liked the walking, and it was easier now that he'd worked out the kinks in his muscles and his feet were used to it.

"Tik," Ava called. "Are you staying here or coming to find supplies?"

Half of them were heading back to the last town they'd seen. It was large enough to have one of those giant hardware stores and a good warehouse. "Who's going?" If Mellow stayed, he'd stay.

"Keith, Scott, and Lena. We need one more. If you want to stay, I'll join them."

Keith and Scott were enough to do the scouting. There hadn't been anyone guarding the stores in the last few places, but Tik knew it might happen. If he stayed, it would help to have someone protect the camp. "I'll keep an eye on the kids and help set up," he said.

Ava waved and hung the gleaning bag over her shoulder. It was a deep bag with handles just long enough to hang an inch or so below the armpit. They all wore them and you could stuff a lot of food into them.

Tik joined Jason at the wagon, helping to pull out the bundle of tarps. Jason grunted under the weight of his end of the load.

"Hey, Tik. You think we're far enough away?" Jason asked.

"From what?"

"The gangs. Are we far enough away that they won't catch us?"

There was a quaver in his voice. Tik had no idea the kid was that scared. Mostly he kept to himself, learning the skills they all taught each other, but not standing out.

Every time sounds of people had come from behind them, Tik had braced for the fight. For days, he couldn't sleep for more than an hour without waking up sure that someone was about to stick a knife in his gut, but he'd thought he was the only one. Basso might send someone after Tik just out of spite. But no one had come.

He tried to figure out when the threat had disappeared, but couldn't. It was as if he'd just let it go somewhere on the road. All he knew was that he could sleep at night now, and Jason was right.

"They would have come right away," he said. "Following us now is too much work for them."

And that fight on the bridge the night they left might have been a sign of more trouble. Basso probably forgot all about his missing lieutenant right away if there was a full-blown gang war. That might explain why they'd slipped away so easily.

Tik and Jason dumped the tarps in the center of the grassed area. Each one was fitted to a tent, Tik unrolled the first one and placed it near the center. Then the fire could be laid outside the camp. It meant they didn't have the heat of it overnight, but it also meant they weren't attracting anyone or anything to the middle of their camp in the dark. And it was hot all day anyway.

Mellow and Maya were sorting through the remaining supplies. Some meat from the last hunt, a few half-rotted vegetables they'd pulled from a garden. It would be stew for dinner again.

Mellow was like an angel as she bent over the sack of ingredients, her hair hanging like a golden curtain. She judged each piece before tossing it into the bowl for preparation, or as far as she could away from camp because they were too far gone.

"If you keep staring at her, we'll never get this straightened out," Jason said, drawing Tik's attention back.

"I was thinking," Tik said. He didn't want Jason to figure out what thoughts were going through his head.

"Sure, thinking." Jason laughed.

"Yeah, about how it might be nice to go back to that big garden and see if there's any fruit." It would be a nice change from stew.

"We checked. There won't be any that got ripe since we were there." Jason snorted. "You like Mellow; why don't you just tell her?"

"It's complicated," Tik said.

"Yeah, grownups always say that when they don't want to talk about something," Jason aligned the last two tarps. "Let's get the tents done next."

Was it really that complicated? Tik thought when they'd finished setting up the tents. He hated to think it was cowardice that kept him from telling Mellow how he felt. It wasn't like he was in love with her, but he liked being with her. And there was only Mellow anyway and if he left it too late, she'd hook up with Scott, and Tik would have to find another girl.

He wandered over to where Mellow was alone cleaning vegetables. "Can I help?" *That was stupid.*

"No, I'm good. There isn't enough here to take long," she said.

She hadn't even looked up when he spoke. That was hard to take. "Where's Maya?"

This time Mellow did look up. Frowning she scanned the area. "She said she was going to practice sewing. Deb showed her how to suture a wound, so she's been practicing on scraps of rabbit skin."

"Shouldn't you be watching her? I thought you were responsible." Tik couldn't stop the words. He didn't know why he was accusing Mellow of not doing her job. He'd stayed to protect them; she wasn't responsible.

"She wouldn't wander off," Mellow said. She stabbed the paring knife into the potato she'd been peeling and left it in the bowl. "I'll go find her if you're so worried."

He reached for her arm as she stood. "No, you are probably right." Maybe it wasn't too late to be nice. "I guess I'm just worried."

Mellow pulled her arm away. "No, because now I'm worried. Where's Jason?"

"Gone down to the stream to see if he can get a couple of fish," Tik said. "He's old enough to be on his own."

"He's eleven. He's not old enough," she said.

An eleven-year-old in the gang would be in charge of recruiting. He'd be able to fight and win against older men. "Maya's only eight," he said.

Something flared behind Mellow's eyes. Tik stepped back, realizing too late that he'd gone too far. "Sorry," he said.

Mellow turned away. "No, you forget that none of us are used to this. You had to grow up fast in the gang. Maybe, in the future, eleven will be old enough but right now it's not. Go make sure he's okay. I'll check on Maya."

Tik wasn't given a chance to repair the damage. He'd meant to say that he liked her and ask her if she'd be okay with hanging out with him. But it had all gone sideways when he tried to sneak up on the words.

He watched Mellow search around the tents then enter one. Maya was probably inside.

Turning, he followed the path toward the river. This campground was set up so people didn't have to go far for activities. Doing some fishing was probably a good idea. It would give him the chance to rehearse in his head what he'd say next time. And that would be soon, he wasn't going to let Scott get in with Mellow just because she was playing hard to get.

Jason was sitting on a rock that jutted out from the shore to create a shadow on the water. He looked up as Tik arrived. "Hey, I thought maybe there'd be some fish in the shade."

"I'm going in," Tik said, kicking off his shoes and dropping his jeans. "If they are down there, we need to pull them out. Remember what Keith said."

"Me too!" Jason jumped up and let his pole fall to the stone.

"No. The current is too strong," Tik said. It wasn't, but he didn't really need to start competing with Jason for a fish.

He ducked under the water and looked to see if any fish were lurking in the shadows. Nothing, but it felt good to be in the river. He stood. "There's none. You go up stream. I'll keep trying here." He heard a snap in the words that he hadn't intended.

Jason picked up his pole and strode toward a narrow place in the river. His lack of retort confirming that Tik's tone had been as nasty as he feared.

"Not too far," Tik called after Jason. He also didn't need to lose the kid.

Stretching out to swim to the far shore, only about a hundred feet, but enough to give him a few strokes. The water chilled his anger and some sanity returned.

Mellow wasn't looking for a relationship. She hadn't shown any preference between him and Scott. It was up to them to make her see the sense of pairing up.

It was up to him.

He swam back to the river bank and pulled himself onto the rock that Jason had vacated. Laying down, he glanced to his right. Jason was there, standing in the middle of the river, pole in the water patiently trying to get a fish to bite.

There were probably none there either.

Footsteps broke through his daydream. Tik spun grabbing for his walking staff.

"I thought you were fishing," Mellow said.

She was standing on the other end of the rock, the sun shining on her blond hair. Her hand was shading her eyes. "Where's Jason?"

Didn't she trust him at all?

"He's up there." Tik pointed and looked.

Jason wasn't in sight.

"Damn. I'll go look for him." He grabbed his jeans and pulled them on, realizing his skin was dry. He must have fallen asleep. Not a great idea in the sun. His skin was light enough that he'd burn. His dad had been Irish, his mother from Mexico.

Nothing hurt as he got dressed, so, maybe he'd avoided a burn.

"Maya and I'll get the fire started."

So, Maya wasn't missing. What was Mellow insinuating? "Good idea. I'm sure there's nothing more important to do."

Mellow frowned and he realized he'd done it again. What the hell was wrong with him?

She nodded downstream. "He's there. It looks like he was lucky."

Tik looked and saw Jason holding a handful of fish strung together. He'd been working with Keith to learn this skill and he had a talent.

"Don't get out of my sight again," Tik yelled as soon as Jason got close.

"You were asleep, and nothing bad happened," Jason said. "Look! Mellow, can you cook these?"

"You can learn to cook them too, Jason," Tik said as Mellow reached for the fish. "We all need to learn everything. You can't expect the women to just clean and cook."

Mellow took the fish and glared at Tik. "We all take turns, and you know it. It will take a while for everyone to learn enough. I don't think you can cook that well, Tik."

"I don't have to learn. It's my job to keep you safe. I can't do that if I'm concentrating on a fry pan."

"I thought you said everyone needs to learn," Mellow said.

"Yeah, just start with Jason." Tik wanted to bite his lip so he couldn't talk. The swim had cooled him down, but as soon as Mellow arrived, here he was fighting again.

"Geez, Tik, relax," Jason said. "I know I gotta learn. I guess I figured if I got the fish, I wouldn't have to learn cooking today." He grinned. "Shouldn't that be a rule? If you bring in the food, you've done your job?"

Tik knew the kid was trying to avoid a blow up. The problem was that Tik was the only one starting anything. Mellow just looked at him like he was crazy. Jason actually caught some fish. All Tik did was cause problems. Maybe that's what Basso saw in him. Tik would never let anyone get away with disrespect. That was the kind of thinking that he hoped to leave behind.

He tried to form the apology, but he couldn't quite figure out what to be sorry for. Maybe it was all in his head.

"You can take over protecting the kids," he said to Mellow. "I'm going hunting. We can't count on there being anything in that town."

She shrugged. "Yeah, maybe it will change your mood. If you have to be mean to anyone, don't pick the kids. They are always trying to do what's needed. I don't see you trying anything but to hurt people."

"And all you do is pretend to be nice," Tik snarled. This time it was easy to see why he was mad. Mellow had no idea how hard it was to keep watching out for threats. Keith was always hanging out with Deb so she didn't annoy people and Scott just talked to anyone and everyone. Tik was the only one who knew that you had to be on alert all the time.

"I'm going to get the traps," he said.

As he ran off, he heard Jason say something and then Mellow laughed.

There would be nothing to hunt; Tik knew that when he told Mellow he was going.

It didn't matter. He wasn't going to spend time tracking through the woods. He was going to spy on the camp. If he could learn why they were laughing at him, then he'd know what to do. He wasn't going to be able to dig himself out of this hole unless he knew what was going on.

He knew three things for sure. One that he'd been an ass, but didn't know how it had happened. He also knew he didn't want to run away from this group. He might not get Mellow to like him, but this was his family. More than the gang had ever been, this group of strangers looked out for each other. It was what people said families were like. Parents didn't abandon their kids because life got hard. They worked it out and stuck together.

That's what Tik wanted. Because the third fact he was sure of was that he had no place to go. The gangs hadn't cared enough to come for him. He didn't have the skills he needed to do what Scott did — wander out here alone. He had to figure out why he kept being mean to Mellow and then stop doing it.

He knew that was easy to think, out here alone with no one to piss him off, but he had to figure it out.

The campground wasn't really set up for spying. The trees were cleared back far enough that no one had to pitch their tent where the branches could fall and the insects were thicker. Tik got as close as he could and crouched behind a huge fir tree. Sound carried pretty well, and if he focused he could hear what people were saying.

"What's wrong with Tik anyway," Jason asked. "He can't take a joke, or have any fun today."

Mellow must have cleaned the fish at the river, because now she was cutting them into chunks for the stew pot. "Yeah, he's kind of cranky. He was okay this morning. Maybe he's just tired."

Maya appeared in Tik's range of vision. She handed a scrap of fur to Mellow. The stitches she'd been practicing, Tik thought.

"He's scared," Maya said. "He looks behind us a lot."

Mellow tested the stitches and said something to Maya that Tik couldn't hear.

"I guess he's worried that someone is going to come after us," Jason said. "But earlier he told me that wasn't going to happen now."

"Yeah," Mellow said. "We're far enough along that we only have to worry about the people around us. Maybe he's got that thing you read about, Maya. Like he doesn't know what to do with the feelings he had in the gang?"

Maya shrugged. "Maybe, but I think I know what the problem is."

Mellow filled the pot with water and placed it next to the fire. "What?"

"Don't you know?" Maya asked. Then she leaned down and whispered something to Mellow.

Tik struggled to bite back a curse.

"No I don't think so," Mellow said. "If he liked me, he wouldn't keep snapping at me for no reason."

Tik's shock was drowned by Maya's giggles. "He keeps looking at you. I don't believe you didn't notice."

"No," Mellow said. She poked at the fire. "Why would he like me?"

Jason laughed this time. "You are pretty and he's a guy. Of course he likes you."

"You don't know what you're talking about." Mellow poked the fire harder. "You should both go read your books. I'll keep an eye on the fire until it's ready for the food. Everyone will be back soon and I don't want them to think we're just lazing around. And don't tell anyone what you think about Tik."

Tik watched as the kids ran to the wagon and picked up the books they were studying. Ava made sure they kept learning, not just the skills they'd need, but also real school work. He glanced back at Mellow. She was staring at the fire as if she could convince it to burn hotter.

Tik's stomach turned over with dread. Had he been so mean that she'd never look at him again? He could tell she was thinking by the way she shook her head every once in a while, like she couldn't believe someone like Tik would think of her that way.

When she'd poked the fire into embers in one spot, Mellow placed the stew pot on top to cook their dinner.

Should he go and tell her he was sorry? It would be a problem for her to know he'd been listening, but maybe he'd be able to wing it and she wouldn't think he was spying.

CHAPTER TWENTY

No, Tik decided. It was still early enough that he could go hunting. Rabbits, maybe some eggs, anything to take his mind off Mellow. It would be better to pretend nothing happened today and find another girl somewhere when they were settled on the farm.

The traps were on the ground beside him. He picked them up and slowly stepped backward until he was deep in the trees. A few rabbits would definitely help Mellow forget he'd been a jerk.

The woods thinned and thickened periodically as though something had been harvesting them sporadically. There were a lot dead leaves, and twigs on the ground; it made it hard for Tik to be quiet. He'd found a way to avoid most of the hunting trips, but Keith had made sure that everyone had learned the basics.

Tik knew that if he couldn't be quiet, there'd be no game to bring back and that was starting to feel like the only way to get over his fight, bring back food. It was always short in supply and they spent more time foraging than traveling some days. Tik wanted to get to the farm. That was where he could start his new life. The constant need to get supplies was hard to take. It was also hard to argue against. If they didn't have food, they couldn't keep going.

It was no good, he knew that every snap of dry wood was alerting all the animals in the area that he was on the prowl. He stood still in the shadow of a tree that had fallen across the path. He kept his eyes on the gaps between trunks ahead. A long ear swiveled. The rabbit was trying to be cautious.

He reached into his pocket for one of the round stones that fit into the slingshot. It was faster than trapping, and more interesting. Aiming the slingshot, he pulled back on the elastic and then let go.

The stone bounced off the tip of his thumb on the way to the forest floor a few feet in front of him. He dropped the slingshot, swore as the rabbit bounced away, and then held his thumb. It took time, but eventually it stopped throbbing with pain.

He should have practiced more. He'd forgotten to make the angle right. Bending to pick up the stone and slingshot, Tik wondered if he was ever going to be more than just a glorified bouncer. The only thing he had talent for was guarding the group. And that didn't guarantee he'd actually win a fight if anyone came at them.

"Might as well go back," he said to the dead air of the forest. Back to where? Camp, yes, but maybe he should go back to the gang. Not Basso's — that wouldn't be possible — but any one of the others would take him.

He'd get back faster than they'd come here. He didn't need to find food for nine people, and he could move at his own pace. Two weeks, maybe a bit more and he'd be back where he could feel useful. Even if it was helping someone to get hooked on the latest drug.

No one would come after him from the group. They couldn't afford the delay, and it wasn't like they'd miss him.

Tik knew he was being stupid, but that didn't chase away that hard feeling of being useless, any more than knowing that he'd been a jerk had changed the words that spewed out of his mouth.

He turned to follow his tracks back to the camp and saw another rabbit. This time he just let it go.

"No luck?" Keith asked then stepped from behind a tree.

So, I don't even know how to creep around as well as an old man.

Keith had seen him ignore the rabbit. It would have been easy to lie, but Tik just pretended it hadn't happened. "There's not much out here. What about you? Was there anything in those stores?"

Keith was keeping his eyes on the forest around them. Tik always forgot to be that alert. It's not like there were any people out here to attack. And any animal would make noise, and maybe stink up the place first. Tik walked past Keith, headed back to the camp.

"We got some stuff, but not much food. There were things we'll need at the farm though. And some ammo." Keith moved to follow Tik.

"So, Jason's fish will have to do?" He knew the answer; they'd have to hunt before moving on. He just wanted Keith to say the words. Maybe it wouldn't feel so hopeless coming from him.

"The kid did a good job, but we need more. That's why I came looking for you. We can fish for an hour while the rest of them get things sorted."

"I'm almost as bad at fishing as I am at hunting," Tik said.

"Then it's a good job I'm here to teach you." Keith pulled two fishing rods from behind the tree. "These are better than what we had."

"I should go back to camp." Tik didn't want to look like he was hiding from Mellow. If he had to apologize, then he'd rather get it done and over with.

"I heard you were feeling a bit cranky," Keith said.

"Did Mellow tell you that?"

"No, Jason. His actual words were, 'Tik is being mean to everyone'. Fishing is a good excuse to sit and talk."

Why was everyone being so reasonable? In the gang, someone would have retaliated and they'd be thrashing it out with fists. Maybe this was another thing he'd have to get used to. "Okay. It's better than going back and facing them."

They set up downriver from where Jason had made his catch. Tik followed Keith's instruction and soon had his line in the water. Now all they had to do was wait for a bite.

"Why are you cranky?" Keith asked.

"I don't know."

"If we were back in town, I'd leave it at that, but we're out here, we have only ourselves to count on, and someday soon we'll need to trust each other or die."

Tik lay back, his eyes still on the fishing pole. If he could hook some fish it would go a long way to making him feel useful. It couldn't hurt to talk, especially if he was going to leave. "I didn't mean to be nasty," he said. "I was trying to get Mellow to like me, and suddenly I'm sniping at her."

"You sure you approached her the right way?" Keith pulled a package of something from his pocket and handed it to Tik. "Trail mix. I'm guessing you haven't eaten much today."

Tik's stomach growled. "I was okay until you handed me food." He ripped open the package and tossed a handful of nuts and dried fruit into his mouth. Chewing gave him time to consider Keith's question. He hadn't thought of it as an approach. He'd moved in on her because he felt like he didn't need to worry about the gangs, and then he started thinking about Scott getting there first.

"I guess I didn't have an approach." He told Keith how he'd felt when Jason asked about the gangs.

"It's something we've all worried about," Keith said. "Not the gangs. Most of us worry about the authorities coming to get us. We all reached the point when we felt safe. But most of us weren't in there with the gangs. You are bound to feel something more complicated."

"Yeah, well that's true. If I go back, I'm dead. Is that true of anyone else?"

Keith checked his line before answering. There were no fish, the bait was still there, and Tik didn't see any of that changing soon. When he settled back in the shade beside Tik, Keith said, "Me, Deb, Ava, and Lena, we'd be put to work on the farms and roads. Hard, but we'd be fine. You know why Mellow left, and why Ava wanted to go. All the kids will be in danger of becoming what you wanted to leave behind."

"So, I should just get over myself?" Tik tried to keep the bitterness out of his voice, but it was there.

"I didn't say that, Tik." Keith sat up. "We got fish."

By the time they sat in the shade again, there were four fish in the creel. Tik was relieved that he'd contributed to the catch.

Keith continued the interrupted conversation, "I'm just saying you aren't the only one going through it. What you feel is real. We all have a taste of it. That means we all get it and you don't have to feel alone."

Tik watched the river flow past. Before he could work through what Keith had said, the fish started biting again. They each brought in four more and then Keith told him to pull in the lines.

"So, what approach did you use on Deb?" Tik asked.

Keith laughed. "Different circumstances, kid."

"Why did you marry Deb? She doesn't seem to be like you." Tik figured that was as tactful as he could manage.

"You mean she's kind of whiney and unwilling to change?" He grinned. "I was kind of antisocial and unwilling to change. I've learned how to be part of the group. Deb will find her way. I might need to give her a nudge if she doesn't find it soon before one of the women strangles her."

Tik hoped he'd nudge Deb today; if she tried one more time to ride in the wagon because she didn't like walking, he'd strangle the woman himself. "So, what should I do with Mellow? I don't want to lose her to Scott." There it was out. That felt like the right problem.

"If Scott was interested in her, or Mellow was interested in him, she'd already be with him." Keith jerked his head toward camp. "Let's get back. I think with Mellow you just need to be clear. The girl is smart, but I don't think she's noticing anything subtle right now. Be nice and don't try too hard."

Be nice and don't try too hard.

Tik had no clue about how to do either

They stepped through the last of the trees to see their camp. Tik felt like he was coming home. It wasn't the first time he'd returned to a camp, but this one was different. It wasn't the first time Lena'd thought to stay in one place for more than a night, but this time people had unpacked more than the usual. With a couple of days, there was time to clean and mend clothes, inventory all of their supplies and make a wish list. Things that filled the clearing with more than just a few tents and bedrolls.

It was this that made him see the anger from the morning for what it truly was. Keith had almost got it right. Everyone was going through something. The difference was that he didn't have any family with him, and neither did Mellow. And if she didn't like him in the same way, or liked Scott more, then Tik would be the only one who was truly alone.

"Go apologize." Keith handed Tik the creel full of fish. "This might help open the conversation."

Tik thanked him and made his way to where Mellow was tending the fire. The stew from earlier was sitting on the edge of the fire, keeping warm. She was making pan bread, not paying attention to anyone.

"We caught these," he said passing her the fish. "There's enough for us to have a full meal."

She looked up from the fire and smiled. "Thanks." Mellow returned her attention to the flames.

Tik smothered the feeling that she was ignoring him. Pan bread was tricky over an open fire. She just didn't want to burn it.

"About earlier," he said. Then, crouching to her level so she wouldn't have to turn away from her cooking again, he added, "I'm sorry about what I said."

"You were pretty nasty to everyone," Mellow whispered. "Are you going to apologize to Jason and Maya too?"

This wasn't the direction he wanted the conversation to go. "Yeah, but I wanted to ask you something."

"Go apologize to the kids. Then come back," she said as she turned the bread in the pan.

Was she doing this on purpose? Keith said she might not even know that Tik liked her, then again, maybe this was the kindness part.

"Be back in a minute," he said.

"Do it properly," Mellow said. "It's not a race. I'm here all night." She laughed when she said the words, but Tik was stung by her assumption that she didn't think he'd do a good job.

He found Maya and Jason helping Ava to sort through the pile of clothes the group had accumulated.

"Can I talk to the kids?" he asked. Ava looked surprised. He hoped it wasn't because he was being polite.

"Sure. Just don't be long."

Tik followed Jason and Maya to the side of the wagon. It wasn't far, but gave him a feeling of privacy.

"What do you want to talk about?" Maya asked.

"I need to apologize to both of you. I was cranky this morning." It wasn't getting easier with practice.

"Yeah, you were, but you were mean to Mellow," Maya said.

Jason stared at Tik. "Are you going to apologize to her?"

This was not how Tik liked things. Keith's voice rang in his mind. *Be kind.* Tik knew he was going to have to learn to do things a whole new way. "I have, and now I'm saying sorry to you."

"Sorry is easy to say," Maya said as though she was parroting someone — probably Ava.

"So, what do I need to do to make you forgive me?" This was more in his expertise, negotiating a way out.

Maya whispered to Jason who nodded. "Okay. You have to do our chores for the whole time we're camped here," she said.

That would be easy to agree to, but impossible to do. "We are all loaded with chores. How about I do one chore each for you?"

Maya looked at Jason who let her take the lead. Tik realized that Maya was going to be a strong woman and maybe lead the group eventually. She was smart, and wily and willing to get her own way. "Okay, you can do the dishes for Jason, and you can get the firewood for me. But one more thing."

She stood there, hands on hips, her brown eyes focused on his. This was important to her. Tik waited. How much would she humiliate him in the name of payback? Even at eight-years-old, she wasn't someone to be defied.

"You have to tell Mellow that you like her."

Tik felt his skin warm. "Even if I don't like her?" He held up a hand to stop the response. "I know what kind of like you mean."

"You do like her that way. If you tell her, maybe you won't be mean to everyone."

"What if she doesn't like me?" Tik figured he'd get some help from Maya if she was so determined to set him and Mellow up.

"You'll just have to deal with it," Maya said.

Jason snickered and ran back to help his mother.

"Fine, we have a deal," Tik said. He held out his hand to seal it.

Maya looked at him, spat in her palm and waited. He followed her lead and they shook hands.

Every step back the fire and Mellow felt like a wade through mud. Tik's heart started to race and he considered running away, but he knew Maya would find him. Running away wasn't going to solve anything.

Mellow was tearing the bread into portions as he approached. Looking around, Tik noted that everyone was busy. There was no audience for him to worry about if it went wrong.

"Okay, the kids are fine," he said.

"What did you have to agree to?" Mellow said with a chuckle. "I'm guessing Maya set a price."

Tik smiled, but regretted that he seemed to have missed a lot about people while they were on the road. From now on, he'd spend more time getting to know everyone rather than worry about what might be coming after them.

"Two of their chores and one promise."

"Not bad. The first time I had to make a deal with her, it was a day of chores. So, can you tell me the promise?"

Tik sat beside her on the grass. He tossed a small branch into the fire to keep it going and then cleared his throat. "I have to tell you that I like you."

Her eyes widened. "Oh, so Maya was right."

Tik thought back to when Maya had whispered in Mellow's ear and then they'd laughed.

"So, you don't like me in that way?"

She blushed. "I didn't believe her when she told me. I don't know, Tik, I haven't really been thinking of that kind of stuff."

It was better than a flat no.

"I get it. So, would it be okay if we hung out and maybe... I guess dated is the wrong word."

She laughed again. "Yeah. Why don't we say get to know each other better?"

The worry was gone. Tik wasn't sure when it had left, but telling Mellow had opened a door in him. Where there was only worry and anger, now something warm lived.

CHAPTER TWENTY-ONE

Ava rubbed dust from her eyes. They were in Millerville. The store wasn't air conditioned, or if it had been, the system had broken down. At least they were out of the sun. Ava picked a few cans off the shelf, checked them for dents or bulges and then placed them in the cart. They'd lucked out and this store hadn't been stripped clean, just the perishables were gone. That was a blessing considering the amount of time that must have passed since everyone left. The stench of rotting fruit, meat, and dairy would have made it impossible for the kids to help her forage.

The others were sorting through the hardware store, or setting up camp in one of the empty houses. It would be nice to have a real roof over her head for a change.

Beans. There were plenty of cans to take that were still safe. A few cans of salmon were in the back of the shelf. Pasta sauce; maybe there was some pasta still left. Maybe they'd find some wild garlic. She walked toward the next aisle where Maya was going through the baking supplies. The thought of a sit-down meal in a house made Ava smile.

"Yeah. My mom is here too," Maya said.

Ava's daydream shattered. There was a strange man talking to

Maya. The girl knew better than that, but maybe she thought the rule only applied back in New Surrey.

He was holding out something in his hand. Was he trying to take Maya?

"Maya, come here," Ava called. She tried to keep the panic out of her voice, but Maya gave her a curious look before obeying.

Ava kept her eyes on the man. She saw him consider running, in the way his glance flicked to either side as if searching for allies, or enemies. But he relaxed and started walking toward her. Ava moved between Maya and the man.

She wished that they'd brought Tik, or Keith, or Scott, but Millerville had looked deserted, so she'd just come with Maya.

"Hey, mom," Maya said. "This is Julian. He used to work in this store."

Ava pushed her cart forward, it would make a good ram if needed. "That's nice."

Julian smiled and reached toward her, wanting to shake hands. "Yep. I stuck around when everyone went farther west. I figured there was enough in town to keep me alive and there's a library a few blocks over for entertainment."

Ava glanced at his hand but didn't reach out to shake it. "How did you know we were here?"

"You didn't exactly keep it a secret. Don't worry, I'm happy for the company." He turned and then stepped a little closer to Ava.

Ava had heard the same noise that Julian had. Footsteps. Was it his partner? Now Maya seemed to get that her mother wasn't glad to meet a stranger.

"Mom, he's nice."

The footsteps got closer and Tik rounded the corner of the aisle behind Julian. Ava felt safer. She told herself it was more that she wasn't alone than that it was a guy who came.

Ava looked at Tik and hoped that he'd stay in place. "We don't know that, Maya. I've told you a million times not to talk to strangers."

"Yeah, I know, but this is the country. We haven't met anyone for ages." The creep of a whine in her daughter's voice set Ava's nerves on edge.

"I meant why did you approach her here, in this store, and why did you talk to my daughter instead of me?"

Julian blushed, but it didn't feel to Ava like it was embarrassment. Had his jaw tightened? Was he holding back anger?

"Hey, answer her, man." Tik shifted his weight a little and showed the knife he kept in a sheath on his belt. "Why talk to a little girl?"

"I didn't mean any harm." Now he was whining.

Ava wanted to get away from the situation. This guy wasn't right somehow. But they couldn't just beat up anyone who seemed off. Living alone for a long time was bound to make anyone a bit odd.

"When did they leave?" she asked.

Julian backed away then leaned against the shelving. "A bit over a year, I guess. Most people held on for a while, but no one was coming in from the highway, and supplies stopped. There was no fuel for the farm equipment."

It was a stock answer, Ava thought. Would the truth be more of a story? Was Julian even an original resident? Had he killed off the last few people living here?

"Where did you live?" Tik asked.

Ava was glad that he was suspicious too. It meant she wasn't being a crazy mother.

Julian's eyes widened, this time in fear. Ava figured he'd just realized they weren't buying his story. "Over the store, when I worked here. Now I live in the old Randall house. I figured they wouldn't mind."

Maya tried to get around Ava. "We should take him back to the house. He probably has a lot of advice for us. Come on, Mom."

It would help to have the others weigh in. Ava couldn't stop herself from feeling there was danger, but Maya was her daughter. When Julian answered the questions, there was a second when she believed him. But now that Tik was on alert too, she couldn't turn off the fear.

"That's a good idea," she said. "Tik, why don't we come back later. There's a lot to scavenge."

Maya and Jason would be safe in the house with the rest of the adults.

Tik motioned for Julian to move past. Tik's knife was in his hands. Ava hoped that he'd have no reason to use it.

She scooped some more cans into the cart then left it near the abandoned checkouts for retrieval.

Taking Maya's arm, she followed the two men out of the store. "Maya, that rule about strangers is always in effect. We don't know anything about this guy, and we need to be really careful."

Her fear must have shown because instead of arguing, or making a smart comment, Maya nodded and walked along in silence.

Ava had to admit, Julian was smooth. By the time he'd finished talking, even Tik was making him welcome.

She didn't buy it. There was no reason for Julian to approach an eight-year-old girl when her mother was just in the next aisle. He had to have known that she was there. If Maya hadn't spoken, they might have been gone before Ava knew anything was wrong.

She'd sent Maya and Jason to bed as soon as they'd eaten. It felt like they were safe out of his sight.

That was another thing: why didn't Julian object to them foraging? He might not need much, but everything they took was coming from his future meals.

Keith had asked Julian to stick with them for the night. Ava knew it was to make the most of the time they had with him. He'd survived out here for long enough to know something useful.

It was different from Scott's advice. When things got difficult, Scott moved on. Julian knew about staying put.

She was afraid they would invite Julian along on the journey. That would put him too close to Maya. Ava couldn't keep watch on her every day forever.

If they wanted Julian to be part of this group, Ava was going to have to leave. She took her glass of wine — they'd opened all of the bottles left in the store — and went to sit on the porch. She knew it wouldn't be long before Lena came out to talk to her. Keith and Scott were managing to get information. Mellow and Tik had gone off to be alone together after dinner. Deb was sitting and drinking on the stairs to the bedrooms. She'd promised Ava to keep Julian from going up.

Ava had been surprised, but then Deb had worked as a nurse, so maybe she'd seen the results of abuse enough to be cautious. Or maybe she was just humoring Ava, or maybe judging her parenting skills.

There were a million stars to light the sky. Sitting on bare ground looking up was a very different feeling from sitting on a porch swing with a glass of wine.

"Shove over," Lena said. "I've brought a bottle."

"I thought you'd be happy inside talking to the new recruit." Ava regretted the tone, but not the words. She felt betrayed that Lena seemed to be okay with Julian. She held out her glass for a refill anyway.

Lena stretched and then settled back on to the swing, starting it rocking with a gentle push of her toe against the porch floor. "I'm not recruiting people."

Ava turned to look through the window. Keith and Scott were still with Julian, and the edge of Deb's skirt was visible, proving she'd kept her promise.

"If no one believes me, why are they standing guard?" It did little to get rid of her fears that they were showing some sense around the stranger. It would have helped, maybe, if Tik hadn't disappeared with Mellow as soon as Julian had been introduced.

"I'm not stupid. Ava, I'm just being cautious. It's hard to turn down someone who might help. Especially when we're taking supplies from him. You may be right, but that doesn't mean we can't get some value before we move on."

Ava couldn't let go of the fear. "Maybe we should move on tomorrow morning, early. You'll be able to get whatever information you need by then. We'll have our supplies."

Lena sipped her wine. Ava hoped that she was considering the idea of leaving.

"We need to rest. You know we were in pretty bad shape when we got here. We need a couple of days." She held up her glass. "This won't help. We'll all have hangovers tomorrow."

Ava knew that was true. It hurt to agree with Lena, but she couldn't put her kids in more danger by dragging them back to the road before they were ready. She just couldn't see how to get through a few days here while making sure Julian didn't get near Maya. "We could stay here," she said. "I mean; it will give us a chance to figure out what Julian is up to. I can protect the kids better if we settle in, and they have a routine."

Lena topped up the glasses and placed the empty bottle on the floor out of the way. "One minute you are trying to get away from him, and the next you're suggesting we stay."

"Yeah, I'm a bundle of contradictions," Ava said. "I'm tired. I worry about what's ahead of us. We've been lucky so far, and that can't last, right?"

"Maybe it's not luck, maybe it's how the world is now."

"Will the farm be like this? Can I look forward to sitting on the porch at night and dreaming?"

Lena chuckled. "The sky is bigger at the farm. It's just a big house and then fields. It's like the stars are a billion nightlights."

They sat in silence as they sipped their wine. Eventually, Ava said, "Why do you think Julian didn't go when everyone left?"

"I didn't buy his story on that, but the world is a big place and we're going to run into a lot of people with hinky stories. I guess we need to think about how we'll deal with it in the future." Lena stood. "I know we'll have to make hard decisions so we can survive, but I don't want to start now, okay?"

Ava nodded and hoped Lena wouldn't regret the choice.

Her worries about Maya wouldn't go away, or be drowned in wine. Ava went back inside the house, taking Deb's place on the stairs. Maya was her kid. She had to be responsible for protecting her.

Deb went up to bed. Ava knew it wasn't to avoid Julian, she just didn't have the interest in socializing with them. It was going to be hard for Deb when they settled and people started to expect more of her. Ava dismissed the thought. It wasn't her problem.

Mellow and Tik returned a few minutes after Deb left. They brought more wine with them. One of the neighboring houses had a wine cellar. Ava wondered why Julian, who seemed to be enjoying the drink, hadn't consolidated it in one place. That way he'd know exactly how much he had left. The little voice inside that kept her suspicion of him alive, suggested it was because his story was a lie. Had he lived here before, or had he wandered in and decided to stay until everything was gone?

Ava refused another refill and placed her glass on the stair beside her. She didn't need any more; she needed to be alert.

After handing over the wine bottles to Keith, who stored some and opened two, Tik left Mellow's side and joined Ava.

"So, they don't see him as a threat?"

Ava shook her head. "Maybe I'm seeing a threat where there isn't one. Mothers can be like that." She didn't believe it, but voicing a thought was a good way to test its power.

"No. I got the same feeling." He tapped the sheath holding his knife. "There's something wrong. In the gang, we had all kinds of people. Most of us were just trying to get along, and the gang provided some structure, so we closed our eyes to the damage."

He laughed. "I didn't know that when I was part of it. Distance kinda gives you a different perspective. Anyway, some guys are off. You can tell. Some of them liked to cause pain, some were greedy for things, some just liked to destroy everything. I never knew what they would do, but I knew they were wrong."

Ava glanced up again to see where everyone was. The stairs were the only way to the bedrooms, at least from inside the house. There was a tree outside the kid's bedroom. Julian was still talking with Keith. Mellow and Scott were playing some card game, Lena was going through the kitchen cupboards making a small pile on the counter of things they would take. Ava's eyes lit on the chef's knife in the pile.

"We need to do something, Tik." Ava whispered. It was a surprise that she trusted an ex-gang member more than her best friend. "I don't care what anyone else thinks."

"You planning to act first?"

"I can't wait until he's done something," Ava said. "I won't let him hurt Maya or Jason."

Tik patted her knee. "I didn't mean that. I just want you to understand that if you go after him, it will change everything. It will change the way the rest of the group feels about you. It will change how you feel about yourself."

Ava kept her eyes on the knife. "What do you mean?"

"We have to wait until he acts. If he leaves the kids alone, then we all move on and no one has done something they can't get over. If he tries to get at them, you and me will be ready. I'll sleep outside the bedroom; you sleep inside."

"I won't be able to sleep." Ava watched as Lena placed the pile of kitchen equipment in a sack.

Tik nudged her. "I put something in the dresser. You don't have to take that knife. It will do more damage to you than to him."

He hadn't just run off to do whatever with Mellow. Ava finally felt like she wasn't alone. "Thanks."

"Keith and Scott won't let him do anything either," Tik said. "They may not believe you, but they aren't easy around him." Tik lifted his chin toward the group. "Check it out. Keith is armed and Scott is only half paying attention to the game."

Ava realized that the tension in the room wasn't coming from her. Everyone was on edge. "It's because he's unknown, Tik. They don't think he's a danger to my kids."

He shrugged. "I'm not sure that's right, but does it matter? They aren't going to relax around him."

It did matter, but not as much as she thought. "Then why won't people move on? Why are they hanging around?"

"Shit," Tik said.

Ava looked over to meet Julian's gaze. Keith was talking to him, but Julian wasn't listening. She'd kept her voice low, but how much had he heard?

CHAPTER TWENTY-TWO

The night had been hard for Ava. It hadn't cooled down after the heat of the day, but she'd refused to open a window. Maya and Jason had moaned in their sleep because of the heat, and she was covered in sweat soured from her fear. In the shower, the flow was weak, but it was enough to refresh her. Ava knew from experience that she'd need to sleep later or the day would be spent fighting off the crankies.

When she opened the door, Tik was sleeping against it. No one would have been able to enter without waking him. He moved inside when she said she needed to get some exercise.

It was early; the house was silent. She decided to make break-fast for the group. It might help them get over her paranoid behavior yesterday. And maybe bring them around to her point of view.

She descended the stair cautiously, expecting to see Julian sitting in the living room, but it was empty. At least she didn't have to worry about him watching her every move.

Today Ava was going to get another weapon. Tik had hidden a gun in the dresser, but that wasn't enough. During the night, she'd thought over Tik's words. She wouldn't go on the attack, but there was no way she was going to let Julian do what he wanted just because she couldn't stop him. A knife was quiet, but a gun was more likely to give her a permanent solution. And maybe after a night under a roof, they would be ready to move on. The longer they delayed, the later they would arrive at the farm, and the less harvest there would be.

She took the eggs they'd liberated from a brood of neglected hens out of the fridge. The electricity was out, but it worked to keep food a little cooler than in the cupboard. There was some dried salami, but no milk. So, no pancakes. Maybe they should start keeping their eyes out for loose livestock. A dairy cow or two would be useful, even if it slowed them down.

"Morning, Mom," Maya said. She was rumpled with sleep wrinkles and her hair was a tangled mess.

Ava kissed Maya's head. "What do you want for breakfast?"

"Cereal with milk and strawberries." Maya looked at the eggs. "Oatmeal?"

"We should go back to the store and see if there is any oatmeal. That's easy to make when we're camping. But there's no milk."

"Yeah there is," Maya said. Then she ran to the front door and into the street.

Ava's heart stopped.

She dropped the bag of coffee onto the counter and ran after her daughter. This was exactly what Julian could be waiting for. "Maya!"

By the time Ava got to the bottom of the steps, Maya was back with a bag of something in each of her hands. The street was empty.

Ava's heart started beating again.

"Dry milk, we just add water. And there are some cans of condensed milk too. Lena says we won't mind the taste so much after a while. I don't know what this tastes like, but it's better than water. And here's some oatmeal."

Maya handed her mother the food and ran back into the kitchen.

Ava looked around again. There was no one in sight, so she followed her daughter.

Jason was in the kitchen, and Ava could hear people moving around upstairs. If she was going to make breakfast, she needed to get started. And they might have hangovers, so greasy would be good.

She set Maya and Jason working with the dried milk to see what dilution was best, put a pot of water on to boil for the oatmeal, and a kettle to make coffee.

The others wandered down over the next few minutes. Keith seemed the worse for wear and the happiest to see the food.

"Where's that guy Julian?" Maya asked as she put a jug of milky water on the table.

"You and your brother go up and get ready. Brush your hair, Maya." Ava didn't want them there when she asked that same question. Mellow grabbed a mug of coffee, added milk, and then grimaced at the taste. "Not great, but not the worst. I'll go up and see if I can help Maya with her hair."

The kids taken care of, and breakfast ready to plate, Ava asked, "So what happened to Julian?"

Keith took a helping of sausage and eggs before answering. "I'm guessing he's passed out somewhere. I got him too drunk last night to do anything, in case you were right about him."

Scott pushed away from the table. "Keep some food for me, I'll go check on him."

Ava wished she'd thought to make tortillas. Then Scott could have taken breakfast with him. "I still think he's going to be a problem," she said. "I want to leave this morning. We can forage again for a little while and then leave."

"It was nice to be in a house. I think we should stay a few days," Lena said. "There's some stores we haven't looked in."

"We need a break. I say we stay one more day," Keith said. Deb nodded and nibbled at her food.

"If we stay, I need a gun," Ava said. "I won't let him harm my kids."

Deb poked at her scrambled eggs clearly unhappy with the food. "Why are you so sure that he's a danger? All he's done is talk to Maya."

Before Ava could answer, Tik jumped in. "You weren't there. None of you were. I'm with Ava. If we stay here, we won't rest. He's bad news."

Lena put her dishes in the sink and then turned to address the group, "I don't know what we should do, but we can't keep hashing this out."

Scott returned, shaking his head. "No sign of him."

Ava clenched her hands under the table in an effort to keep the anger out of her voice. "If you all want to stay here, I get it. We're exhausted. I can't stay. Even if I'm wrong and there's no threat, I'm not getting any rest. And I'm making some of you nervous enough that you're not either."

Ava knew that Lena was right. She wasn't so far down the rabbit hole that she didn't see the other side. What Lena didn't seem to understand was the risk. Ava only came along to save her kids from a future of violence and fear. If they were just going to spend their lives fighting about who to trust, it was better to leave.

Lena pushed away from the counter. "What would make it work for you, Ava?"

Hadn't she been clear? "We leave and find somewhere else to rest."

"What about the next person we meet?" Scott asked. "Anyway, you didn't seem to have a problem with me? What's different?"

Ava didn't want to talk about it anymore, and the kids would be down any second. But she couldn't just storm out and leave.

She needed supplies; she needed to get the kids together. Then she could get back on the highway and keep moving forward.

Then Scott's question sank in. Why hadn't she been worried about him?

Keith saved her from trying to answer. "You offered help. You didn't start with someone who couldn't defend herself." He rubbed his temple, clearly still hungover. "The more I think about it, the more I'm coming to Ava's point of view."

His words gave her some comfort. She wasn't over-reacting. "Look, I'll just go on ahead. You'll catch up with us in a couple of days. I'll take a gun and some supplies and then we don't need to talk about it any longer."

The sound of running feet on the stairs warned that the kids were on their way.

Mellow herded them into the kitchen, picked up their plates and suggested they eat outside. She winked at Ava as they walked by.

Tik waited until the door was shut and then spoke quietly, "I'll go with them. We can't just send Ava alone."

Lena looked out to the backyard where they could hear Mellow laughing with Jason and Maya. "If you go, then Mellow will want to go with you. We'll be broken in half. If you go, you should take the wagon and Starbuck. That means Scott will probably want to go."

Ava felt like she was fighting Lena for control. She didn't want to lead the group. Lena was better at it, and Lena didn't have kids to think about. "I'm not trying to break up the group."

"I know," Lena said. "It's not really my decision. We should all agree."

Keith stood and picked up a gleaning bag. "Let's get supplies, keep our eyes out for Julian and decide when we get back. We can go out in pairs."

It wasn't what Ava wanted, but a few hours of scavenging

wouldn't make a difference to her decision. "The kids stay with me."

"Fine," Keith said. "I'll come with you. Lena and Scott and Deb can go as a team. Tik and Mellow can go together to that store she was talking about. Is that good enough?"

Ava nodded and grabbed another bag. "I still want a gun."

Keith touched her shoulder. "I'll have a gun. You keep the kids together."

There was no sign of Julian. Ava didn't feel any of her fear lessen. It was almost worse that he'd disappeared. She knew he'd been listening when she and Tik had talked last night. Maybe she'd scared him off, and maybe he was just biding his time so they would forget the threat he posed.

Ava knew to her core that Julian was a danger. The others didn't agree, but they all had doubts. Even Keith had been hyper-alert all morning. It had been hard to stop Maya and Jason from running through the hardware store. The aisles were narrow and the shelving was tall. There was plenty of shadow for Julian to hide in.

Keith had solved the problem by splitting the kids up. He took Jason through one half of the store, and she kept Maya with her in another. They'd found fishing supplies and a few tools, but the grocery store had been their best location.

Ava wouldn't return there. It felt like Julian's lair.

When everyone returned to the house, the story was the same. Julian was gone.

They made another pot of coffee and cooked the last of the perishables they'd found. The kids sat at the table eating, so the conversation had to stay vague, no mention of a threat.

"Are we ready to vote on leaving?" Lena asked. "I don't know that we'll get any more supplies, so it's more about resting."

Maya held up her hand. "Hey, do we get to vote?"

Lena glanced at Ava for an answer.

"Sure," Ava said. It didn't matter what anyone else decided unless it was to leave. She'd made sure that the supplies were packed so she only had to take one bag. The hunting knife she'd slipped into her pocket while they were in the hardware store was good enough for defense.

"So the choices are to leave now, or to stay a few days," Lena said. "Unless anyone wants to discuss it, why don't we have a show of hands."

Everyone voted to leave.

For the first time Ava felt safe. The others must think she was right.

They cleaned the dishes and tidied the house before gathering at the wagon. It seemed both needless and civilized to Ava. It did put a finality on the time they'd spent there. It was a pity; the house would have been her dream home in other circumstances.

Scott had hitched Starbuck, and everyone just started walking, no ceremony, no goodbyes.

The exit was at the end of the main street. It curved up toward a two-lane road, which Ava knew was an hour's walk to the highway. There she'd feel safe.

No one chatted, and the heat of the day had sent birds into the shade. The town felt oppressive. Ava looked behind as they turned the last curve of the road.

Julian stood in the middle of the street, watching them. She was dizzy with relief. He was staying in the town. At least his threat was over and her kids were safe.

CHAPTER TWENTY-THREE

Lena trudged along beside the wagon. If she had known how mind numbing the journey would be, she might not have left New Surrey.

There had been two more encounters since Millerville. In a town two days along they'd found a group of twenty people who had set up in a summer campground. They had given Lena's people shelter for the night, and news, but were politely insistent they move on in the morning.

The following week, they'd seen what appeared to be a fort. The walls surrounded what looked to be about six blocks in a town nestled in the hills. There were guards on the top of the wall. Keith had urged the horse past, waving to the guards, and making sure they saw his bow. For a few nights, they had kept a careful watch for raiders, but no one had come. Either they didn't see the point in attacking armed people for a few scraps of food, or they simply didn't want to mingle with outsiders.

There had been some reports early on about plague avoiders. People who withdrew into what they called safe zones. Afraid that the measles plague had been just the beginning, they didn't want to risk infection. Maybe the fort was one of the safe zones.

Lena calculated that at their current pace, they'd get to the farm in another month. It would be hard work to prepare for winter, but at least they'd all have beds. The farm must be able to support them, and maybe a few more people. Lena knew that the dairy cows were probably gone, but surely, they'd find some live-stock once they settled.

"We have company," Scott said.

Lena came out of her daydream to see two men standing in their path. They were dressed alike. Camouflage, heavy boots, bandanas around their necks. They stood at ease, their rifles at their sides, which probably meant that they weren't going to start trouble, but were able to finish whatever someone else started.

She stepped forward, leaving the others to stand with Star-buck, knowing that Keith, at least, would be ready to act if these men attacked.

"We're just passing through," she called out as soon as she was close enough to see any details. Both men were clean shaven, hair cropped close, one had blue eyes the other green. They hadn't missed a meal in a while either.

"To where?" the older man asked.

"My name is Lena Custordin. I have a farm west of here."

He looked at his companion and received a slight nod. "I'm Max Wells, this is Evan White. We're from a community up the road. Our job is to make sure no trouble comes in."

"Do people get to pass by?" Lena asked. She couldn't imagine that any community would bar the road to everyone. "Is there a toll?"

A sneer crossed Evan's lips, but Max was the spokesperson. "No toll, ma'am. We likely just need to escort you on your way."

It was late afternoon and they'd been thinking of camping soon. Lena knew that they couldn't travel more than an hour before they would need rest. "How far before you feel safe?"

"Depends. We need to know more about you." He looked over

her shoulder. "You, and that lady in the wagon, come with us. You'll talk to the mayor and she'll decide what happens."

Lena looked around even though she knew who was riding the wagon. She hoped that someone had switched places, but no, Deb was perched on the bench. "I'm not sure her husband will be happy for you to take her away."

"I assure you that there's no danger. Your people can rest here. We'll be back in no time. If you don't come, we can't let you pass." His stance changed as he spoke. Where he was relaxed before, Max tensed. His hand went to the stock of his rifle, ready to swing it into action.

"I'll talk to them, but I don't command them. We all decide." She bit her lip as she thought of a solution. "I'm sure they'll agree if Evan stays behind. That way we each have a hostage. If you don't harm us, no one will harm him."

Evan flushed and then sneered. Apparently, he didn't think anyone was much of a threat.

"That's acceptable," Max said. "You go get her, and then Evan will join your people."

"No, Evan comes with me. He leaves his rifle here, and one of my people will search him for weapons." Lena had no idea what she would do if Max refused, but it felt like stupidity to just go along with his orders.

He turned to Evan and nodded. The younger man placed his rifle on the ground and started walking toward the wagon, not waiting for Lena.

They'd been walked along a street. A few people glanced their way, but didn't linger or approach. The presence of so many people after being alone for months unsettled Lena.

The brick building they'd entered must have been some kind of warehouse before, but now it was a headquarters. Lena sat beside Deb on a leather couch in an office where they'd been left by Max. The first floor was partitioned into rooms, and this office had a wall of windows so that anyone here looked out over the whole area. Lena could see people working, sorting, and storing items. A few people were walking between the rooms.

"They shouldn't have left us here without offering us something," Deb whined. "It's rude."

"I guess they aren't worried about the niceties," Lena answered. "Let me do all the talking. If they ask you questions, please try to be pleasant, and don't lie. And don't tell them any more than they need to know."

Deb sighed and rolled her eyes. "It's not like we have anything to hide." Lena gave her a glare. "Okay, okay. I'll be nice. I won't tell all of our secrets."

Lena shook her head. The woman was like a sulky teenager. If she wasn't the only one of them with medical training, Deb wouldn't be there.

Footsteps on the metal stairs cut off Lena's reply.

The door opened. A woman stepped inside, and sat behind the desk they were facing. She was in her thirties at the oldest. It was odd to see someone so young in charge, but then maybe Lena had it wrong. Maybe this woman was just asking questions.

The woman touched her short black hair as though it was in need of tidying. It didn't. She wore a black suit and heels. Her face was made up and her understated jewelry spoke of restraint.

She gave a tiny cough and then her eyes focused on Lena. "My name is Abigail Blackson. I am the mayor of The Community of Truth. My job is to ensure we are safe from all enemies. I will ask you some question. Please answer fully so that I can assess our options. Let's start with your names."

It wouldn't hurt to play along, Lena thought. "I'm Lena Custordin; this is Deborah Boatman."

Abigail nodded and made a note on a pad of paper that she pulled from a drawer. "The names of the people in your party, and their relationships."

"Deb's husband Keith. Mellow Jannsen, Tik Allan, Ava Walker and her two kids, Maya and Jason. Ava is my best friend, and Scott Haverst." This was the oddest interview. Abigail didn't react to any information, just made notes.

"Very well. Now, tell me why you are on the road." She looked up from the notes with an expectant expression.

Lena frowned. "We all have our own reasons; I can't speak beyond what I know."

"I do understand that, Lena. Tell me what you know. Deborah can add any information you miss."

"Why do you need to know all of this just to let us pass through?"

Abigail put down her pen and leaned her arms on the desk. "I don't, but my man says your people look worn out. I'm assessing whether to let you go on your way, or whether to let you rest in my community."

Rest would be nice now that it was too late to go much farther before dark. No matter how weird it was, the community clearly thrived. It gave Lena hope for her own plans.

"Most of us left New Surrey because we wanted to control our lives. Scott joined us on the road. We're looking to set up our own community to the west."

Abigail scribbled a few words. "Have you harmed anyone?"

"No. We have only met a few people along the way."

"How would you defend your group if threatened?"

Lena wasn't about to tell Abigail how they were armed. She'd likely learn it from Evan. He didn't seem like the type to let a little hostage situation stop him from snooping. "I don't know what we will do. No one can know. I do know that we don't intend to harm anyone. That we aren't the type of people who look for trouble. We came here to meet you, so that should say something."

Lena watched as Abigail took in the answer. She was clearly trying to be fair, but Lena knew how they'd felt about Scott. It hadn't taken long for him to fit in, but that first night, she couldn't help wondering if he was a threat.

She felt Deb fidgeting beside her and looked. Deb clearly had something to say. She'd promised to be polite, so maybe it wouldn't hurt. Lena gave her a tiny nod.

"I'm a nurse," Deb said. "If you have anyone in need of care, I could do that if you let us stay."

Abigail smiled. "We have medical personnel, but a nurse is always useful." She made a last note and then stood. "Welcome to The Community of Truth. You can stay a few nights. We'll talk again later. One of you will be escorted to bring your people in, the other can start setting up your camp." She walked out of the room.

CHAPTER TWENTY-FOUR

Lena stretched and rolled over. The temptation to stay in bed was strong, but with a groan she flung the covers off and headed to the bathroom. Yesterday Abigail had been all welcoming host. They'd offered to help with some of the work, but she'd waved them off saying they looked like they needed rest. Lena's attempts to insist they pay with work had been feeble.

Now, rested and ready move on, she went in search of the rest of the group. They were all sitting around a large table picking at the remains of a breakfast. Ava got up and pulled a plate from the oven for Lena.

"They have electricity," she said. "And radios — short wave. We heard some broadcasts from England. It was fascinating. Does the farm have a generator?"

Lena sat and poured a glass of milk, not the reconstituted powder, but real cow's milk. "There was, but I'm not sure how we get the fuel. Most of the stores of gas are useless because they gelled after a while. Some sort of chemical additive."

Keith kept his eyes on the door, always alert. "They use pedal power. I'll check on how to convert it. It would be better to know what's going on around the world when we're at the farm. Just in case all hell breaks loose."

It felt unlikely to Lena. Most of the people in New Surrey were happy to stay where they were for the few luxuries they could get their hands on.

She finished her breakfast and was getting ready to bring up the subject of leaving, when Evan marched into the room.

"Abigail wants to see you now," he announced then stood waiting for them to rise.

"All of us?" Mellow asked the question, but Lena knew others were thinking it.

"All of you." Evan scowled. "I said now."

Lena sighed and then got up. It wasn't going to be worth the effort to argue. She wanted to thank Abigail anyway. It didn't make much sense that they were in a such a hurry, but maybe there was something about community living that the group needed to learn.

In Abigail's office, the entire group crowded around the desk. Max stood beside Abigail who sat erect behind it. The mood was all business.

"I want to thank you for your hospitality," Lena said when no one spoke. "We'll be out of your hair by this afternoon."

"Perhaps not," Abigail said. Standing, she looked at each of the members of Lena's group. "I have an offer for you."

Lena didn't respond. There was nothing to say until they heard the offer.

"The Community of Truth needs more people like you. Hard working, talented, willing to learn. I'd like to offer you membership."

Did she expect an answer right away? Lena looked around. Deb and Tik looked like they were thinking it over. They needed time to discuss. But first she wanted to find out the details.

"We were planning to continue with our journey, but we'll give your offer consideration when we know what that would mean to us." It was as tactful as she could make it. Part of her wanted this. It was like her dream for the farm. Another, bigger part, recognized the parallels to New Surrey. Someone in charge would always make decisions.

"I'll leave you here for an hour to discuss what you would like to do. Our rules are simple. You contribute to your ability and you receive the basics. You can earn more by contributing more. If any attacks come, you will defend the community. Is that sufficient?"

It wasn't the whole story; Lena would bet her life on that.

Abigail asked if anyone had questions, and no one did. "Are we confined to this room?" If they could get out, then there was still time to get some information, like converting the generator. She was sure that if they said, no thanks, there would be no time to wander around, they'd be escorted out of town and on their way.

"You fear that we will listen in?" Abigail laughed. "You may leave. Please be back in one hour with your decision." Then she left with Max two steps behind.

When they were alone, Keith spoke up. "Don't start talking now. I think we all have to take a little while to think over what she offered. Why don't we meet back at the house in a half hour? We'll have time to hash through our ideas and still be back by the deadline."

The others agreed. Keith held Lena back while they drifted out. Lena could see Deb waiting in the hall outside.

Keith leaned in so they could talk quietly. "I'll be over at the machine shop getting what information I can. Deb will scope out the medical center to see if she can learn something fast."

"So, your vote is to go?"

Keith shook his head. "I'm not sure right now, but you and I both know we'll be marched out if we say no. That generator and a functioning hospital are two things we won't see again any time soon."

Lena went back to the house. Mellow and Tik were there already. "I thought we could pack our stuff up," Mellow said. "Even if we stay we're probably not living in this house. We can bring our bags back to her office when we go."

Lena nodded and said she'd help. Going to Ava's room, she started packing the kid's bags while she thought. Keith was right about doing what they could to learn how these people managed. Where did they get the cows for instance? In Millerville, Julian had kept chickens, that wouldn't be hard, just getting some chickens might be a challenge. But cows took care. Maybe she should send someone to check out the community's farms if there was time. Being the leader wasn't her plan, and she'd stop as soon as she could hand it over. Today, she'd take it on, and get a feel for how people were organized here.

Maybe they could stay for a while. A month would be good, a year would be better but the farm wouldn't wait forever.

As she packed Ava's belongings, Lena realized she'd already made her decision. She didn't want to trade New Surrey for another hierarchical community. The farm was going to be run by everyone and if that meant she had to leave by herself and gather another group, that's what she would do.

She moved on to her own things, leaving Ava's bags on the landing. She hadn't unpacked more than what was needed for a night's stay. Jamming her pajamas in, she turned to go.

Tik was standing in the doorway. "We're all back."

Her stomach turned. This was the first time they'd faced a decision that could tear them apart. The first real time. Millerville didn't count. She would never have abandoned Ava, and neither would anyone else.

In the living room, they all sat in chairs waiting for Lena to join them. She wasn't going to tell anyone what to do, but someone had to start the discussion. "So? Anyone ready to start?"

They looked at each other, no one seemed willing to take a stance. Maya held up her hand. "Do we have a vote again?"

Lena laughed. "Yes, but I'm not sure your mom will be happy if you vote against her."

"But that's supposed to be how it works, right?" Maya seemed genuinely puzzled.

"Yep, but she's your mom. We need to talk about it first anyway." Lena checked that Ava wasn't having a heart attack. She was hiding a smile from Maya.

"I think it's too good to be completely real," Scott said. "I'm not staying. If you all are ready to go, I'll keep tagging along, but towns don't feel right to me."

Deb was the next to speak. She flicked a glance at Keith first, but Lena could see she wasn't going to be discouraged. "This place isn't perfect, but it's here. The farm is another month away and who knows what state it's in. I vote to stay."

"I checked the school out yesterday," Ava said. "They are very specialized in what they teach, but I can't say it's wrong. It's probably more important to learn how to survive than to learn Shakespeare. I just think we need to keep going. At the farm, we get to decide how we live. Here, we are just following directions."

"One thing going for it," Tik said. "No gangs. I could fit in with the security guys like Max and Evan. Mellow can do a lot of different things here. It's safe."

Lena could almost hear Brian's voice giving his opinion. It was safe. It was a place he could thrive. A place Lena could teach, or help manage. Brian would have loved it. Is it inevitable? Will the farm community become like this?

"I want to go on," Keith said.

Ava looked to the kids. Neither of them seemed willing to give her a hint how they were going to vote. She shrugged. "I don't know, even though I said we should keep going, I don't feel strongly either way. I guess I'll go along with the majority vote."

It was odd for Ava not to have an opinion. "If you stay, you'll have a way to contribute, and the kids will have friends." Lena didn't know why she was trying to sway Ava.

"Yeah, but I'm getting used to the idea of being more than just a teacher. At the farm, I can learn more and we'll have more people join us eventually. And maybe there'll be some other people living around on farms of their own."

"I want to go," Maya said.

"Me too," Jason added.

Ava grinned. "Why?"

"I don't like it here. No one was nice to us when we visited the school." Maya folded her arms over her chest as if the discussion was over.

"I guess that's my vote then," Ava said.

"Mellow?" Lena asked. She wouldn't let Tik speak for the girl.

"If I was making the decision for just me, I'd say go. This place is fine, but we could have stayed in Millerville if we wanted something like this. I'm with Ava. There's more opportunity in a place we build ourselves."

"How do we want to decide?" Lena asked. "We can do it as individuals, or as a group."

Keith might have something to say to Deb if she really wanted to stay, but losing anyone at this point was going to be a blow.

Keith stood. "We're a group. We don't need to vote, most of us want to go on. I can't force Tik to come, and if Deb really wants to stay, I guess she will. But I'm going with the group. We agreed to go to the farm and start over, and we should do that."

Deb's pout deepened. It seemed to Lena that if she could get Keith alone they would be having one hell of a fight.

"So, we get our stuff back and we leave," Lena said. "I think Abigail wanted to hear it from all of us."

Deb crossed her arms and glared at Keith. "If everyone is

going on to the farm, I'll come." She turned to stare at Lena. "You need a nurse, and I'm not going to abandon my marriage vows that easily."

Lena bit her lip to stop the smile. It was weird how people changed, or maybe it was just the way she saw them that had changed. Keith might be curt and grouchy sometimes, but he knew how to be part of a team, and she was glad of his presence. Deb on the other hand seemed determined to make sure everyone knew she was coming under protest.

"Do you know where the horse and wagon are?" Lena asked. "We'll let Abigail know what we've decided and then I think it's best if we just get our belongings and go."

Scott picked up his pack and said, "They are both in the barn at the end of the street. Last time I checked nothing had been taken. Can we go?"

No one seemed willing to linger. No matter what they could learn from this community, they all wanted back on the road.

CHAPTER TWENTY-FIVE

Abigail didn't react when they told her. She stared at them as though willing them to change their minds. It felt like an hour passed while they waited each other out. Lena didn't know what she'd expected, but it wasn't this silence.

Eventually she broke the standoff. "Then I guess we'll go."

This time Abigail spoke. "Yes. You'll be free to leave as soon as you've earned the food and lodging you have used."

"How will we do that?" Lena wasn't ready to argue yet. Maybe they just wanted an hour of labor, something they could simply do and then leave. Or payment of supplies, not that they had any to spare.

Abigail reached into the drawer and pulled out a sheet of paper. She ran her finger down the page as if reviewing the contents, but Lena knew that the woman was just stalling.

With a small sigh, Abigail rested her arms on the desktop. "You have consumed a day's worth of food and lodging. Your efforts to learn how this community works has delayed my people in their duties, so two days of labor in the fields will clear your debt."

She said it like they were getting a deal. Lena didn't need to think about it. This was a never-ending debt because every day they paid for required another day of payment. "Thanks, but there must be another way. We can't ever catch up to that deal."

A smile flashed across Abigail's lips. Lena knew she'd just asked the question they were leading her to. "There are other ways. Perhaps it would be better if the rest of your people waited outside. I prefer to speak to the leader in this negotiation."

"We make our decisions as a group," Lena said.

"Then we'll place you in the fields. I will not sit and argue the merits of our deal with a rabble."

Lena felt a hand on her shoulder. She turned to see Ava shaking her head. "Just do it her way, Lena. We'll be outside. We trust you."

Looking at the others she saw agreement in their faces. She didn't want to take this role. Keith or Ava would be better at it, but there was no room for her to deny their trust. Lena swore that the next opportunity she had, she'd let them all know that she wasn't going to be the one responsible for the whole group.

In moments Lena was alone facing Abigail and Max. Did the woman always have him by her side? Was he a guard, advisor, or was she his puppet?

"Well," Lena said. "What are the other ways we can repay your hospitality?" She didn't care if the words came across as sarcasm. This was hostage taking.

"You can leave someone here," Abigail said flatly. "I'll take the nurse or the girl, Mellow. We're short on breeders and healers. Leave them and I'll get you an escort out of the community with all of your supplies."

The woman was insane.

"I don't trade people for anything. You're free to ask them to stay, but it's not my decision to make."

Abigail huffed. "I thought you'd say that. Wait until you've run your farm for a couple of years. You'll feel differently."

It would never happen. People had to be free to make their own choices. If that wasn't true, they might as well all go back to New Surrey.

"I can see there's no changing your mind," Abigail finally said. "Very well, I'll take the horse and wagon. They'll be useful."

There was no negotiation going on. Lena didn't want to sit here all day listening to one after another of Abigail's prices for their freedom. Since she wasn't planning to stand by her agreements, she just needed to sound like she was being serious. "No. I think you need to listen to my offers now. I get that we used some of the food you've saved up, but we also used ours. No one got in the way of your people. We observed and answered questions. We still have some supplies we can give you to replace the food we ate."

"Unacceptable."

So it was Abigail's way or nothing. There was only one thing that Lena could think to do. Find something the woman would accept and then find a way for the group to escape with everything they brought with them.

"Is there another option?" she asked.

"It's the horse and wagon, and if we don't come to an agreement soon, I'll take all the supplies you have."

"I don't seem to have a choice. Look, how about if we give you a day's hard labor, and the wagon? It'll set us back, but won't kill our plans. Do that and I won't find a way to let all the travelers who come behind us know that you're trapping people."

Abigail looked at her list of things that Lena's group had consumed again. Lena figured she was just biding her time so she didn't look weak in front of Max. As crazy as Abigail was, she must know that there was a point beyond which no one would follow her. If she used this tactic a lot, then there was a good percentage of the population of the community who weren't here by choice. It probably wouldn't take too much to get them fighting. In fact, it might be a good way for Lena to get more people who would help on the farm.

"Fine," Abigail said. "The children will also work. It's not what we normally expect, but if you are determined to go, I must have decent payment for the things my people have provided."

She stood and flicked her fingers at Max so he moved forward. "Return to the house you stayed in. I will have a guard placed with you to ensure you are still with us in the morning. Tomorrow you will work from sunrise to sunset and then you will leave us."

Leaving tired and in the dark wouldn't be the easiest, but Lena knew they would find rest as soon as this community was behind them.

The group followed her back to the house without question. When they arrived, Evan was standing on the porch.

"Please stay out here," Lena said. "We don't need watching that closely and we do deserve some privacy."

Evan shrugged and stepped aside. It was a small victory, but having him outside gave Lena time to explain and plan with her group.

Inside, Lena whispered to Scott to check for other guards. When he came back to report there were none to be seen from inside the house, she ushered the group to the kitchen.

"Maya, Jason, we need you to be quiet and listen to us for a while. This is really serious." Lena kept her voice low enough that everyone had to lean in to hear.

"What if we have an idea?" Maya asked.

It was always Maya pushing at the envelope. Jason wasn't quiet, or repressed, but Maya was never willing to be left out.

"Then you need to do it like the adults, quietly get our attention and tell us." She wasn't willing to discount any ideas.

"Maya, just hold up your hand," Ava said. "In fact, we should all do that so we don't end up yelling to get heard."

It felt like they were in detention to Lena and she started to giggle. "Sorry, I guess it's getting to me." She took a deep breath and then told them what Abigail said. "So, I thought we should try to get out of here tonight. Even if she was planning to stick to our deal, we can't get by without the horse and wagon. And it's not ours anyway."

There was silence. Lena hoped they were all thinking of a way to escape rather than a way to try to reopen the discussion with Abigail. One of the others could probably have negotiated something better, but even then, Abigail likely didn't stick to any agreement that didn't favor her.

Maya's hand went up. "Can we sneak out a couple at a time?"

Tik nodded. "We can't go as a group because Evan might see us, and we'll be too loud."

"We have everything we need from here," Deb said. "If we go in groups of two then the others can talk and pretend we're all here. The first ones at the wagon can hitch the horse and get ready to go as soon as the last arrive."

Where had that come from? There was no whine in Deb's voice. She didn't complain about having to leave, she just put the best plan on the counter.

Lena saw Keith smile and realized that the sulky Deb that everyone else saw might not be the one he stuck with.

"Okay, who goes first?" Ava asked.

"Keith and Maya," Scott said. "Me and Jason, then Deb and Mellow, You and Ava, Tik can be the last, but right behind you."

No one had anything to add. So Lena crept back to the living room to look out on the porch. Evan stood guard looking straight out onto the street. Lena opened the door and said, "We're making some tea, can I get you a mug?"

"No, ma'am. I don't need anything."

"Okay." He probably didn't want to be in their debt. "We'll be turning in early. Don't want to hit the fields too tired to work."

He nodded, never taking his eyes off the street.

. . .

They spent the remainder of the afternoon resting. It wasn't easy for Lena to be patient, but there was nothing for it. As soon as it was dark enough to cover their movements, she put the plan in motion. "Send the kids to bed for a nap, loudly. Maya and Jason, stomp upstairs and then creep back down."

When that pantomime was over, Lena sent Keith and Maya on their way, starting a conversation with the others so that Evan would think they were all getting ready for bed.

A few minutes after Keith and Maya, Scott and Jason left. Another short pause, and then Deb and Mellow slipped out of the back door.

"I guess they're getting to the barn," Ava whispered. "If they'd been caught, surely someone would have come to get us."

"Yeah," Lena said. Unless Abigail was playing some demented game. "See you in a few, Tik." She took Ava's arm and crept down the back stairs into the night.

There was no one about, and that made sense to Lena in a community like this. Everyone rose with the sun and went to bed with the moon. She let herself feel hope as they kept to the shadows of the back lanes. Tik was only minutes behind them, the limit of the town was less than a mile away. The trick would be to get there with Starbuck and not rouse the guards that were surely in place.

The barn was quiet when they entered. It took moments to get their eyes to adjust to the dimness, but when they did, Lena was happy to see the horse hitched, and the mounds of supplies under the tarps in the wagon didn't look any different from when they'd left it.

Ava ran to hug her kids, and Lena moved to the back of the wagon to check under the tarp.

The barn door opened.

Lena looked up expecting to see Tik, but instead three men stood outlined in the moonlight.

"Stop," the middle one said. "Those belong to the community now."

She could see Tik approach from behind, and then Keith marched past her with a crowbar in his hands.

"No, it's ours," he said raising the crowbar. "We're leaving now, and no one is getting in our way."

Lena couldn't move. It was like she was watching a play. This wasn't happening to her people. They were almost away.

The three men moved to attack Keith. He swung the crowbar low, taking out the middle one at the knees. The other two kept coming at him, then Tik waded in.

It all happened in a blur.

Tik kicked one of the attackers, and then got shoved into the barn wall by another. He struggled to get back into the fight.

Mellow grabbed something from the wagon. Lena saw the blade of a shovel swing and catch a new attacker on the shoulder. Unfortunately, the momentum of her swing carried it to the side of the wagon with a jarring clang. Mellow dropped the shovel and cradled her arm to her side.

Keith punched his opponent who dropped to the ground and then turned to take on another man who'd run into the barn.

Lena, still frozen, was only able to witness the fight. Then one of the men who'd come in leapt onto the back of the wagon and started tossing bags out.

They couldn't afford to lose any of the supplies.

Now she had to act.

She ran to the wagon and jumped in, swinging her fists for lack of any other weapon. The man was unbalanced and her fist connected with his shoulder. He tipped to the side and Lena pushed him. Her hand hurt, but not so badly that it might be broken. He landed on the ground, his fall cushioned by the bag of dumped supplies.

Lena looked around as he gained his feet. There were no new attackers, but another man was free from the fight. He heaved himself into the wagon, and tossed two sacks out.

Starbuck was starting to fight the harness. Lena moved into the driver seat.

"Get on the wagon," she yelled. If anyone wanted to get in front of a panicked horse, they were welcome. She felt Deb land beside her on the driver's bench, and then a few thuds as others made it into the back. A grunt and then a rock of the wagon let her know someone was ejected. A quick look around gave her the plan. Everyone except Tik and Keith were in the wagon. Those two were finishing off their opponents.

She snapped the reins struggling to turn Starbuck's rearing into forward momentum. Tik and Keith would catch up as she passed.

Starbuck ran without encouragement. The smooth road helped them to gain speed, even though the wagon rocked a bit, Lena was confident they would make it. She heard a shout and turned to see Keith running beside the wagon, reaching out his hand to Tik. They were all together.

The noise of the fight hadn't carried out of the barn, but now the horse was creating enough commotion with its hooves on the road and a high-pitched neigh. Lights flicked on in a few bedrooms, but she had faith that no one would be able to catch them.

Lena saw the last of the buildings in the distance ahead. Two men were standing in the middle of the road. She hoped they had the sense to get out of the way. She couldn't stop Starbuck even if she wanted to. He was panicked and it took all of her strength to hold the reins.

The two guards held position until the horse was almost upon them, then they ran to the side of the road. Neither raised his rifle.

In moments, they were free.

. . .

It took some time to get Starbuck under control. In fact, the horse ran out of energy before Lena could slow it enough to pull to the side of the road.

"Is anyone following?" she asked as she dismounted.

The others left the wagon and joined her on the grass.

"No. We're clear," Scott said. He went to the horse and started murmuring quietly and running his hands along the shaking animal. "He'll be okay. I'm going to walk him a bit, and then rub him down."

Lena turned to the others. Tik was holding his side, Mellow still cradled her arm.

"Let me look at that," Deb said. "I hope we still have our medical supplies."

"I'll check to see what we lost," Ava said.

They pulled the wagon into the shadows of the trees to set up a camp. Half of their food was gone, but nothing else of importance. Lena was grateful for that small cost. As soon as Starbuck was ready, they continued putting distance between them and Abigail.

CHAPTER TWENTY-SIX

"It feels like we've been on the road forever," Deb said. Keith was walking beside her, but she might as well have been alone for all the company he was. "My feet hurt, and I'm getting sunburned."

He shifted his rifle to the other shoulder. Ever since they'd left that horrible town, everyone had carried guns. Well, not her. Deb didn't want to start any trouble.

"I'm beginning to wonder if there's even a farm at the end of this," she said, hoping to get him talking.

Keith grabbed her arm and pulled her off the road and into the trees. "Look, Deb. I think you'll be fine when we get there, but we're all feeling the effects of the journey. Harping on about how hard it is won't make it feel better, and it won't make you any friends."

She pulled her arm away. It wasn't like him to get physical. He'd killed that guy for beating his wife after all. But the others had changed Keith. The man she'd married would never have dragged her into the shadows and spoken to her like that.

Forcing her lips closed on the response she really would like to give, Deb huffed. "I don't need friends," she said. "I'm a nurse.

They need me. I should be able to ride in the wagon, not have to trudge along like everyone else."

Keith shook his head. "If you really don't want to be here, you should just leave."

"You would do that for me?" That was more like the man she loved.

Keith glanced around as though a monster was about to jump out of the woods. "You can leave. I'm staying with the group. I want you to stay, but you keep saying how hard it is. I'll get over it if you go back to The Community of Truth, or if you stay with anyone else we run into."

She couldn't believe what she'd heard. "You would abandon me out here. After dragging me away from New Surrey. After making it too dangerous for us to stay at home?"

Keith looked down at the ground.

At least he was ashamed of what he'd done. He would apologize. Maybe not now, but soon.

"Would you have preferred I let Josie get beaten up?" He turned his gaze back to her. "No one could stop him. I didn't mean to kill him, but he wouldn't stop fighting. It was an accident."

Why was he still talking about that? "Then you should have told the police."

"There were no witnesses. I would have been put on the road gangs during the day and prison at night. You would have been alone. I didn't want to do that to you."

How would alone have been worse than this? They were walking toward a dream. If the farm wasn't there, or wasn't able to support them, they would be back on the road and begging for someone to take them in.

"I don't want to leave you," she admitted. "I don't want to keep doing this, but I don't want to be alone."

Keith reached for her and pulled her into a hug. "You don't have to be. If you want to go, you'll find someone. If you want to stay, you have to stop whining all the time. Even the kids don't complain."

She sighed. "We should get back to the group. They'll be out of sight by now."

Keith led her back to the road. The wagon was still visible as it crested the hill. Deb suppressed a sigh, knowing it would annoy Keith. Did she want to leave? Even if he came with her, would she be able to fit in anywhere else? There was no way she could go back to what they had.

She adjusted her sunhat and hurried to catch up with the wagon. They'd be setting up camp in a couple of hours. She'd think about how to get Keith to agree with her by then.

This time they camped by a little stream. Deb preferred it when they camped near water. It meant she could have a bath, even if it was just ankle deep and with a washcloth. It was good to be clean. She also had a chance to apply some of the creams she'd brought. Moisturizing was holding off the worst of the sun damage, but not all.

She'd offered to bring water for boiling so she could have some time alone. Now in the cool of the stream, listening to the birds in the trees and the bubble of the water, she tried to put aside her conversation with Keith.

He hadn't meant what he'd said. She wasn't always complaining. They'd been grateful when she'd bound the wounds from that fight. And when she'd known which of the nearby leaves would help heal the burn that Maya had gotten when she reached for the pot on the fire.

She turned at a rustle of the undergrowth. If it was a wild animal, she was in trouble. Keith had told her to take some kind of weapon, and she had. But the crowbar was sitting on the bank of the stream beside her clothes.

Keith stepped from behind a tree.

"I'm glad I volunteered to come and help," he said. "If it had been Tik or Scott, you would never have forgiven them."

Deb laughed. Keith was back to the man she loved. "I was just going to get dressed anyway."

"I'll fill the buckets; you take your time." He picked up the two buckets and walked a few yards upstream. "You look happier now," he said.

Deb smiled as she dried herself. "It's cooler, my feet don't hurt, and I'm in the shade. What's not to be happy about?"

"When we get to the farm, it will be hard work. For all of us," Keith said, spoiling the moment.

"We might find a place to stay before then. Not all of them will be like Abigail's town."

"Now we've crossed the border, we're in farm country. I don't know if there'll be many towns."

Deb ignored the comment

Keith returned to her as she pulled her dress over her head. The others were eager to get into their night clothes as soon as they made camp. Deb liked to keep some sense of civilization. As her dress slipped over her hips, Keith wrapped his arms around her from behind. She leaned into him. There had been few opportunities for privacy since they'd left. It was wonderful to feel him against her.

"We could take a little longer," she murmured twisting in Keith's arms to face him. "It's been a long time."

He nuzzled her neck. "Yes, a long time, but if you are leaving, I don't want to... I guess I want to start getting used to it."

She pulled away. "You were serious? You'd let me go just like that? Is it Lena? Or Ava? Yes, she has kids. That would be a draw for you." She bent down and picked up the crowbar then started to leave.

Keith reached for her wrist and gently brought her to a stop.

"I don't want any of the other women. But I can't be part of a community that I didn't build. You knew it wouldn't be the end, when I killed Josie's husband. You know I can't just sit by and let people hurt others."

Deb pulled her wrist away. "Fine, let's get back to the camp. I'm sure everyone is waiting for the water." She left him to carry the buckets.

After eating her share of the oatmeal and vegetables that constituted dinner, Deb sat next to Mellow. She wasn't going to just let this go. If she could make some allies, Keith would understand she wasn't the only one who might regret the choice of coming with Lena.

"How's your arm," she asked knowing full well that the bruise was healed.

Mellow rubbed it and then smiled. "It's fine. That ointment did a great job of getting rid of the bruises. Thanks for that."

"You must be missing your friends," Deb said.

Mellow reached for a small branch and poked the fire. "I didn't really have any. I was more interested in studying than partying."

Maybe she'd chosen the wrong person. Wasn't every teenage girl into parties, and dresses, and boys. "At least you had nice things. Do you miss home at all?"

Mellow sighed and hugged her knees to her chest. "Sometimes I miss my room. But it's nice out here. Clean air. No one to threaten you. Oh, I guess that's not always true, but back there, I couldn't go out at night. I just mainly went to school, did my stint on the work teams, and went home. Being out at night meant I had to deal with guys who thought they had a right to touch me, or worse."

This really wasn't working out as well as Deb planned. She tried another, more direct subject. "But out here, you have a future of hard work. Maybe having a few babies with Tik. And being subject to all kinds of dangers."

Mellow looked at her. "It's still better."

It was clear she had to get more pointed in her questions. Mellow wasn't as bright as everyone thought. "What had you planned to do after graduation?"

"I wanted to work in the gardens, or maybe be a teacher. But it wasn't up to me," Mellow said. She shifted onto her hip and looked Deb directly in the eyes. "You don't know what it was like for people like me, do you?"

Now her interest was piqued. Mellow was pretty, she shouldn't have had any problems. Pretty girls got the good-looking guys. "What do you mean, people like you?"

"Orphans. Particularly girls. There was no one to protect me. No one was going to talk to any of the team leaders so I could get a place. All of the other kids had at least one parent. The other orphans dropped out. I was the only one who made it to graduation."

Had the world changed that much? When she was a high school student, the lines were clear. She was a cheerleader; Keith was a jock. They were in the cool group. "But you were skilled. Lena saw potential."

"That wouldn't have been enough. After graduation, I'd be all alone. It wouldn't be long before some gang member would take me. Tik knows. Even if it had been him, it would be Tik the gang member, not the Tik we know."

Deb started to shake her head, but Mellow put her hand on Deb's leg.

"It's true. I'm glad you didn't know. It's nice to think there were some people in New Surrey who weren't part of the problems."

"You could have gone to the police," Deb said. It was a strange echo of what she'd said to Keith. And it was what she would have done.

"They wouldn't have done anything. The cops used prostitutes too."

Deb wanted to reach out and hug Mellow. It was an oddly maternal feeling; one she'd never had before. Mellow was rigid and there was no way that Deb could act on her feelings. "I'm sorry I brought up the topic," she said.

"Don't be," Mellow said. The tightness left her body and she smiled. "It's never far from my mind. When I get tired on the road, it helps me to keep going. Whatever happens on the farm, it will be better than anything waiting for me in New Surrey."

Deb stared at the fire for a while. Keith couldn't be right. She had tried hard not to be annoying. The others must like her a bit.

The flames had no answer for her questions, and Deb was determined to prove that Keith was exaggerating. Mellow had left to sit with Tik. The young couple had formed quickly and seemed to be inseparable in the evenings. Deb remembered when it was like that with Keith. And she wanted it back.

She pushed herself off the ground. If Mellow wasn't going to be an ally, then she needed some straight talk. Ava and Lena were as blunt as it got.

She found them together sitting with some mending outside the tent where the kids slept. It bothered her that the whole group was always on alert since the brawl. She blushed at the realization that she hadn't been. That she'd relied on everyone else to keep her safe. She hadn't even learned how to defend herself properly.

"Hi, can I help?" she asked. At least she could sew. And maybe she could try to be nice.

Lena tucked the garment she was mending into the sack at her side. "We're just about done." Her tone said, *as you probably knew.*

"Okay, is there anything else I can do?"

Ava rolled the rest of the mending and shoved it into another sack. "Everything is done. Is there anything you can do, Deb.? I mean other than nursing?"

"Nursing is important," she snapped back. "I can do a lot of things. I just don't know what needs to be done."

Lena stood and tossed her sack into the wagon. "We've been on the road for months, Deb. We've all kind of found a rhythm. No one else has to ask what needs to be done, they just know."

So, there was no way for her to help? That didn't make sense. "So how do I figure out what to do?"

Lena sighed. "Look, Deb, you haven't been interested. We need you as a nurse, but you've never wanted to get involved before. You need to give us a little direction."

She wanted to ask outright if she was part of this group. It was feeling more and more that she was just on the outside. That she was only good when things were bad, but other than that she was a freeloader.

Why are they being so hard on me?

"Maybe I can do more to teach people about healing?" It was a place to start.

"We have books, but it's always a good idea to get practice. Who were you thinking?" Ava asked.

Why didn't they just tell her who to train? "Mellow is good, but maybe Maya could learn some of the easier things — and I taught her how to stitch up wounds."

Ava looked to Lena before saying, "Let me think about it. She'll probably want to, but I think she's too young to learn anything useful."

Deb nodded and headed back to the fire. So, maybe Keith had a point. How would she be able to fix this? It wasn't just about being nice. It was about getting into the cool group. And she'd been part of that before; they didn't let anyone in for free.

She hadn't slept much. Keith was on guard first shift, but he hadn't come back to their tent all night. Deb knew her husband thought she was going to leave the group. Last night she'd learned how easy that would be; they had books to help them when people got sick or injured. It wouldn't be as good as having a nurse, but that was the only thing she brought to the group.

It wasn't fair. She wanted to help and they had shut her out. It wasn't her fault that she didn't jump in and try things. She liked to be good at something before she did anything.

Laying in the tent wouldn't help. Deb crawled out into another hot and dry day. She pulled her robe on and went to the fire. She could help make breakfast. It wasn't as though they were eating complicated stuff.

"Morning," she said. Trying to be pleasant was the first step. "Can I help?"

Mellow stirred the pot. "Yeah, can you get me the dried fruit from the wagon? It's still oatmeal, but maybe a few cranberries will make it taste better."

She had no idea where the dried fruit was, but it wouldn't take long to find it in the wagon. It was good that her first attempt at helping had met with success.

At the wagon, she felt the contents of each bag to avoid opening them all. The dried fruit was in the sixth bag, but it was small and she should have thought of that first. Maybe later she'd investigate what was here so she'd know next time.

Taking the fruit to Mellow, Deb noticed others were starting to gather. Her husband was nowhere to be seen. "Where's Keith?" she asked no one in particular.

"He went hunting. I'm sure he'll be back soon." Mellow poured a few handfuls of fruit into the oatmeal.

Maya was sitting nearby, dragging a brush through her hair. "Deb, help me."

She preferred the children to call her Mrs. Boatman, but Deb figured it wouldn't help her new image to say so. She went over and took the brush from Maya. The girl had straight hair, black and coarse. It should have been braided, but Ava let her daughter run wild.

"Maybe you could cut it off," Maya said. "Then it wouldn't get tangled."

"It would be hard to grow back," Deb said. She regretted the tone when Maya's eyes widened. It wasn't supposed to sound like a reprimand, but maybe that's how she'd always talked. "I mean, you have pretty hair and you'll regret cutting it. Let me fix this and then we'll braid it. That way you won't wake up with so many knots."

"Will I get curls?"

Deb grinned. No woman was happy with the curl in her hair. "Maybe a few waves, but you don't want curls. Believe me, they are never where you want them."

Starting at the bottom of Maya's hair, Deb worked out the knots carefully. It didn't require her to talk, and she could see her progress as Maya's hair went from a mare's nest to a shining fall. The actions were almost meditative. Her bad mood faded as she completed the work.

"Wait here," she said handing Maya the end of her braid.

Running to her own pack, Deb found a ribbon she'd been using to tie back her hair on windy days. She took it and finished Maya's braid with the bright red material.

"Thanks. That's better," Maya said. She flipped her head so the braid swung around. Deb had a moment's fear that the girl would use it as a weapon against her brother.

"When we are at the farm, maybe you could show me how to look pretty too."

"We'll let your mother decide that. You are pretty enough for an eight-year-old."

Maya laughed and gave her braid one more toss before running to get a bowl of oatmeal from Mellow.

CHAPTER TWENTY-SEVEN

Keith had been at the front of the group all day, leaving Deb to walk alone. No one seemed to want to be with her. It was lonely now that she noticed. Up until today, she'd seen it as a break when Keith wasn't with her. A little solitude in the group.

As they'd started looking for a place to camp, Deb decided that she'd offer to cook dinner. The rabbits that Keith and Scott had killed would be great grilled. She'd stake them with some of the wild rosemary twigs she'd picked and maybe Lena would let her use some of the potatoes.

They pulled into a clearing about mid-afternoon. The fire was made up and burning down to embers when she brought the skinned rabbits with her.

"Is it okay if I cook?" she asked, not quite willing to just start.

Mellow looked up. "Uh, sure it would be nice to have a change. Can I help?"

Deb held out the rabbits. "Can you butcher these?"

"I'm not great. What do you want to do with them?"

Deb was glad that she had skills that Mellow didn't. It was petty to think that, but it felt good. "You know what? I'll do the butchering. Can you ask Lena for some potatoes?"

Mellow nodded and then left.

Deb stripped the meat from the bones and then pushed a skewer through each chunk. She looked for something to use to hold the skewers above the heat. It wouldn't take long to cook the rabbit; it would be easy to overcook too.

Mellow returned. "Do you want to cook them whole, or boil the potatoes?"

Deb told her to bake them and then wondered what to add for a veg. This was how a meal should be.

She asked Mellow how to set a spit on the fire. The girl said she'd take care of it.

"I'll look for some greens, I'm sure there are some around," Deb said.

In amongst the trees she found some wild asparagus that would do, and a few mushrooms. If only they had olive oil, and sea salt and fresh pepper.

When she returned to the fire, Mellow had a spit ready and the potatoes were soft. They heated water for the asparagus and a pan for the mushrooms. It was going to be perfect.

The others started to gather. Drawn by the aroma, Deb was sure.

She helped Mellow dish out the food when it was ready.

They were sitting happily and Keith was by her side. And everything was perfect.

Then Ava yelled, "Stop."

Deb watched as she grabbed Jason's plate and scraped off the greens. "What's wrong?"

"He's allergic to asparagus. Everyone knows that."

"I didn't know," she said. "I'm sorry."

"Well, you could have been his nurse for the ten seconds before he went into shock," she snapped.

Deb put her plate down. Now she'd screwed everything. They would never forgive her. It wouldn't matter that she was nice, that she was capable of more than just nursing, they would be happy if she left. If she was gone, then everyone would be safe.

They were huddled around Jason, making sure that there was no contamination on his plate. Deb wanted to go over and see if she'd done any damage, but knew they would start blaming her again. She looked at Keith for support. There was no help from that direction. He was tossing the discarded asparagus into the fire. If Keith wasn't going to stand up for her, then everything was lost.

Deb felt her stomach tightening and then her chest. She struggled to her feet and ran to the trees. She couldn't let them see her cry. She already knew it would be ugly. This wasn't her usual tears, the ones she shed to get Keith to do as she wanted. These were already making it impossible to breathe or even stand up straight. The heat on her cheeks was still dry, but it wouldn't be long. Her face was swelling and her lips were pulling into a grimace.

She made it to the trees before the first tears fell. Then a few more feet in before her body convulsed in a sob. She crawled to the closest trunk and hid behind it. She was far enough away that no one would hear her pain, at least she hoped that was true. It wasn't about getting people to like her anymore. It wasn't about braiding Maya's hair. She was a nurse; how could she not have found out about the allergies?

Another sob wracked her. Deb bit her lips closed. Tears were falling because she realized the answer to her question. She hadn't been thinking like a nurse. She'd been thinking about herself.

The violence of her crying bout was waning when she heard someone approaching. Whoever it was wanted her to hear them. She knew that everyone had been trained to walk quietly and not scare off the game. Even she'd been given lessons, but here she was bawling in the woods and scaring off anything that might be food.

"Deb," a voice called from the other side of the tree.

It was Scott. He was being kind by not coming around to see how badly she looked. It didn't matter. The fact that it wasn't Keith hurt more than she could have imagined.

"You don't need to check on me," she said. "I'll be fine." She wiped her eyes and nose trying to make her words the truth.

"I'm sure. I just thought you'd like to know Jason was okay. He didn't eat any of the asparagus."

"I'm glad," she said, muffling a gasp of air. "I should have known."

Scott made his way around the tree and sat opposite her. He handed her a tissue. "We found these in the last town."

"I must look a mess," she said wiping her cheeks dry.

"You look like you've been crying. Most people look kind of wrecked after that." He turned away as she continued to dab at her eyes. "I guess you're wondering why Keith didn't come looking for you."

She shook her head, knowing that if she tried to speak, the crying would start again.

"He wanted to, but I thought it might help if I came instead. I get the feeling you're mad at him." He raised an eyebrow, but didn't ask for details.

"Not really, but I guess we'd be arguing anyway."

"So, what's gotten into you? We were kind of used to your bitching and stuff, but the last couple of days, no one knows what you want."

At least it was in the open. "Keith told me that I need to start contributing, or leave."

Scott grunted and then patted her knee. "He didn't mean that you had to run away."

She sighed. It felt like she would never get enough air again. A deep breath threatened to jerk into a sob. Deb dabbed at her eyes and then made her decision. "I was trying to be helpful, but everyone has done everything. It feels like there's no room for me. Like I've chosen my role in the group forever and I won't be able to change."

"It's a group of determined people, that's for sure. Some days I wonder if they just want me along for my horse and wagon." He laughed. "I'm betting everyone is still trying to figure out what it's gonna take to survive."

"I thought my nursing skills were enough." She tucked the tissue into her pocket. "You know I was given no warning about leaving. Keith just came home, handed me a backpack, and said we were going."

"What would have been different if you'd known before?"

She thought about who she'd been in New Surrey. "I would have done everything I could to stop him from leaving."

"So, you're feeling a little trapped? It sounds like you've got some grounds for being..."

"A sulky teenager?" Deb tried to chuckle so that it didn't sound petulant, but it hurt to say that out loud.

"I was going to go with resistant, but you know your motives." He turned at the sound of flapping wings, then looked back at Deb. "So, you can't change what's happened, what are you planning to do now?"

There was no way she'd survive on her own. "Do you think a heartfelt apology and a promise to do better would help?"

"The apology is a good start, but your actions are what will count." He stood and held out a hand to help her up. "Let's give it a try."

As she followed Scott to the camp, Deb tried to think how to apologize without making herself feel worse. It wasn't going to help to go through a list of her mistakes. And she needed to explain why she'd been that way, so that they would believe her when she said she'd change.

She stalled at the edge of the trees.

Scott gave her a gentle push. "Don't overthink it. Just say what you feel."

She nodded and stepped forward.

Keith moved toward her as soon as he noticed. He looked worried, and Deb couldn't help the thrill of satisfaction that he missed her and worried about what she'd do.

While she'd been crying, everyone had finished dinner and the plates were cleaned and stacked near the fire to dry. Maya and Jason were braiding a rope from the rags of old clothing. Mellow was singing quietly and Tik was sharpening his hunting knife.

Ava and Lena were talking, something they always did and it made Deb feel like she wasn't a part of the group. She was the only adult woman who wasn't involved in that conversation. No wonder she didn't feel like offering help.

"I'm sorry," she said before anyone could speak.

"For what?" Maya asked. "You didn't know about Jason's allergy. You didn't do it on purpose."

That simple statement was all it took for the words to start tumbling out. "I should have known, Maya. I haven't been doing anything all this time. I should know how to hunt, how to mend. I should be getting ready to help plant a crop, or something for our new life."

Lena was looking at her now, actually listening. Deb noticed that she had the attention of the entire group. Something that hadn't happened before. They'd been polite, but this was the first time anyone had actually listened.

Keith put his arm around her, but Deb shrugged him off. She didn't need comfort right now, later yes, but right now was her chance to make a difference.

"I know I'm kind of spoiled, but no one ever tried to make me be any different. It's like you all made your mind up about me before we left." She held up a hand to stop the words she knew were coming from the others.

"I'm not blaming anyone. I'm a grown woman. I should have noticed before. So, from now on, I'll try to learn more so I can contribute more."

Lena stood and looked around at the others. She must have been hoping someone would step in to answer, because she sighed before turning back to Deb. "You are more than a nurse. You can dress the game that's brought in. And a nurse is important," she said the words quietly. "Maybe we did shut you out. I know it seemed easier than trying to get you to stop bitching. But let's put that behind us."

"Someone has to point out the downside," Deb said, the words out before she could stop them.

"Yes, but it doesn't always have to be you," Lena said.

"Okay," Deb agreed. Then she laughed. "I'm really good at it. Maybe I can train someone?"

The rest of the group laughed with her for a change. Keith hugged her and this time she let him.

Ava stood, picked up a pile of books that she'd been flipping through every night. "Start with this. We have a ton of information and everyone is doing their best to absorb what they can. It needs to be organized. Lena and I are too busy with everything to do it. I know. We're teachers. The irony is not lost on us."

Deb took the stack of books. It was heavy enough to make her flex her knees. "Can you give me a hint about organizing this?"

They pulled her over to the fire and started explaining lesson plans and learning goals. Deb tried to keep up, but it was difficult to follow the tips. "Stop," she said. "Too much too fast. What's the first thing we'll have to do when we get there?"

Ava and Lena looked at each other. Lena grinned. "Okay, maybe you don't need a teaching certificate. We'll need to harvest any wild crops and get things ready for winter."

Deb nodded. "I'll start with finding that information and we can go from there."

CHAPTER TWENTY-EIGHT

It would only be a few weeks now. Lena reminded herself as the aches of walking on the hard road surface drew her attention. They'd stuck to the road since Abigail's attempt to trap them. It made for faster travel, but it was harder on her joints than going along the fields. Most of the team had a tough time getting started in the morning now. She wasn't fully convinced of their plan. Yes, they probably made more progress during the day, but they had to get off the road to find a place to camp, and then get back on the road in the morning.

But she wasn't going to bring the subject up again. They'd argued about it enough and it was more important to keep going.

She was walking beside the wagon while Ava drove. Deb and Keith had scouted ahead so the group wouldn't get ambushed. That was another practice they'd started. Sending someone to look for likely resting places.

"It looks like our scouts are coming back," Ava called. "It's early."

Lena didn't know whether that was good or bad. She just kept walking, willing to wait until they caught up to Keith and Deb. What they really needed was more horses so they could move faster. But that would leave them saddle sore until they got used to it. There really was no better way to get to the farm. It was just taking much longer than she'd expected when they planned their escape from New Surrey.

A few minutes passed as the distance between the main group and the scouts closed. Lena watched as Maya and Jason were helped into the bed of the wagon, and then Mellow. Tik and Scott moved in closer. They'd refined their defenses starting the night of the fight. Now that everyone was healed, the adults all carried weapons and were trained to use them. Lena's pistol was in a holster under her arm.

Keith waved everyone to stand down as he got close enough. Deb trailed him just like she'd always done. At least this time, she was alert and checking the area for threats. She still sulked occasionally but learning a few skills had given Deb a new outlook.

"There's a school ahead," Keith said. "It's deserted, but there's a games field that we can set up camp on. Someone built a fire pit in the center of the track, but they must have moved on a while ago."

It would be nice to be in the open tonight. Lena liked it when they found a campsite in the trees, but she was always alert to anything approaching. And a school wouldn't be too far off the road. A benefit in the morning.

"I think we can send a team to check out the town," Deb added. "It's across the river. The bridge is still clear, and I could see a few stores. Maybe we can still find something to scavenge."

They all looked to Lena. She would have to talk to them about this need for her to be a leader, to be the one to make decisions. Tonight, might be a good time. Right now, someone needed to give the go ahead. "Fine. Did you try to get into the school? If there's a gym, maybe we can get a shower."

"I looked around. No one was there," Keith said. "If the water is hot and running, we just need to shower in turns."

It had been a week or more since they'd been near a shower. Lena told Keith and Deb to lead the way.

The school was empty. The glass cabinets in the halls were still filled with the trophies and pictures of school teams. Most were dated ten years ago. They'd checked the library. Ava was always willing to gather more books, half of the contents of the wagon was knowledge. This one didn't have anything useful other than a box of notebooks stashed in a cabinet.

There was no way to bring the horse and wagon into the school, so they'd be sleeping in tents again. Scott and Keith had checked the boiler in the basement of the school. There was enough fuel to run them for a few hours. The water would be hot soon.

Tik, Mellow and Ava had gone across the bridge to search through the stores for anything useful. Even a few cans of beans would help fill out their dwindling food.

"Let's set up camp while we wait for everyone to get back." She followed the others out to where they'd left the wagon in Deb's care.

Starbuck was happily grazing on weedy patches of grass that was all that remained of the center of the track oval. It wasn't enough, but it would keep the horse going.

It didn't take long to set up, and start a fire in the pit. They'd cook over the fire again, because no one had been able to get the school's kitchen equipment running. Maya and Jason were repacking the wagon, placing items inside the large pots Lena had scavenged from the kitchen.

Looking at the sack of beans, made her hope that the town hadn't been scoured clean. They needed some variety, and there'd be no hunting here.

"Mom!" Jason called.

Lena looked up to see the three foragers coming through the

chain-link fencing. They had found some items. All three gleaning sacks bulged.

"Some food," Mellow said. "We found a garden too. So we have some lettuce, carrots, and beans. And this," she said smiling and reaching into the sack. When she pulled out her hand it held ripe tomatoes. "I'll dry them on the fire so we can keep some."

The thought of fresh produce filled Lena's mouth with memories. Showers forgotten, she helped prepare the meal.

When they were done, they took turns getting clean. Lena waited until last, wanting to stay under the water as long as possible.

Scott waited outside the locker room to keep watch and the others went back to camp.

The heat of the water soaked into Lena's body. It felt like comfort and peace. The only thing that would have been better was a bath, but no school had those.

Eventually she stretched and washed herself. Her joints were loose again and her muscles didn't ache anymore. They'd do this tomorrow before they left, she promised herself.

Dry, dressed in clean clothes, hair wrapped in a towel, Lena left the showers and walked down to the camp. It was peaceful, the fire casting a glow around the tents, but not into the dark night. She'd been in there longer than she'd thought.

The refreshing scent of tea floated toward her and Scott as they approached. She saw Ava rise and head toward the kid's tent to say goodnight to Maya. Well, that's what she always gave as her excuse, but Lena suspected that Ava was checking to make sure they were safe. Jason trailed her, always determined to stay up longer than his baby sister.

She reached for a mug to take a cup of tea and dropped it as a scream tore into the night.

Ava ran from the tent, Jason on her heels. She was holding a scrap of paper and her eyes were shining with fear.

"Maya." Ava gasped. "He came and took her. Julian. He has my baby."

Deb took the paper from Ava. "Oh god," she whispered. "It says, 'Thanks. Julian'. He followed us."

CHAPTER TWENTY-NINE

"Stay here," Lena said, pushing Ava to sit near the fire.

She sat, but gained her senses immediately. "No! I have to go get Maya!" Ava struggled to rise against Lena's pressure.

"No, you're too upset. Stay here with Jason. The others will protect you." Lena looked at them and met Keith's eye. "Keith and I will get Maya back."

Keith went to the wagon. Lena hoped he was getting their rifles. The best outcome was to avoid a close-in fight.

"Scott, Tik, Mellow." Lena pointed at each one. "Guard the camp. Deb, I need to talk to you."

Deb, who was hugging Jason to her side, handed him over to Ava and then joined Lena as she walked to meet Keith. "Do you have anything that will calm Ava down?"

Deb shook her head. "We don't have any sedatives, and I don't think you want her passed out, right?"

Lena watched as Keith loaded both rifles. "No. She needs to see Maya when we bring her back. I just don't want her running after us if she gets a chance. I don't want her getting shot."

"I'll talk to Mellow. She's been studying the herbal medicines. Maybe she's got something we can brew into a tea." Deb looked back to where they could hear Ava arguing with someone. "Whatever it takes, we'll keep her here. I'll make sure Jason stays too."

Lena hadn't thought of Jason. He was just a kid, but they all knew how to handle guns. Would he go after his sister? Probably.

"Okay, if anyone tries to come after us, you stop them. We'll get Maya."

Deb walked past Lena and gave Keith a kiss. "You both need to come back, whatever happens." She gave a laugh, but it held no joy. "Be careful." She hugged Lena and then walked back toward the fire.

"I didn't expect that," Lena said. The hug had caught her by surprise. If this was the new Deb, maybe it was a good thing.

"She'll come through." Keith handed her a rifle. "Do you have your handgun?"

Lena patted the holster. "It's loaded. So, let's get going."

"Anything else?"

Lena hoped they wouldn't be fighting close, but she lifted her pant leg to reveal the skinning knife strapped to her calf.

Keith pointed toward the bridge. "The prints leading from the tent go that way. We can't sneak up, so let's be fast. Julian is probably too busy finding a place to hide to keep watch."

Lena started her run to the shadows beyond the bridge. It reminded her of their flight from New Surrey.

Keith kneeled beside her at the far side of the bridge. "You know this is likely to end in bloodshed."

"I'd rather it didn't." She shifted the rifle in her arms and undid the strap on her holster. "If one of us has the opportunity, we should just take the shot, right?"

Keith was scanning the area. He bent to test a depression in the grass. "If we have time to decide, it should be me."

"Why? Because you've killed before?"

He took a few steps and bent again. Then he waved her to follow. "To be honest, that was more of an accident than a killing. I only meant to scare him out of hitting his wife again." He held up his hand for her to stop. Then after finding some clue that Lena couldn't make out, pointed to a large building. "Don't get me wrong. I would have killed him, but that's not the reason. I'm a better long range shot. And hunting has taught me how to take down a target."

"Okay." Lena followed him to lean against the building. "But I'm not going to hold back. There's no way we can leave him alive. He'll just keep following us."

Keith leaned slightly to scan the street without losing his cover. "It's hard to make the kill shot."

"I can do it."

Keith waved her to the next building. "I didn't mean aiming. I mean, it's hard to pull the trigger when you know what's going to happen. Shoot for the widest part of his body. I'll finish him off if needed."

Lena didn't argue. She'd seen death on the farm. They killed the stock when they needed food. She'd been shown how it was done.

It was taking too long. Lena followed Keith from building to building, trusting he was on a trail. It was hard to keep quiet when she couldn't see any of the markers he noticed. They were almost at the end of the main street of stores and there was no evidence that Julian was anywhere nearby.

"Tell me what's going on," she whispered.

"We're catching up," Keith said quietly. "Maya is doing a good job of leaving clues."

He pointed to the center of the road. Lena saw a ribbon lying at the edge of a pothole. Finally, Keith's tracking lessons started to surface. They were walking beside the trail he'd found. She'd only been looking ahead. Lena felt her fears recede. She'd been worrying about the possibilities and whether Keith was taking her to Maya. Tracking required focus and calm.

She took in a deep breath and started searching ahead and to the center of the road. Julian might have stayed there because it was fast travel. He could have taken Maya as soon as she entered the tent. That would give him twenty minutes' head start. At the pace Keith was setting, it would be a miracle if they caught up.

"Can we go faster?"

"I said we were catching up. I think he's planning to stay in town tonight. Maybe he's twisted enough to think we'd just keep going without Maya. Whatever else is going on, she's probably not helping him get away."

"We should have believed Ava," Lena said. "Sorry, I know you need to concentrate."

Keith pointed out a footprint at the edge of a puddle. "We're almost on them. Get over there." He indicated a dark doorway in the last building. A movie theatre.

Lena wanted to keep going, but she wasn't the hunter. She had to believe that Keith knew what he was doing.

"We have a couple of ways of doing this," Keith said. "You need to decide how we'll go about it."

"You probably know what's best," Lena said. Keith had more experience than she did in hunting.

"No. You need to decide; the others see you as the leader. The way this goes down will tell them what kind of leader you are."

"Fuck! There's no time for this. I don't want to be the leader."

Keith grunted. "You don't have a choice. That's how we see you."

She'd make sure the conversation happened soon. People needed to understand that decisions should be made by the group, with the most competent person casting the final vote. "What are the two options?"

"We get Maya back and then kill him, or we kill him and get Maya back."

"I'd like it if Maya didn't have to see him killed."

"Yeah. She'll see death soon enough. Okay. Can you smell that?"

Lena sniffed and caught the faint scent of wood smoke.

"They are somewhere in that orchard." Keith jerked his head to a small grove of fruit trees. "You can go straight in and try to talk him into letting Maya go. I'll come around from the back and take aim."

"What if... what if he won't let her go?"

"You shoot him in the leg. I'll go in for the kill."

Lena's stomach dropped at the thought that they could plan to kill another human being so coldly. "I think we should both see what's up before you go."

Keith looked like he was going to argue, then his face cleared. "It's risky, but fine. Do everything I say, so we don't give away our approach."

She nodded and checked her handgun. Feeling like a western gunslinger, Lena followed Keith into the first line of trees. The smoke in the air was thicker and the scent of overripe apples flooded her senses.

CHAPTER THIRTY

Be silent. Don't worry about speed. Don't worry about what you can't change.

None of that helped when the image of Ava's face rose in her mind. How would she live with it if they were a minute too late to save Maya?

Keith tapped her shoulder, and when he had her attention, he pointed ahead. Lena could see movement and then a breeze brought the smoke toward her.

There was only one person in the gap between the trees. She couldn't call it a clearing. The rows were still orderly even though the undergrowth reached her knees in patches. It was more like a place where a tree was missing. The dark did more to cover their movements than the orchard.

Keith leaned in close, his words just a breath in her ear. "The fire isn't doing anything but smoke. I don't think he has any skills."

"Maya?" She matched the volume of his voice.

He shook his head and drew Lena back a few paces and behind a low apple tree. "I can't see her. The fact that he hasn't got light is in his favor too. We need to get close, but it's time to split up."

Now that they were about to act, Lena wanted Keith to stay. She knew his plan was the right way to go, but it left her alone and solely responsible for whatever happened.

"If she's not there, we need to get information out of him. We need to find her, no matter what's happened." Even if it was just a body, they would take Maya to Ava.

"It'll take me about fifteen minutes to come around the back," Keith whispered. "I think you should wait for five minutes and then go in to talk."

"You'll give me ten minutes?" As she said it, the time seemed both too much and too little.

"I'll get there as fast as I can. I figure five minutes is all you'll be able to stand waiting."

He knew her better than she thought. "Okay, I'll count to three hundred before I move."

Keith glanced over his shoulder. "Don't rush it." Then he disappeared into the dark.

Lena listened carefully but there was no sound of Keith's movement. The silence made her feel alone in the universe. She glanced toward where they'd seen Julian and noticed he'd managed to get some flame going. If she was very lucky, he'd lost his night vision and she'd have a tiny advantage.

She started her count, concentrating on the pace, aware that she would speed up the count in her impatience. Lena moved two trees toward Julian as she counted the last hundred seconds. He was talking, but it looked like his audience was the fire.

She moved forward, still making no noise, as she completed her count. In her heart, she wanted Maya to be sitting across from Julian. Her darker instincts expected to see her harmed.

Just outside the ring of glow thrown by his weak fire, Lena kicked some leaves aside to warn him. He jumped up and spun toward the sound.

"I'm armed," he shouted.

Lena saw no evidence of a gun or a knife. He was lying and didn't even know that she could see him.

"It's okay, Julian. It's me. Lena. Remember?" She stepped into the light. Holding up her hands, the rifle grasped in her right.

He was holding a tree branch. "Drop the gun."

She placed the rifle on the ground, raised her hands again and stepped forward. "No need for anyone to get hurt."

"Why are you here?"

He was insane. "I want to talk to Maya."

He glanced to the other side of the fire, then turned back. "She's not interested in talking."

She followed his movement. Maya was slumped against the ropes tying her to the tree. Lena could see her hair swaying as her chest rose and fell.

She was breathing.

"I'll just wait until she's ready. Do you have any water?"

She needed to get closer to Maya. If she could play on his crazy idea that nothing was wrong, he'd let her get to the fire. Her gun was useless in its holster while her hands were up. He'd have plenty of time to get to Maya if she tried for her weapon.

"No. You should just go." He stepped toward Lena menacing her with the branch. "Maya is happy with me."

It was too soon. Keith would still be getting into position. Lena had no idea whether Keith was still approaching, or whether he was standing in the shadows ready to act.

"I just need to talk to her, so I can tell Ava that she's okay. I'm sure you're right, but you must know that Ava will want me to check."

Julian lowered the branch, and looked at Maya again. "Okay. But she's asleep. You can wait here." He pointed to a bare patch of earth across the fire from Maya.

He may be insane, but he wasn't completely stupid. She'd have a hard time getting to Maya from there.

"You followed us all this way?" Lena asked.

She had to wait for Keith. There was no way she could do anything to resolve this alone without getting hurt.

"I thought I lost you in that town," he said. Another glance at the tree where Maya was still slumped, and then he sat between Lena and Maya.

"It must have been hard," Lena said. She wrapped her arms around herself hoping he wouldn't notice she'd reached inside her jacket. The gun felt reassuring in her hand. Now she just needed a chance to use it. He had to move away from his position. If Lena shot now and missed, the bullet would go past and hit Maya.

"Not so bad. I knew I'd find you and Maya would come with me."

She nodded. The fire had caught the wood now. Its crackle and pop masking any sounds that Keith might be making. Lena remembered to keep her gaze to the side of the flame as much as possible. She needed her night vision.

Julian stared at the flames.

Lena took the opportunity to withdraw her weapon and hold it to her side. If Julian wasn't going to move, she would. All she needed was to change the angle a little, taking Maya out of the range of a miss. Keith would have to take care of himself.

"Did you —"

Her words were cut off as Keith stepped out of the shadows and grabbed Julian by the throat. He dragged the man away from the fire.

"Cut Maya free," Keith said. "I'll deal with him."

Julian was fighting back now. Catching Keith off balance, he managed to get his feet under him.

Lena ran to Maya, releasing the knife from the strap on her calf. She cut the ropes, and Maya slumped forward. Lena caught her, dropping the knife, feeling the dead weight land in her arms. She checked for a pulse. It was there, strong but slow. She'd be fine if they could get her awake.

Lena moved Maya a few paces away so that she'd be safe from the fight. It would take Julian time to find her if he won.

The thought of Julian winning chilled her. She checked Maya, who gave a small moan. Whatever Julian had given the child was wearing off fast. Lena whispered, "Stay here, I'll come and get you in a few minutes." She could only hope that the words had sunk through Maya's confusion.

Lena wrapped her jacket around Maya, picked up her knife, and ran to help Keith.

Julian had landed a punch that stunned Keith. Lena saw him push Keith to line him up with the fire. She rushed across the clear space and rammed into Julian.

Julian spun and grabbed Lena's arm. "You can't have her."

Lena stared into Julian's eyes. There was anger and fear in his gaze. Even in his madness he must know that he couldn't win against two attackers. Two people who would never stop until Maya was safe.

She heard stones rolling in the shadows across the fire. Lena kept her focus on Julian.

"She belongs with her mother," Lena gasped, as she freed herself from him.

Julian bent to pick up a rock, his other arm swinging toward her.

She moved in close knowing that distance was going to work in his favor. He was taller. If she moved back, there might be no other chance to get within his guard.

He lost his balance when the rock didn't lift easily. As he stumbled, he reached for another weapon. Lena crowded him, hoping that the threat would make him think twice about attacking.

Julian swore as his hand wrapped around a branch that burned at the edge of the fire. He seemed not to notice the pain after the first shock. Julian regained his feet, swinging the burning branch toward her.

Lena could smell the flesh charring. She knew he was trying to get enough distance so that he could run. She could see it in the way he twisted his body toward the darkness. She couldn't let him go.

He swung the branch toward her. She jumped back instinctively. It gave him the chance he needed. Julian threw the branch at her and ran toward the shadows.

Lena dodged the branch and ran after Julian. Her knife grasped in her hand, she was grateful that he was running away from Maya's position. Her night vision was gone because of the fire, she had to follow the sound of Julian's feet pounding on the packed earth. If he got too far, she would be crashing into trees rather than after him.

She heard footsteps behind, but put them out of her mind. Then the sound of Julian's flight changed. The crack of dry branches breaking on contact replaced the crinkle of dry leaves underfoot.

Then an impact. She struggled through the shadows, her vision getting better but not enough to see more than shapes.

Julian was flat on his face, his foot trapped between two large branches on the ground.

He turned to her. "I promise I won't take her again. Just help me out of here and you'll never see me again."

Lena shook her head. She couldn't trust herself to speak. Walking up to him, she knelt, gripped her knife firmly, and sliced his throat.

Blood covered her hands and chest when she was unable to dodge it. Her mind recoiled at what she'd done. Her stomach roiled. Then Lena heard the scream.

"You need to clean up," Keith's voice cut through screaming.

Maya was pulling away from him, trying to get as far as she could from the sight of Julian's death. Lena reached for Maya, then pulled away as she saw the blood on her hands and Maya's look of terror.

Keith held Maya's arm, but allowed her to pull to the extent of his reach. "There's probably a place in town. I think you should go ahead. I'll talk to Maya. We'll come find you."

"I didn't mean to..."

Keith handed Lena a rag that he pulled from his pack. "I know. You meant for him to die, but not like that, and not in front of Maya."

She tried to wipe the blood from her shirt. It just made the rag wet and sticky. She needed new clothes as well as a long shower. Another long shower.

"I'll go ahead, but I don't have anything to mark where I go in." Lena said, standing, and moving away from the body.

Keith looked at Maya before answering. Lena followed his gaze. Maya was staring at Lena, her terror still there. Lena wished the price wasn't so high, but there was no doubt in her mind that Julian would have kept coming if she'd let him live. If only it had been a bullet. The knife felt too personal. She never wanted to do that to a fellow human again.

"We'll find you. Just get clean. Toss the clothes, I'll find something for you," Keith said. Then after another glance at Maya. "I'll get her calmed down. Ava will help her understand."

Lena wondered if Ava could help her understand her own actions. That disconnect from her feelings and razor focus on the goal needed to be controlled. She'd never acted like that before. Brian wouldn't know her if he saw Lena today.

The second building she broke into was an apartment block. Inside the first suite she flicked the light switch and one bulb lit in the entryway fixture.

There was enough water pressure in the first-floor suite to wash the clotting blood from her body. There was some in her hair, but most of it was on her clothing. It didn't wash the stink from her memory. Under the cold water, she closed her eyes. The last seconds of the chase ran through her mind. Seeing Julian caught in the trap had flipped something in Lena's head.

At the time, it had felt like someone else was operating her body. She hadn't thought about what to do. She'd told Keith that she was willing to do whatever it took to make Maya safe, and that's what she'd done. Lena tried to feel remorse for killing Julian, but there was none. Only fear that she hadn't been in control.

Now, as she dried herself with a threadbare towel from the linen closet, Lena still tasted the blood. It was in her body, and in her mind. She worried that it would always be there. She worried that now she'd crossed a line it would be the start of her descent into Abigail's madness.

She couldn't let the group put her up as the leader. This violence would not end in a good place.

Lena heard noise in the hallway and reached for her gun. Before this she would have assumed the noise came from Keith and Maya. Now, she couldn't take the chance. There could be more people like Julian around.

"Lena," Keith called from the hall.

She held a towel across her chest and walked the few steps to the apartment door. She checked the peephole before opening it for Keith and Maya.

The girl kept Keith between them and wouldn't meet Lena's gaze.

Keith held out a t-shirt, black with a green peace sign over a marijuana leaf. She turned around and pulled it over her wet hair. It felt better to be wearing a clean top. "We should head back. Ava will be frantic."

Pointing Maya to sit on the sofa, Keith opened his pack. "You need to eat. Your body used up most of its reserves in the fight."

He handed her two energy bars. "It won't hurt to sit for five minutes."

"I want my mom," Maya said. "I don't want to wait here." She glared at Lena.

Keith had been right, as soon as the food was in her mouth, Lena felt the pinch of hunger. She barely chewed the first bar before swallowing it. She ate the second bar while she checked the kitchen for supplies. They couldn't turn down a chance to forage. Their journey wouldn't bring them this way so it was the only opportunity.

There was one chipped glass in the cupboard, not even crumbs anywhere else. She filled the glass with water to wash down the last of the energy bar. "Did you find anything in the stores?"

"Not much. I got a couple more t-shirts, but we didn't find any food."

"Then we should head out." Lena didn't want to be anywhere near the place. She knew Maya wouldn't listen to any explanations. The sooner she was with Ava; the sooner Lena could hope that she'd understand.

The sun was clearing the hills when they finally rejoined the group. Maya hadn't been able to walk much. Whatever drug Julian had given her drained her energy. Keith carried her piggy-back while Lena lugged all of the supplies. It had taken everything Lena had to keep moving. If the group reacted the way Maya had, it might be the last time Lena travelled with them.

The silence weighed on Lena. She tried not to worry about what had happened, but her mind kept running a play-by-play every time she stopped thinking of other things.

Ava saw them first.

She yelled something that Lena couldn't make out, and started running toward them, Jason at her heels. Too late Lena realized that it looked like Maya was hurt badly by the way she hung limp from Keith's shoulders.

"Maya's going to be okay," Lena said. She dropped the supplies and helped Ava take the sleeping girl from Keith.

She barely moved until Ava pulled her into an embrace and cried into Maya's hair.

"Mom." The word was groggy, but there was no terror in it.

Lena's body flooded in relief; there was no permanent damage. Then Maya looked at her and the ice of fear glazed her eyes. She buried herself deeper in Ava's arms, muttering something.

Ava looked at Lena and then Keith. "I don't know what happened, but thank you."

Keith picked up the guns. Deb ran to him, planting a kiss as she continued on to see to Maya.

Lena couldn't stay to hear Ava's reaction when she learned what Maya had seen. She bent to pick up the dropped bags and started to return to the camp, her steps dragging with exhaustion. Scott passed her with a makeshift stretcher.

She heard them convince Maya to get onto the stretcher.

"Something happened," Ava said. She'd caught up with Lena as the others hurried to bring Maya to the campfire.

"You should be with Maya," Lena said.

Ava took Lena's arm and gently pulled her to a stop. "Let me get some of those bags. I can tell you're about to drop. I need to know what made her so scared of you."

There was no blame in Ava's voice.

"He didn't do anything but drug her. At least I'm pretty sure she isn't hurt in any way." Lena battled with the need to unburden her own guilt.

"Stop dodging me," Ava said. "The sooner you tell me the sooner we can get Maya back to loving you."

Lena tried to keep the sob inside, but Ava's caring and her own guilt at the damage she may have done to Maya over-whelmed her self-control. And worse, no matter how much she tried to justify what she'd done, Lena couldn't stop thinking about Julian's last moments. She dropped to her knees and sobbed, unable to speak.

Ava knelt beside her, patting her shoulder, and murmuring comforting words until the crying stopped.

"She saw me kill him. It was bloody, and I'm pretty sure she didn't see much of what led up to it. She was so afraid of me. I don't know if it can be repaired."

Ava wrapped her arms around Lena's shaking body. "Kids get over things. It will take some time, but we all know you. We all know you did only what had to be done. Even Maya knows that inside. She's just scared, and you were the closest person she could direct that emotion at, and she's probably feeling guilty for thinking Julian was a good guy."

Lena couldn't stop shivering. Even with the sun warming the world for another hot day, Lena felt like she was sitting in a snowbank.

Ava pulled her to her feet. "You need food and sleep. You and Maya will be riding in the wagon today. Come on, I promise everyone will be grateful for what you did."

"I don't want their gratitude, Ava. I don't even want to tell them what happened. Can we just let it lie for a while?"

Ava took all of the packs and said, "When you are ready."

CHAPTER THIRTY-ONE

There was too much room in the wagon. Lena pushed aside a few sacks of supplies, only enough food for a day, and the farm was at least five more days away at this pace. They'd only managed a few hours of travel today. The group was already running on short rations, and they'd be in no shape to do anything but lay down and hope for food by the time they got to the farm.

That's if they all made it alive.

This area was too good a campsite to pass up; the giant flies didn't swarm so thickly. Lena had forgotten the bugs in the summer here.

Keith, Scott, and Mellow were out trying to find some game to hunt. There hadn't been any for days, and their supplies had never been enough for more than a few meals anyway. Not since the fight to leave Abigail's Community of Truth, when they'd lost half their food in order to escape. The tools had been replaced, but not the food.

This wasn't supposed to be how it went. The trip was over a month longer than she'd expected. There were no small communities along the road where they could work for a few meals. It was hard to believe that the only community left was Abigail's

218

P.A. WILSON

town, which was more like a prison for indentured slaves. The rest of the world couldn't have run to the closest city. There must be something of a community left. But that was for after they settled in at the farm.

No one else seemed to notice how bad it was. They looked to her when the subject came up, but Lena had no answers either.

"May I have a gleaning bag, please." Maya had stopped flinching away from Lena, but this formal politeness was almost as bad.

Lena handed Maya one of the long bags. "Did someone find a town?"

"No, Deb said we should see if we can find some wild vegetables. She's coming with me and Jason so we don't get any poisonous ones." Maya flashed a tiny smile.

Lena counted the smile as progress towards healing their relationship. "We'll get set up," she said. Then, handing a second bag to Maya she added, "Maybe you'll get lucky and find lots."

The girl took the bags and returned to where the others were pulling open the bundles that made up their tents.

Lena sighed and grabbed the sack of oatmeal. Unless there was some meat to supplement the grains, it would have to be enough for two meals.

Ava and Tik were putting the first tent up as she approached. They moved efficiently and quickly, but Lena could see the strain on Ava's face. It was taking too much energy to set up their usual camp.

"Why don't we just sleep in the open," she said. "It's warm. We won't have to take down the camp in the morning."

Ava looked from the half-erected tent to Lena and then shrugged. "Sure. I guess we can have one night without the pretense of privacy." She glanced at Tik.

He laughed. "Sure, it'll save us time and maybe we can get farther tomorrow. I'm looking forward to a real roof over my head. I don't know how Scott does it all the time."

Neither did Lena. If she never slept under the stars again it would be too soon. The other two packed the tents and left Lena alone as they stowed them in the wagon.

She knelt at the pile of stones they brought from camp to camp for making a fire pit and started arranging them. They'd have a cooking fire ready if the hunters were successful.

The process of arranging the stones was like a meditation. Each one fit next to the other snuggly so that no embers would slide out and create a fire that they couldn't control.

The quiet movements allowed her to think through the problem. There were only a few solutions, and the best seemed to be leaving people behind. If two or three of the group went ahead quickly, the food would be enough. Then they could return with supplies. It was risky. The people who stayed would have to forage, but if they didn't have to trek all day, they wouldn't need as much.

In fact, two people on the horse would be at the farm in a little more than a day — if nothing went wrong.

Who would go and who would be left to wait it out?

The fire was in full flame when the hunters returned. Lena didn't need anyone to confirm that it wasn't successful. There was nothing slung over their shoulders, or hanging from their belts. Not even a rabbit or squirrel.

Keith shook his head. Mellow went to sit beside Tik. The normal conversation was gone, no one had the energy for small talk. If Deb and the kids hadn't found anything, Lena would have to talk about the problem. She didn't want to tell them what she'd decided.

Ava came from straightening the bedrolls and sat beside Lena. "Is there anything that we can eat from the seeds we brought to plant?"

So, she's noticed how low we are on food. Not that anyone would think they were knee-deep in groceries, but if Ava was asking about the crop seeds, she knew how bad it was.

"They are too dried out for eating. It will take a couple of days of soaking to get them even close to edible." If they started now, it would be something. "We could probably use a quarter of the crop seeds without causing problems next year. It wouldn't make a lot of sense to eat it all and then starve later."

Ava poured oatmeal into a pot and then took out a small sack of dried fruit. "This is the last of it. We'll hold off on the crop seeds. Maybe there's game to hunt farther along."

Lena left Ava to her cooking. The water jug was low too. They'd need to fill it as soon as they came to a building with running water. There weren't many of those left either. At least the farm had a well. There were probably some wells serving houses in the back country, but it was a couple of day's travel to any of them, and they wouldn't make it.

She walked away from the small group, trying to find some quiet where she could let her mind turn over the problem. Maybe she was like her students, the ones who skipped breakfast, and probably dinner, they couldn't think through a simple problem.

Leaning with her back against a rock, she closed her eyes. There wasn't much noise to disturb her, or keep her awake. This was one of the few places where there wasn't a stream or a river to cool the air. The heat sat on her skin like a cloak. Her exhaustion and hunger kept pulling her into a drowse, and that wasn't what she came here to do.

There was a buzz of insects in the air. It occurred to her that they might be able to eat bugs, but she had no idea which ones would be edible, how to cook them, or how to catch enough to satisfy eight people. Although the bugs were definitely dining well on them.

"Deb and the kids are back," Scott said. Waking Lena from another shallow sleep.

"Anything?"

"A few mushrooms, but nothing substantial." Scott sat beside her and stretched out his legs. "How bad is it?"

Of course, he'd know they were in trouble. When he was on his own, he'd be careful not to run low on supplies.

Should they have stayed at the last place they found food? Long enough to strip the fields? Lena hated the cost of staying. Any extra day they dallied meant a day later in the season. A day closer to winter. A day longer they'd need to find enough supplies to survive.

"Bad. There's just not enough food to get all of us home."

Scott grunted as if he were agreeing. "What are you going to do about it?"

Why me? "We need to decide together." It felt like a phrase she just kept repeating and everyone never listened.

"Yeah, but you've got a plan. I know you Lena, you don't want to deliver bad news without some kind of hope." He shook his head as she tried to deny it. "It's good. You keep everyone hopeful. But there's a time when we have to make hard decisions. I've heard you every time you've said you don't want to be the leader, but you know why everyone keeps looking to you, right?"

"No."

He laughed. "You act like the leader. You do what needs to be done. You got everyone out of New Surrey. You got us out of The Community of Truth, you dealt with Julian. You can't expect people to stop noticing."

"I can't just let everything go to hell." She sat forward, stretching her back. "I think we have to split up the group. Send two people ahead, maybe on the horse. Then we wait for them to come back. With food."

"There's other options," Scott said.

"I can't think of any," Lena said. "If I'm such a great leader, why am I drawing a blank?"

Scott was looking toward the camp. Lena followed his gaze. It wasn't the camp. It was the wagon and the horse.

He was planning how to leave them. If he took the horse, they were lost. She didn't think that he'd take the last of their supplies, or not more than his fair share, but the added burden of their gear would slow them down enough to mean they'd die on the road. She knew there was a small town near the farm, but the rest of the distance between their camp and the farm was unpopulated and used for range. They'd die looking for a ranch house.

"We need you, Scott." She couldn't bring herself to say they needed his horse and wagon. It wasn't just that. His experience of being on the road had saved them more than a few times when they were looking for a campsite.

He looked at her and then back at the wagon. "I wasn't planning on leaving. I was wondering if we need to sacrifice Starbuck. We could eat him. It would be hard to pull the wagon, but we'd have meat."

A little revulsion, a little guilt, and a lot of hunger turned Lena's stomach. "I hope that's a long way down the list of options."

"Don't like horse meat?"

"Don't like the idea of Starbuck meat. He's the reason we've made it this far." She looked over the horse again. "He's finding enough food. If only we could live on grass."

"I'm sure the kids would rather starve too."

Lena knew that there were probably other solutions, but doubted that there was a best one. Only the least bad. "What about my idea?"

He gestured to encompass the entire clearing. "This is the worse place to leave people. The best case would be us getting to the farm in two or three days. Starbuck would be pushed to his limit."

"Us?" Lena hadn't wanted to think much about who would leave.

"I'm not letting Starbuck out of my sight, and you know where the farm is located."

"Okay, so two days there, one day for Starbuck to recover and two days back — only one person needs to come back."

Scott pushed himself off the ground brushing the dirt and dried grass off his jeans. "That was the best case. And what happens if we run into trouble? What if we lose Starbuck? What if there's nothing for us to bring back? There's nothing here to support six people. Laying down to starve is worse than moving forward even if the outcome is the same." He walked to the camp without waiting for her answer.

Lena stayed where she was and watched as Scott joined the rest of the group. She couldn't help but notice that they all moved slowly, there was none of the usual chatter. The kids sat close together poking at the fire.

Scott had become one of them, something that she didn't think would happen. He was practical and looked at problems as though everything had a solution, without being annoyingly optimistic. He didn't talk about leaving them, but had never really committed to staying. She wondered how he was feeling about the group now that they might not make it. Was he really planning to go? Had he deflected her concern so that he wouldn't give her warning?

He was different from Brian, more than just being comfortable outside a town. Brian would have found a way to turn the group against each other at the first challenge. He'd be pressing her to return to New Surrey at any bump in the road.

It was a blessing really, that Brian wasn't with them. Lena knew they wouldn't have gotten this far if they hadn't worked as a team. But was she doing the right thing? Brian liked to make all the important decisions. Look at how he'd assumed she was willing to give up her work to support him. He would be telling the group what to do right now. And it would be whatever made Brian the most comfortable.

The thought startled her. It was the first time that she'd thought about him without feeling a little longing that she tried not to acknowledge. The first time she didn't mentally excuse his behavior.

. . .

Her thoughts kept her away from camp until she noticed that the darkness was making it increasingly harder to see the details. If she didn't return soon, then she'd be stumbling into every stone and broken branch between her and the fire.

She shifted her weight to loosen the tightness in her back and legs. Tomorrow would be another day of trying to walk out the pains in her body. Lena started to push herself off the ground, and then noticed Scott approaching again. Even in the twilight it was easy to identify him. Tik strutted. No matter how tired he was, the swagger of the gang member never stiffened or slowed. Keith's walk was the low steps of a hunter. He was always looking for something, either attack or game.

Scott walked quietly, but always seemed to be about to break into a lope.

"Food will be ready soon." He joined her on the ground, close enough that she could have leaned on his shoulder. "There's talk of pulling out the last of the whiskey."

There was nothing to celebrate. "I'd rather they left that until we are at the farm."

She felt him shrug beside her, but kept her eyes on the camp.

"You know; you should just talk to them. A real leader would listen to everyone before making a decision."

She thought they'd moved past that discussion. Scott was deliberately pushing at her buttons. Was he angry that she hadn't followed him? "I don't want to be a leader."

"That would sound more true if you weren't sitting here trying to figure out how to leave people behind. You can't stop yourself from making plans, but you can stop shutting everyone out."

Lena suppressed a sigh of frustration. It had annoyed her when her students sighed, it would annoy Scott. Right now, even at this moment, he was the only person she could talk to. "I don't get it. One minute you are telling me I can't avoid being the leader, now you're happy to criticize my skills."

"Why are you still out here?" He didn't let her answer. "While I was gone, what were you thinking? I'm guessing it wasn't about how to tell the group that we have to split up. You were trying to work out how to tell them they had to stay behind."

That was uncalled for. She'd decided to follow his advice. There was no need to pick at her for taking a few minutes to think.

"They know," he continued. "Everyone can see how low the supplies are."

"I know that," she said. The anger she kept pushing away was getting stronger. "You don't know anything about leading people. You were alone before we met. If you think you can do a better job, then I'm happy to step aside."

Scott leaned away from her. "I don't want your job. I didn't realize you wanted it that much either."

Lena clenched her fist to stop the anger from spilling out. "I don't, but someone has to do it."

"Yeah, it's hard," he said. Lena could tell he was reining in some emotion, just as she was. "Look, you're right. I'm used to being alone. Or, I was. But I wasn't born traveling. We've all been forced to do things we'd never have thought possible."

"Like kill a man in front of a child?" The words were out before she could stop them. Everyone had acted like killing Julian was the right thing to do. But inside, Lena couldn't pretend it wasn't a horrendous act. Every time she thought about it, she felt sick. And it was never far from her thoughts.

Scott shifted to face her. He looked sad, not angry or as if he was blaming her. "Like doing what you had to do so that Maya was safe. You have to let that go. If you are very lucky, you'll never have to do that kind of thing again."

"It's not easy," she said. "When you're responsible for people, even if you don't want to be, you have to know that you are the good guy."

He rubbed his face. Brian had done that sometimes when he was contemplating something he knew would piss her off.

Lena turned away from Scott's gaze and glanced at the fire again. Dinner must have been ready a long time ago. Were they waiting for her? Was she ruining their last meal together?

"What did you do before?" Lena asked.

"A different life," he answered. "Maybe someday I'll talk about it. It was the right choice for me at the time to head out on my own."

He couldn't be much older than Tik. How had he become so sure of life? "Maybe this is another one of those times. Maybe you should leave. We'll figure out a way to survive." There was so much bitterness in her words that Lena felt acid burn her gut. How had she gone from admiring his poise to wanting to hurt Scott?

"I'm sure it's not one of those times. You need me, anyway. Starbuck is mine, and so is the wagon. I feel kind of obligated to help." His voice was soft. Whatever he'd been feeling moments before had gone.

"You were the one who suggested eating your horse."

He laughed. "Yeah, well he's getting fat."

It was not the time for a joke. She wanted to yell at him that this was life and death and that he needed to take it seriously.

"That's a good reason to ride him to the farm. You just don't understand what I have to do. I know that whoever we leave behind will have a hard time. I don't want to come back to find them dead. It's more important that the group survive than the individuals."

Brian had probably thought he was doing the right thing too. It had been so easy to tell herself that he was wrong. That the individual people were important. The only comfort she could dredge up was the fact that she wanted the right thing for the group, not for herself.

She rose and dusted off her jeans. It was as good a time as any to start the discussion. "We should go back. I don't want them holding dinner any longer."

He stood too. "So, you'll listen? You'll tell them how bad it is, and then let them help solve the problem?"

That's exactly what she would do. Why did he keep harping on it? "When we were in New Surrey, I thought that the worst thing in my life was going to be the rules and restrictions. I promised everyone that we wouldn't do that when we got to the farm. Now I wonder if it was just a lack of voice. We all know that things will get hard, no *if* about it. I don't know why I try to fix things."

"Tell them that, it's a good start," he said.

"It's going to be a long night. Is it okay with you that we eat before we start talking about starvation?"

He took her elbow and started leading her toward the warmth of the campfire. The days might still be broiling, but lately the nights had cooled as a reminder that the year was passing.

In the end, Lena let them eat.

After she explained how short their rations were, and how far she thought they had to go, the discussion heated up. The only ones not offering ideas and arguments were Maya and Jason. They stuck close to Ava, and watched the adults plan their future.

Deb disappeared into the dark in one of the few lulls in conversation. She came back a few minutes later with their final sacks of food.

Even knowing the reality, Lena's heart sank at the sight of the few sacks. The group was silent as they looked over the meals. Lena thought they were all trying to do the math, and not liking the answers.

"You can last a long time without food if you don't expend a lot of energy," Deb said.

"That's why I thought it would work if some of us stay here." Lena still didn't like the choice, but no one had come up with a better plan.

Deb looked around the group. "No one wants to stay here, Lena. But you've missed the point."

Lena search the faces of her friends. No one seemed to understand Deb any more than she did. "I'm too tired for guessing, Deb."

"We can use Starbuck to carry some of the stuff in the wagon. Set up some kind of saddlebag thing. If we make enough room, most of us can ride the wagon."

Riding would be much the same as waiting. "It will still take us too long to get to the farm." Lena tried to work out the fastest they could travel.

"We have water, and we can get more," Deb said. "If we only have one small meal every day, those of us in the wagon. Then we can give more to... say Keith and Tik. They can range ahead. Looking for game, looking for stuff to forage."

"And one of us can drive the wagon," Ava added. "We'll keep a rifle up there, just in case. It could work."

They looked at Lena. The words formed in her mind to tell them she wasn't willing to be the leader, but they disappeared under the trust that came her way.

She could think of a hundred ways it could go sideways in the space of a day, but that was true about everything. "Does anyone think this is a bad idea?"

No one spoke.

"Okay, we need to sleep. We leave as soon as we can in the morning."

CHAPTER THIRTY-TWO

They arrived at the farm with barely enough energy to walk up the porch steps. Lena knew there was no way the supplies would have held out, but that hadn't stopped her from hoping. Right now, she was shaking with the effort to keep from laying on the ground and sleeping, scared that it would be forever.

The wagon waited at the bottom of the dirt road that led to the barn. The farmhouse was in sight, right beside the barn, just as she remembered. The only problem: light shone through the windows.

"I guess it was stupid to think no one would have found the place," Lena said, her voice barely carrying to the group. "You stay here; I'll go see what's going on."

"I'll come," Scott said. "You won't get anywhere alone."

She was glad of the company. In the last day, apathy had taken over as her primary emotion. Lena knew it was because her stomach was so empty it felt twisted. She could see the same need reflected in the dull expressions of the others. Alone she might just give up, but with Scott beside her, she might just find the strength to take the farm away from whoever was staying there.

Keith handed Scott his rifle and then turned Starbuck to the side so they could clear the road. She knew it meant they would be able to escape if things went wrong, but this was their home, and she was going to stop here. There really was no option. If they had to go back on the road, they wouldn't last more than a day.

The steps creaked as they headed for the front door. A curtain twitched and then the door opened. A man stood there. His shirt clean and pressed, his pants were neat, and he was wearing slippers. Lena's feet protested in the worn boots. The man was in his fifties, but there was healthy vigor in his blue eyes and clean-shaven face.

"Hi," she said. "I'm Lena Custordin. This is my aunt's farm. I mean, it's mine."

The man looked her over. She knew what he saw. A dust covered woman with gaunt cheeks, and dull eyes. Someone with no fight left trying to pretend she could take away what he'd stolen.

"It's our farm. We been here for a while. You need to keep moving on."

Scott stepped into the square of light. "It doesn't seem hospitable for you to steal our home and not tell us your name."

"I wasn't planning on being hospitable. I said you need to keep moving on." A shadow moved in the room behind him.

Lena stepped in front of Scott, trying to keep the rifle from sight. There was no need to escalate the situation. "This is Scott. Did you know my aunt? May?"

"No." The man stepped backwards and reached to close the door.

"Larry, there's a bunch more of them," a woman's voice called.

The man pressed his lips together. "Ellen, you stay inside."

"But there's kids with them," Ellen said and then appeared behind Larry. She was thin, and her hair was faded blonde.

The words seem to penetrate Larry's stubbornness. Lena hoped Scott would stay quiet while she negotiated.

"Yes, we have two kids. Are you alone here?" She tried to look around them into the house.

"It's just us, and that's all the farm will support." Larry had regained his resemblance to a brick wall.

Lena just needed a toehold. "My aunt was able to make it produce much more than that. You could use help. There's no need for any of us to leave."

"I don't want trouble, and people bring trouble." Larry said.

She looked over his shoulder to find support from Ellen, but the woman was watching her husband. He was making the decisions. She may not like it, but Ellen wouldn't go against Larry.

"We aren't trouble. We're looking for a safe place to settle. The kids need a home." Her voice wobbled on the last words. It was hard to stay calm this close to the end of the journey. These people didn't seem bad, like Abigail, but they weren't going to share without a good reason. Pity didn't seem to be enough.

Scott touched her back with the rifle. Lena tried to see what he wanted her to notice, but nothing had changed.

"Should have thought of that when you took them on the road." Larry peered over her shoulder. "We'll take the horse."

Not on my watch. "If we stay, the horse stays. The wagon too. It will be handy for bringing in the crops." She just needed him to agree to one thing; one yes and she'd have a trail to follow that would end in them inside the house.

"That's true. I guess you'll be walking when you leave," Larry said.

"If you only use the farm to feed yourselves, you don't need either," Lena said. "Do you have neighbors? Someone to trade with?"

"Haven't looked."

This was going nowhere. Lena's mind was fogged with fatigue and hunger. There must be a way to get past this. She glanced over her shoulder at Scott. He was watching Larry and Ellen.

"Look, Larry. I guess I can understand your position," she said, taking a step forward, but careful not to get too close. "I was probably stupid to think that the farm would be unoccupied after all this time."

He nodded and took a half step back. "I guess you figured it was your aunt's farm so it was yours."

She nodded at him, knowing that mimicking his movements would make him more susceptible to her requests. "I know you and Ellen have probably worked hard to make it as fruitful as it is."

Ellen came closer to the door, peering at the action over Larry's shoulder. "That's right. We've earned the farm. You can't take it from us."

"I know that," Lena said, voice low and steady. "We're just exhausted and famished. If we could get something to eat before we go..."

Larry glanced over his shoulder at Ellen.

Lena knew they were half way to agreeing. If she could get a meal, she could get permission to stay overnight. That would give her time to figure out the next step. It didn't matter that Larry and Ellen were here. The farm would need lots of hardworking people to get it back from the years of neglect. She was happy to start out as a farmhand.

"Lena," Maya's voice came from the darkness behind her.

Lena looked, noticing Larry turn to see what was happening. Maya stepped closer. Her hair was a mess, her shirt was dirty and her pants were obviously three sizes too large. Someone had done a great job of making the girl look pitiful. Someone who knew how to pull on the sympathy of strangers: Deb.

"Is that your girl?" Ellen asked.

Lena turned back to the couple. "Her mother is part of our group. This is Maya." Lena pushed her forward. "She's been a very brave girl. The road is hard on kids."

"Larry, get the stove lit." Ellen put her arms around Maya. "You come in here while we get set up, Maya. It's cold out there."

Larry hadn't moved. He looked at Lena, eyes narrowed. When he was finished scrutinizing her, he turned his attention to Scott and pointed at the porch. "You can leave the rifle right there. In fact, you can leave all your weapons with me until you leave." He peered into the night where the rest of the group waited. "How many you say?"

"There's eight of us," Lena said. If they gave over their weapons, it would show good faith. And she wasn't going to let Larry keep them. Even starving, they could take back what they needed. She just didn't want to start life at the farm with violence if she could avoid it.

"I ain't going to be stupid enough to pull you all into the house. You take the horse and wagon into the barn. There's lots of room for you. I'll get Ellen to bring you sandwiches. You can have your weapons back in the morning."

CHAPTER THIRTY-THREE

The barn was empty.

Lena could smell the cows, so they hadn't been gone long. Starbuck had a stall, and Larry tossed a bale of hay in the manger. The bale was small and badly tied, but it was fresh.

They left the wagon outside, but took all of their possessions inside.

Lena knew there was plenty of room in the house, but didn't want to push Larry too hard. They'd slept in worse places. Ellen turned up with a platter of sandwiches, a bowl of bruised apples, and Maya in tow just after they'd settled in.

Ava ran to Maya as soon as she came into sight. She may not have said anything, but the way Ava held Maya tightly told her how tense she was. Since the Julian incident, Maya stayed with her mother.

"Thanks," Lena said. She took the platter and passed it to Mellow. "It's been a few days since we've eaten a full meal."

"Larry's bringing some lanterns. You make sure you put them out before you go to sleep. I don't want to wake up to a barn burning."

Lena needed to keep the couple talking. "Will you sit with us?"

Ellen looked around. "Some fresh news would be nice." She turned to the door. "I'll get a cushion to sit on. You'll need something to drink too."

Larry passed her at the door. He held four lanterns in one hand and a shotgun in the other. "There's enough fuel in these for a couple of hours."

When Ellen returned, she carried a cushion under her arm and two pitchers in each hand. "Milk and water."

So, the dairy cows are around somewhere.

"Thanks," Lena said. She longed to eat one of the sandwiches, but it could wait. "You found the cows, then."

"It took a couple of days to figure out how to milk them," Larry said. "They don't give much even now, but enough to share for tonight."

"If they haven't been milked, it will take a while to get them producing. And if we could find a way to mate them, it would help." She took a long drink of milk that Deb had poured into one of their own glasses.

"We've had to learn about everything since we got here," Ellen said. "We worked out the milking. Well, I did that while Larry went hunting. There are a few stands of trees that the deer seem to like."

"And the produce garden?" Lena asked.

"There's some. Not pretty, and kind of tough, but we have carrots. Some lettuce grows, but it's mostly just leaves here and there."

Larry listened and watched, but Ellen did all the talking. Lena figured it was time for introductions.

"You've met Scott," she said. "This is Keith and his wife, Deb. Mellow and Tik over there, and Ava, she's Maya's mom and there's Jason, her son."

"Nice to meet you." Ellen glanced at Larry then turned back to Lena. "Why are you all here?"

Lena took the sandwich Mellow passed her, but held it while she talked. "We lived in a place called New Surrey, in Upstate New York. The towns aren't good places to live any more. There's too much of the old world still trying to hang on. We came here for a better future."

"You still think that way?" Larry asked. "Even with what you been through? It's obvious you've fallen on hard times."

"We've had some problems, but I think we all still want to create something better." Lena took a bite of the sandwich. The meat was overcooked and under-spiced. The bread hadn't risen properly, and the butter was starting to go rancid, but it made her mouth water.

"We've all got skills to work on the farm," Keith said. "I've taught everyone to hunt. Deb's a nurse. That's something you'll need eventually. Mellow and Ava have worked the town farms; they know how to get the land to produce. We just needed to get here."

"I worked the farm in the summers with my aunt," Lena added. "It wasn't just coming to a farm for me. I loved it here when she was alive. I wanted to make it like that."

"That might be," Ellen said. "But we have to look out for us. We got books and time. The farm will support us for our lives. You have to move on."

Lena thought she heard regret in Ellen's voice, but knew it was probably wishful thinking on her part. There just wasn't enough time to talk them into sharing the farm.

"What about other people?" Tik asked. "You are right about us running into problems. What happens when problems find you?"

"We'll take care of ourselves," Larry said. "No trouble found us until you arrived. I'm betting no trouble finds us when you're gone. Eat up."

Lena had finished her sandwich while the others talked. Every adult in the group had tried to play on the good side of this couple who'd beat them to the farm. Nothing seemed to be getting through and Larry's last comment felt like it was a prelude to 'pack up and go now'.

"You said we could get our weapons back in the morning. Does that mean we can sleep in the barn?" she asked. "Or, can we stay a while to help you out?"

Ellen looked at them. "The kids can stay with us when you go. You said the road is hard on them. They can live here with us."

"No," Ava said. "My kids stay with me."

Larry raised his shotgun, not to aim, more like he was reminding everyone that it was there with him.

Ellen gave him a little shake of her head. "I figured you'd say that. No hard feelings. They're your kids and you know what's best for them. I never took to people who told parents how to raise their children." She rose and picked up her cushion. "We could use the horse. Leave him with us and you can stay the night here."

She didn't wait for an answer. Larry followed her out of the barn.

"You can't leave Starbuck with them," Jason said. "He's our horse. We need him."

Lena checked to see if either Larry or Ellen were hanging around. It seemed like they trusted the group enough to leave them alone during the night. "I didn't agree to give them Starbuck. He's Scott's horse, I can't give him away."

Scott laughed. "I would have come back and taken him anyway. But it's going to be hard on the road with no destination."

"And no food," Deb added.

Lena sank to the ground, the effort of facing the two occupants of the farm had sucked the last of the energy from her body.

Now that she didn't have to put on a brave face for Larry and Ellen, she felt the weight of the last few days as they'd struggled to make the final leg of their journey. This was supposed to be the end of the problems, not another hurdle — one so big it looked impossible. "We need to figure out how to convince them we're an asset. We aren't leaving here. This is our home." She prayed that there was a way to do it peacefully.

"Do you think our rifles are still on the porch?" Tik asked.

They'd handed all the other visible weapons over to Larry when they got to the barn. Too tired to find a way to talk him out of it, Lena had watched Keith and Tik reluctantly place the rifles on the table that Larry dragged out to the porch — the table her aunt had used to hold tiny glass animals. Larry hadn't thought to ask if they had other weapons. Now she was glad of the bargain. If they had guns, she wasn't sure she could stop a fight.

"Don't go looking. This isn't the time to start a war. There's no guarantee we'd win. What if one of us got killed? We are supposed to live here." Lena knew she needed to divert them from that track. She may not have the right answer, but bloodshed couldn't be their first resort. She still woke sweating with the memory of Julian's body going limp, and his blood spraying her clothes.

"We don't know anything about them," Deb said. "We don't know why they left wherever they came from. We don't know if they murdered people, or if they are criminals, or what. We can't take the chance that they'll even stick with a deal they make."

Well, that's all true, more or less, about us. We must look threatening to them in our state.

"It doesn't matter," Lena said. "None of us are angels. It only matters what we do going forward. If we start with killing, what kind of people does that make us? At least Abigail didn't try to kill us."

"Not directly, but we would have died long ago if she'd taken our supplies and Starbuck like she planned." Tik's voice was harsh. Lena could hear the violence of his gang life in it.

She couldn't let him fall back into the life he ran from. "We don't need an enforcer. We need to think this through." Did they have the reserves to fuel a real idea?

Lena looked at each of her companions. There was fear and desperation there. And hope; she needed to touch that, the hope that things would work out.

Ava hugged Maya closer. "We won't last much longer on the road, Lena."

"You don't need to tell me that. Whatever happens, we can't leave tomorrow, with or without Starbuck." Lena wished someone would do something other than just imply they would fight. Where was Keith's wisdom on this? What did Scott feel like doing? He could leave, she hoped he would stay, but this wasn't his fight.

"We need food and rest and a reason to get up in the morning," she said. "I won't let them send us away."

No one spoke for a few minutes. Then Keith broke the silence. "What do you mean us to do?"

Lena wondered the same thing. It would be possible to take the farm back like Tik wanted. Would she wake up screaming about the dead bodies? And if this was their only way to deal with obstacles, how long would it be before they met a stronger force?

Larry and Ellen were only doing the same as her group were doing. They wanted a better life, and they thought they had it. Lena wondered what was happening in the house. She figured Larry would try to stay up watching. He'd be armed. But he wasn't young and if they'd really been living on the same quality of food that had been offered, surely, he wouldn't have the stamina.

"I doubt we'd be able to get our weapons," she said, hoping to put an end to that train of thought. "We need to work with them. The farm can support all of us, and more without too much effort. I don't think they realize how much work it will be. If they've only been here a few months, they've been harvesting wild crops. They don't know what to do so that they'll have food in the winter and next spring. By the state of the meal we got, whoever does the cooking doesn't know the basics. And those apples are what May would feed to the livestock. We can show them a lot. We just have to do it fast."

"You told them we could help," Mellow said. "They didn't care."

Lena smiled. "You are exactly right, Mellow. We need to show them what having us on the farm will do."

She went to the pile of supplies and started tossing bedrolls to the others. "We need to sleep. At first light we get to work. I know where there's likely to be crops to harvest. We present them with an example of what it means to have more people working the farm."

CHAPTER THIRTY-FOUR

It was still dark when Lena woke. Even in the dark, she felt safe and at home. There was something in the feeling of being at the end of the journey that gave her strength. The meal last night wasn't enough to get them through a full day of work, but a few hours would be all it took to show Larry and Ellen that they were valuable enough to keep. If it didn't work, they would try something else. And if that didn't work, then Larry and Ellen were only two people to their eight.

She crawled out of her bedroll and felt for the lantern she'd placed at her side last night. Feeling the cool glass, she patted the ground beside it where she'd set the book of matches. Lena touched the flame to the mantle and blinked as the brightness cleared the dark away.

In her searches last night, she'd found an old plow, and a few hoes. They'd plow part of the field near the house. It would be ready for the seeds they'd brought. No seed would go into the soil until they were moved into the house. Once in there, she'd feel like they were part of the farm.

She shook Ava's bedroll and made sure her friend was awake

before moving on to rouse the next person. Within minutes everyone was up and ready to head out to the fields.

A cock crowed.

"There's chickens," Lena said. "We'll find some eggs. At least it will be protein, and there'll be something in the harvest we can eat raw. It will be good to have breakfast."

They took the pitchers and glasses with them. Lena knew where they could get water. It would be cool enough in the fields this early, they just needed enough food to keep them going.

"Okay, this is it, everyone. Hook the plow up to Starbuck and hope he'll cooperate." Lena showed Scott how to use the harness. She knew how to man the plow from her visits, although it had been years.

The first field was only a few yards from the back door of the house. Larry and Ellen had clearly been living off the self-seeded vegetables. Lena pictured it next spring as the shoots of lettuce, beans, and carrots would be just poking up. She led them past that field toward the far corner. The ground was hard and whatever crops had been planted were long gone to weed.

Lena demonstrated the correct way to get a row plowed and then took Maya and Jason in search of the chickens. They were in the wild pen just beyond the tree line. Her aunt had hated the sight of the chickens pecking at each other. The distance also reduced the volume of the cock's crow.

Someone had fixed the mesh fencing, but the henhouse was in bad need of repair. The hens were pecking at the ground where seeds had been strewn. Lena hoped they weren't crop seeds. The chickens would be better on vegetable scraps and the bugs they scratched out of the soil.

She opened the gate and led Jason and Maya inside. "Don't move too quickly. We want them nice and calm while we find the eggs." Lena headed for the henhouse just in case, but there was no evidence of any laying inside. "They've probably nested on the ground. Take the eggs gently and put them in the basket."

The kids were good egg hunters. They didn't disturb the chickens, and they found a dozen eggs within a few minutes. The first few eggshells cracked as soon as they were moved. "The chickens need some calcium in their diet," she told the kids.

"They are all poopy," Maya said.

"They come out of the chicken's butt," Jason said.

"We'll wash them at the well." Lena walked them back through the fence, her mind turning over all the projects she was seeing. Maybe the kids could take on the care and feeding of the hens.

At the well, her aunt had installed a tap like they used to see on TV shows about African villages. She'd said, "If they don't need to walk buckets of water to the fields, neither should I." The tap had come in handy in the hot summers.

The eggs cleaned, Lena walked the kids back to the field. They could move quickly now that sun was brightening the sky, not fully risen, but enough that a soft white light gave them a clear view of where they walked. There was no sign of action at the house, so they still had time to keep working and surprise Ellen and Larry with their results.

Starbuck had cooperated enough that a few rows of soil was turned over. The lines weren't straight, and there were a few gaps, but it was starting to look like a farm.

"We can plant there tomorrow. I figure one field this year will be all we can manage." She handed eggs to everyone and there was silence as they cracked the shells and slurped the raw contents. It wasn't her favorite way to eat breakfast, but the energy was welcome.

"What next," Mellow asked.

"Potatoes, and if we're lucky some tomatoes and beans. And blackberries." Lena took them to the secret garden she'd planted as a child. Her aunt had kept it up for a few years, Lena hoped it was long enough to ensure there were plants still seeding.

The garden was a small clearing in the woods. Larry wouldn't have come this way to hunt because brambles looked like they barred the way. Lena knew the secret path through the thorns.

She showed the others how to avoid being scratched and led the way. On the other side of the thick bushes was her garden. The fence had fallen over in places, pulled down by the brambles. There were potatoes just as she'd suspected. And the blackberries were heavy on the branches. Along the corner in piles were the beans she'd planted. Her aunt had shown her how to twist the vines so she didn't need to use canes to hold them up.

"Pick as much as you can," she said. "I want Larry and Ellen to be blown away. Then we are going to tell them we're staying."

The sun was fully up by the time they'd gleaned everything that hadn't been nibbled by the deer or chewed by slugs. Their baskets were overflowing with produce as they left the patch.

Lena sent a silent thanks to her aunt for tending the garden for so long. She'd saved their lives with that little act of kindness.

When they came in sight of the house, Larry was striding across the field, a shotgun in his arms. His gaze was kept on the ground and Lena realized he was following Starbuck's hoofprints.

He looked up as Starbuck tossed his head, jingling the harness he still wore.

"You think you can just steal my crops?" Larry yelled, raising the gun.

"Step back, old man," Tik shouted. He pulled out his hand gun.

This couldn't happen. They were so close.

Larry kept his gun leveled and his eyes on Tik. "I knew I couldn't trust you. Get your asses off my farm."

Keith moved to stand beside Tik and then pulled out his own gun. "Think twice before you make your next move. We aren't going anywhere. Now you can figure out how you and Ellen get to stay."

Lena was frozen. The situation was escalating beyond the point of negotiation. She couldn't turn to look at the others, only hope that they would stay there. She had to stop this.

Larry didn't move. At least no one was shooting. If she had known about the weapons, Lena knew she could have done something. Now, instead of just coaxing Larry and Ellen into accepting them, she had to repair the damage.

Lena walked to where Keith and Tik stood and placed her hand on their arms. "Put them away." Then she stepped closer to Larry. Telling herself he wouldn't shoot her without provocation, and hoping there would be no provocation, she said, "You have it wrong. We harvested this to show you what we can do. This doesn't have to be your farm or my farm. There's plenty here for all of us."

He kept the shotgun raised and glanced at the basket she held up with shaking arms. "Where'd you find that?"

It was a good sign that he'd taken his attention off the other weapons. Lena had no idea if Tik and Keith had disarmed.

"It's my aunt's farm, remember?" Lena said. She turned to see the others lining up behind her, the two men had lowered their guns, but still held onto them. "You'll notice we didn't take our other weapons." She was doubly grateful they hadn't gone looking for them. "I'm sorry we kept these, but there are wild animals out here and the kids needed to be protected." It wouldn't hurt for him to think the guns were for anything other than murder.

"What's the horse been doing?"

"Why don't we go back to the house and talk?" Lena put the basket down, knowing she had his attention.

Larry lowered his shotgun and reached into the basket, picking out a handful of berries. The juice stained his fingers as he bruised the fruit. "I didn't think those brambles produced anything but thorns."

"Like I said. Let's go inside and we'll talk."

Larry looked back at the house and then to Lena. She could

see his surrender to the inevitable in his eyes. "I'm not a fool. Hand me those guns. Then you can put the horse in the barn and we'll see what Ellen has to say."

Lena smoothed the sheets on her bed. Her bed! Ellen had been harder to convince than Larry. The kids ran and brought more eggs to show her that the hens were laying. Deb talked about how they could get more meat out of a deer by dressing it properly. Keith offered tips on hunting. Everyone talked about how the hard work felt good when they saw the results.

Now they were in the house. No more barns or hard ground. No more days of too little food and too long walking. Tears raced down her face. It was over. They'd made it. She wouldn't be alone with the hard decisions any more.

EPILOGUE

Maya reached for the stems close to the dirt like her mother showed her. When they came up, she saw a cluster of small beets. It wasn't great but at least it wasn't dry beans again. All winter they'd had to live off whatever was in the root cellar and what they could find in the woods. They'd dried more meat than she ever wanted to see again.

"Hey," Jason said. "You going to pull more, or is that enough?"

She looked into the basket. Peas, lettuce, spinach, and the beets. "Almost done. What have you got?"

He held up a pair of rabbits. "I saw some deer too, but they won't let me go hunting, yet."

She pulled another handful of beets and tossed them into the basket. "You ever miss it?"

"What, the town?" He laughed. "Not really. I guess I miss my friends. It would be nice to have someone to hang out with."

Maya missed her friends too. "Maybe they'll find some more kids when Lena says Tik and Scott can go out and find other farms."

"I want to go with them," Jason said.

Jason would probably get his way. He was good at wearing the adults down so they just said okay to what he wanted. It had been easier to do when they just had mom. Now it was like every adult was a parent.

"Then I'll have no one to play with me."

"I'll make sure we find a bunch of other kids. Maybe there's a school nearby."

Even school would be a change.

"I guess no one is coming here to find us. What if it's just us forever?"

Jason took the basket from her. "Don't think like that. There's someone out there. It's probably because winter was so cold and snowy. Other people will be coming any day."

Maya hoped so. It was kind of lonely for a kid on the farm.

WANT MORE?

Want to know if Lena and family survive the battle to keep her new home? Use the QR code to get your copy of A Fight For Home.

Sneak peek next.

If you enjoyed reading A Need to Breathe, please consider helping other readers to find the story by leaving a review.

CHAPTER 1

It was getting harder and harder to hide the fact that the ingredients she was using to make their meals were coming from outside the shelter. Pallavi stirred the pot of boiling water and added the chopped carrots and potatoes. At least she didn't have to explain the water; her father had gone to great lengths to ensure that they had access to fresh water from rainfall that was filtered to purity.

She glanced over her shoulder to see her brother, Mahir, chatting with her father. At nine years old he should be getting into trouble on the streets, not talking to their father about the best way to protect everyone if someone should breach the shelter defenses. Mahir was small for his age, and she couldn't help thinking that was because he hadn't been allowed to run in the sun for years. He'd been so young when their mother died. Pallavi was eleven when they first came to the shelter. She knew what it was like to feel the sun on her face. And now that she was sneaking out, she at least had some freedom.

"Daughter, the food is starting to smell delicious." Her father's voice was weak. He tried to hide it, but Pallavi knew he was ill. The next time she went out she must find some medicine.

Mahir walked over and took the spoon from her so she could continue preparing ingredients while he stirred.

"He will guess soon," Mahir whispered.

Pallavi ignored him. If her father became suspicious about how fresh the food was, she would think of a lie.

"Our garden has produced more than I could've hoped," her father said. Sometimes he seemed to read her mind. "You children have learned to garden well."

Pallavi had been hoping that the discussion would not come up for months. "It is like Mama is watching and helping us."

Her father liked to think his dead wife was watching over them. It was another sign of his illness, that he simply nodded and didn't launch into a long story about how her mother had been the best wife, the most loving mother.

Pallavi remembered her mother, and every time she looked in the mirror the reflection looked more like the woman her mother had been.

It was easier to keep her dark hair long because the shelter was supposed be sealed. That meant there was nowhere to dispose of clippings. At least as far as her father knew. He was so afraid of what might be going on outside their doors that he seemed to choose to believe they were more self-sufficient than they really were. She had her mother's gray eyes, and it looked like she was going to be the same height, although five and half feet could hardly be called height. The rest of her features she'd inherited from her father, her strong nose, her cheekbones, and her brown skin. And one more thing. Distrust of strangers.

The decision to go outside the first time took so long because Pallavi was convinced the world was full of danger. Only dire need had made her squeeze through the broken slats one night. Nothing bad had happened, but every time she ventured out, her stomach tightened, and her breath caught as she slid the loose wood aside.

"It has been a long time, Papa. Eventually we will have to go outside. When will we know it's safe?"

Her father coughed. It started as though he was clearing his throat, but then developed into a wheezing, compulsive gasp. Talking about going outside upset him, but never this much. She left Mahir at the fire and went to her father's side.

"It's okay, Papa. I'm sure it's not time yet. As you say, we still have a lot of vegetables." She handed him a glass of water and rubbed his back until the coughing subsided.

Ava moved the lantern to the end of the next row of shelves. When they'd found this root cellar, there had been no doubt it was where they would hide all their supplies. Three days of clearing and digging out some fallen areas gave them enough room to store all the harvest, preserves, and their dwindling supply of medicines.

It was a bonus that it was far enough away from the house that if they needed to, they could extend it without worrying about the foundations. And they could use the basement for storing things that needed to be kept dry, at least for now. She hoped, that eventually they would need the space for more bedrooms as more people joined them.

She looked at the next page in the notebook she used to keep track of what was left, so they knew what would happen as they got through winter.

"Four full barrels of carrots, unopened." She looked through the lattice they used to cap the barrels of vegetables and made a note. "I'll have to talk to Mellow," she muttered. "That's not what I call full."

The harvest had been good, but it was going to be tight over winter. With so few people to work the farm, they'd had to limit how much they planted. But if Lena's plan to create alliances worked out, maybe they would end up with some temporary workers from other communities so that they could supply food for the farm and a lot of other people.

She moved on to the next item on the list. *Cabbage, six crates. All full.* At least, that was what Mellow had written in the book. Ava didn't want to open the crates, but the one in front had too much space between the heads. The top was still in place, but if she was going to talk to Mellow about being precise, she needed to do it herself. Placing the book on the shelf, she hefted the crate onto the floor, and then jumped aside as three cabbages fell out.

"Dammit."

There was a missing slat in the back.

"Ava. We need you at the house."

Ava looked up to see Tik outlined in the doorway. His frame had filled out with the hard work on the farm, and he lost that slight edginess of a former gang banger.

"I need to finish in here," she said, grunting as she placed the crate back on the shelf. "And I need a new crate. Can you get it for me?"

Tik stepped through the doorway and walked to join her. He looked into the crate and whistled. "How many missing? Is it gonna be a problem?"

"I have to check all of them to see how many we need to replace. I don't think it's going to be a problem unless a lot of the crates are broken. And the cabbages that fell out might be somewhere under the shelving ready to be put back."

Tik pushed the crate a little further back on the shelf. "I'll help you do it later, but you need to come to the house now. We have a visitor. Lena wants all of us there when we talk to him."

"Someone from Crystal? They've come to tell us their decision on the alliance?" She picked up the lantern and stuck the notebook in her pocket.

"No, we're still waiting to hear from Crystal. I guess their council must hash everything out before they make a decision. This is someone we've met before. Come on."

Ava entered the back door of the farmhouse. She lay her notebook on the kitchen counter as she passed through. There were voices in the front of the house, so she assumed that was where she was needed. As she passed through the dining and living rooms, she hoped that it wasn't some kind of accident that needed medical supplies. Every time they used up some of the supply, it was just a little step closer to relying on folk remedies and herbal concoctions.

The front door was open, and Ava could see Keith and Deb standing just in front of the opening, both holding rifles. Just in front of them Lena stood blocking the stairs. So, not an accident.

She stepped between Keith and Deb, to see her son, Jason, also holding a gun. No matter how often she saw him go armed, it bothered her that such a young child would have to learn how to defend his home. He should be dealing with getting his first girlfriend at age thirteen, not facing down threats. That was the world now, the plagues had wiped out a way of living as well as so many of the children.

"Why should we trust you?" Lena asked. "The last time we saw you, we almost lost our freedom. And we did lose half of our supplies. You realize that almost killed us all."

Ava stepped up beside Lena as she spoke and saw who was standing on the path. Evan. That's the only name she had for him. On their journey to the farm, he'd been a guard at the Community of Truth, and complicit in his leader's plan to trap people and work them to death. Ava was surprised that Lena hadn't simply shot him, but then they would have to dispose of the body.

Ava watched as Evan held his arms out to the side, showing that he had no weapons within easy reach.

"Things have changed. Abigail is gone." He kept his arms out to his side, relaxed.

Ava turned to Lena and noticed Scott standing at the other end of the porch. "Did you check to see if he has any weapons hidden?"

Lena kept her eyes on Evan as she gestured to Scott. "I wasn't sure we would let him get this close. I'm still not sure we want to listen to him. But that's a good idea. Scott, pat him down."

They all watched carefully as Scott searched Evan. It didn't make sense that he wouldn't have some weapon.

"Where is everyone else?" Ava didn't want to take her attention away from Evan. Even though she didn't have a weapon, she wanted to make sure that there were no signs of a threat.

"You mean where are the kids?"

Lena knew her too well for Ava to deny it. "I could only see Jason. Where's Maya? And where's Mellow?"

"Maya is in her room. I suspect she's watching out of her window. Mellow went to the graves this morning."

When they had arrived at the farm almost a year ago, there were two people living there. Husband and wife, both too old to make the best of the farm. It had taken some effort, but Lena had convinced them that they were better off taking in the ragged group of people who had arrived at their door in a wagon, than letting the farm go to ruin. Over the winter both had succumbed to the flu.

"There's nothing," Scott called to the group on the porch. He stepped away from Evan and joined Lena, taking his rifle from where it leaned against the porch rail.

Ava wasn't convinced. Just because he didn't have anything on him didn't mean that Evan wasn't the bait in a trap. "You didn't come all this way without some kind of protection. Where is it? And did you walk?"

Evan lowered his arms, apparently thinking that he passed the test. "I left my weapons with my horse just down the road. I have a rifle, some ammunition, a bow and two quivers of arrows."

Ava could see that Lena wasn't sure what to do. Their history with this man and his community was enough to send him away. But they were so few, they needed alliances. That's why they had approached Crystal, a town a couple of days away, to make alliances, and make them both stronger.

Ava stepped a little closer to Lena to speak quietly. "It's going to be hard to learn what we need if he's standing that far away."

Lena uncrossed her arms, and beckoned Evan. "You're not entering the house. We'll do this on the porch. And anyone who wants to stay can stay."

As Evan walked up to join them, Ava tried to get Jason to leave, but he refused to budge. Scott said he would make some tea and disappeared into the house. Deb drifted away, but Keith stood his ground.

Ava went into the dining room and brought back two chairs. They might as well all be comfortable while they listened to what Evan had to say. Maya ran down the stairs and helped her by bringing another chair.

When they were settled, which meant that Ava and Lena sat at the small table placing Evan across from them leaving him no room to escape, the others shifted their weight, keeping their weapons ready.

"What do you mean Abigail is gone?" Lena asked. "She had a sweet deal there, in the Community of Truth, and no one seemed willing to make any changes when we came through."

Evan looked around, and then relaxed back in his chair. "Like I said, she's gone. Do you mind putting the guns down? I'd hate to have someone shot by accident."

Ava let Lena take the lead. She wasn't crazy about having all the guns around them either, but until Evan explained what was going on, and why he was there, it didn't seem prudent to let down their guard.

Lena considered for a few minutes, and then waved at the floor. "You can relax. We know he's not armed, and he can't get out that easily."

The weapons were placed on the ground with only a little complaining.

When people were quiet again and everyone was around the table, Lena straightened in her chair. "Okay, no more excuses. What happened to Abigail? And why are you here?"

CHAPTER 2

Evan spent most of the journey thinking about how he would answer these questions. When the council sent him, they hadn't given him a formal statement. It was supposed to make him more believable, putting it into his own words, but he wasn't a diplomat. He might just make it worse.

"I guess I should start with Abigail." He rubbed his face, feeling the grit from the road mix with his sweat. "She's the reason we are going out to other communities. Although, yours is the first. We need to get a bit stronger before talking to other groups."

"Stop rambling," Ava said. "What happened to her?"

Lena let Ava take command? Was it because of her schoolmarm attitude? Evan automatically responded to it.

"She's dead," he said. "It happened a few months ago. She just got worse as time passed. We couldn't deal with it any longer. I couldn't be part of it anymore."

Lena glanced at the others in the room. They nodded back, everyone alert. Their guns were near at hand; she hoped they wouldn't be needed. "Abigail tried to make us indebted to the community forever, basically making us slaves. She stole half our rations and we almost died on the way here because of it. She wanted to take our children away. How exactly did she get worse?"

Evan looked at his hands, which were clasped on the table in front of him. The anger and despair at the memory held him back.

"Evan, you have to tell us, so you might as well just say it."

He looked up at her, swallowing the bile in his throat. "After you escaped — yes, we were trying to make you stay no matter your plans — she didn't want to chance losing again. The next group that came, a family, two kids and two dads. She made us put them in the jail and we took their horses and supplies. Once they realized she wasn't going to give them back, they agreed to stay."

"So we escaped, and she used that as an excuse to make it harder to leave? Are we supposed to feel guilty?" Ava asked.

Lena put her hand on Ava's arm. "How many travelers come past?" she asked.

"More these days. We're the first large community people travelling west come to. The cities are failing. The smaller towns are struggling to provide for the inhabitants, so people keep moving on." He stopped speaking for a moment to break what he knew was going to be a list of excuses. "Our community isn't a bad place. There are way worse out there."

"So we're supposed to accept you because you aren't as bad as you could be?" Ava asked.

"No, I'm just trying to explain."

She waved her hands to dismiss his words. "Fine. What happened next?"

He felt the heat of shame warm his cheeks. "The next few groups were the same. Then Abigail said we couldn't take on anyone else. She wanted us to steal the supplies and move the people on. She said it was them or us." He rubbed his face again. "I couldn't do it, so she sent me to the fields. Then I heard she said to kill anyone who came by. Her excuse was they would tell communities down the road about us, and we would be attacked."

"So you killed her?" Lena asked. "That doesn't make me feel like you can be trusted as partners. What happens when we don't agree?"

Her words felt like a slap. "No! We were planning to put her in the jail until we could get her calmed down. She was cool when you saw her, right? By the end, she was ranting. But she got away. I joined one of the search parties. We wanted her gone, but not that way, left to die because she didn't know how to hunt or build a shelter. We wanted her gone, you can understand that, right? We wouldn't kill her."

"It's pretty much what she'd been doing to other people. Why should we believe you are here to make allies, and not to steal what we have?" Ava asked.

Evan felt heat rise in his cheeks again, this time anger, not shame. "All I can say is we've changed. If we wanted to steal your supplies, why would I be here alone? I was the one who found her. She was lying underneath a tree. I thought she was sleeping, but then I saw the blood."

"An animal?" Scott asked.

"A bullet. She'd been shot by someone from the fort. They left a mark, so we would know. They do that with territory markers. They are expanding. Abigail must have run into them. Knowing her, she fought to keep the land in the community."

"So Abigail died. Now what happens to the people she trapped?" Scott's voice was bitter. The Community of Hope had tried to steal his horse and wagon along with their supplies. Evan remembered how Scott seemed to love the animal.

"They all stayed. Like I said, it's not a bad place. They had found friends and purpose, so they didn't want to go on the road again. Especially now that the Fort was stretching its boundaries. And we changed the name. There was too much bad history linked to it. We called the town Prosperity."

"So why are you here?" Lena asked.

"I'm here to ask you to form an alliance with us. We are all weaker than Newton's men. If we work together we might have a chance. You'd get more people here to help defend the farm. We would get access to your knowledge. You've found a way to thrive here. We need to know how to do that. Abigail didn't worry about what skills people had when she trapped them, so we don't have what we need."

It was clear that Lena didn't believe him. He had to admit that the deal was lopsided. The farm stood to gain more from the alliance than Prosperity.

Lena stood up and pointed to Scott. "Put him in Tik's room, it's the most secure. Lock the door."

Evan didn't protest. They needed to talk without him there. He would wait, and he would rest.

"I think he's getting a little better," Pallavi said. She was standing at the far end of the shelter waiting for her father to fall asleep, so she could slip out and get more supplies. Mahir had rushed over as soon as he saw her get close to the secret exit.

"The stew did help," Mahir whispered back. "But you should stay here."

Pallavi bit back the words that surged out of her mind. She was sixteen, and a nine-year-old shouldn't be able to order her around. But there was no room in the shelter for teenage moodiness. This new world made her think about everything she said. She could only hope that Mahir had the same consideration when he became a teenager. If they were still here.

She glanced at her father again; his normally warm dark skin was ashy. And his breathing had a worrying rasp to it. When she touched his forehead earlier, it was hot but there was no fever sweat. He'd dutifully drunk all the water that she passed him. Her hope was, with enough liquid, he would start to sweat, and the sickness would break.

"He needs something more than vegetable stew," she said. "There are medicines, and there were lentils, and rice."

"And how will you explain that? It's easy for him to believe you could grow those vegetables. But he knows how much medicine we brought. And he also knows how much he's taken." Mahir nudged her away from the gap in the shelter wall. "It's too dangerous. There are bad people running around. How do you think Dad will react if you don't come back one day?"

Pallavi hadn't let herself think about that. If she got caught, she would be leaving Mahir alone. Her father wouldn't last long without her care. But he wouldn't last long anyway, and she couldn't let that happen just because it was a little risky. "I'm careful," she said.

"I'm sure everyone thinks they're careful." Mahir's face set with his stubborn look. "Tell me what you're looking for. I can go get it."

"Is it because I'm a girl?" Pallavi regretted the sarcasm in her voice as soon as it was out. "I'm sorry. Look, I'm experienced at this. You need to be trained."

"Then train me. And yes, it's because you're a girl," he said with a shake of his head. "The bad people may be looking for pretty girls."

It hurt Pallavi that her little brother knew about such evil stuff. He'd been so young when the plagues hit. Just old enough to be vaccinated. A few months earlier and he would've died like so many of the other children. She could only think that Dad had told Mahir what he thought the world was like outside. And even though her brother had been out, it hadn't been enough to convince them that Dad was completely wrong. And maybe he wasn't. She'd seen strangers roaming the woods lately. Men in groups of one or two. She'd avoided them so far.

"Stay here with dad, please," she asked. "I don't have time to train you right now. I promise I will. But right now, someone has to watch over Dad."

She put her fingers across her brother's lips as he tried to answer her back. She was losing time by arguing. His fingers clenched in frustration. Then he relaxed.

"Okay, this one time," he said. "But if you don't come back soon, I'm coming for you. And then Dad will be left alone. So you better not stay away too long."

Pallavi leaned against the gap. It was just big enough for her to slip through, but it also allowed her to see if anyone was outside before she left. It was evening, but the sun was still there. If she hurried, she would be back before it was full dark. No matter how urgent the need, being out in the dark was terrifying. Because when she couldn't see, all of Mahir's bad people seemed to be crowding her.

"Okay, I promise I'll be back soon. An hour, that's all I'll need." What she didn't say was if she couldn't find what they needed in the storehouse at the farm, the next trip would have to be days long. Dad had done a lot to prepare them, but it had only been for five years. It had been six since they shut themselves in the shelter. It proved how sick he really was, that he hadn't done the math.

Mahir reached to swing the loose panel to the side until it stopped. Pallavi planted a kiss on his forehead and wiggled through the gap.

Want to know if Lena and family survive the battle to keep her new home? Use the QR code to get your copy of A Fight For Home.

FREE EBOOK

Claim your copy of Running the Game when you use the QR code below to sign up for my newsletter and cheer on Pen as she vies for a commission in the military.

FREE EBOOK

ALSO BY PA WILSON

For more books by P A Wilson

Use the QR code below or go to pawilson.ca

ABOUT THE AUTHOR

Perry Wilson is a Canadian author based in Vancouver, BC who has big ideas and an itch to tell stories. Having spent some time on university, a career, and life in general, she returned to writing in 2008 and hasn't looked back since (well, maybe a little, but only while parallel parking).

She is a member of the Vancouver Writers Social Group, The Royal City Literary Arts Society, and The Surrey Writing Workshop. Perry has self-published several novels. She writes the Madeline Journeys, a fantasy series about a high-powered lawyer who finds herself trapped in a magical world, the Quinn Larson Quests, which follows the adventures of a wizard named Quinn who must contend with volatile fae in the heart of Vancouver, and the Charity Deacon Investigations, a mystery thriller series about a private eye who tends to fall into serious trouble with her cases, and The Riverton Romances, a series based in a small town in Oregon, one of her favorite states. Her stand-alone novels are Breaking the Bonds, Closing the Circle, and The Dragon at The Edge of The Map.

For more information
www.pawilson.ca
pawilson@pawilson.ca

ACKNOWLEDGMENTS

People think that the process of writing is solitary. That's not the case for me. I have help from so many people it would be hard to acknowledge everyone, but I'll give it a try.

The support and inspiration I get from my writer's groups is incalculable. The Vancouver Writers Social Group opens my mind to other ways of telling a story. The Royal City Literary Arts Society gives me the opportunity to meet and share with other writers who have more knowledge than I do. The Other 11 Months group is where I learn about getting the words on the page. And my critique group who helps me find the best parts of the story I want to tell. Thanks to all of the members of these great groups.

Last of all, but definitely a huge part of the process, my beta readers. These are the people who love stories and are willing, and more than able, to tell me if my finished story is ready for you, my readers.

Made in the USA
Middletown, DE
20 January 2024

48230258R00165